Resounding praise for
the incomparable *USA Today*
bestselling author

SAMANTHA JAMES

"NO ONE CAN WRITE A BOOK
QUITE LIKE SAMANTHA JAMES."
Catherine Anderson

"JAMES DELIVERS DELICIOUS
AND EXCITING ROMANCE."
Publishers Weekly

"READERS WILL ADORE HER ENDEARING,
THREE-DIMENSIONAL CHARACTERS."
Romantic Times

"A REMARKABLE WRITER."
Lisa Kleypas

"SAMANTHA JAMES WRITES EXACTLY
THE SORT OF BOOK I LOVE TO READ."
Linda Lael Miller

By Samantha James

A Perfect Hero
A Perfect Groom
A Perfect Bride
The Truest Heart
His Wicked Promise
His Wicked Ways
One Moonlit Night
A Promise Given
Every Wish Fulfilled
Just One Kiss
My Lord Conqueror
Gabriel's Bride

SAMANTHA JAMES

A Perfect Hero

AVON BOOKS
An Imprint of HarperCollinsPublishers

This is a work of fiction. Names, characters, places, and incidents are products of the author's imagination or are used fictitiously and are not to be construed as real. Any resemblance to actual events, locales, organizations, or persons, living or dead, is entirely coincidental.

AVON BOOKS
An Imprint of HarperCollins*Publishers*
10 East 53rd Street
New York, New York 10022-5299

For my family . . .

Kelly and Traegon,
who gave me my precious babies,
Nick and Ashley—who always make me laugh.

Sara and Steve . . . thanks for brainstorming with me
from across the pond, guys!

Jami, who I know will be the best R.N. ever!

And last but not least, for Ed.
My husband, my heart . . . my own perfect hero.

I love you all.

Prologue

London, *1814*

Whispers had begun to circulate in the church. Oh, but it was wrong . . . so wrong. For only moments earlier, all she could think was that no other day could have been more perfect for this . . . her wedding day.

High above, the sunlight shone through the stained-glass windows of St. George's Church in Hanover Square, bathing the interior of the church in a radiant, ephemeral glow.

It was a sign, Lady Julianna Sterling had decided as she stepped from the carriage and approached the church. For too long, a cloud of shadow had been cast upon the Sterlings. She'd viewed the beautiful day as a symbol of her life to come, a good sign. For surely on such a glorious, golden day like this, no hint of darkness would dare come to pass. Her union with Thomas Markham would be blessed, blessed as no other.

And yet, but moments later . . . she battled a low-grade panic. Thomas should have been here by now.

Where was he? *Where?*

A hand touched her elbow. Julianna looked up into her oldest brother's gray eyes. If Sebastian noticed the whispers of their guests, he ignored them.

"You look like a princess," he said huskily.

Julianna struggled for a smile and miraculously produced one. Her gown was of sheer, pale pink silk—her favorite color—draped over silver satin. Matching pink slippers encased her feet. Sheer Brussels lace adorned the sleeves; embroidered on the hem were delicate white rosebuds, shot here and there with glistening silver thread. But perhaps the most striking feature was the long, elegant train, which swirled behind her.

"I feel like one," she admitted softly. "But thank you, my lord. I daresay you're rather dashing yourself."

"And what of me?" Another voice, this one belonging to her brother Justin. "Am I not dashing as well?"

Julianna wrinkled her nose. "Desperate is what you are," she retorted, "if you must seek compliments from your sister."

"Minx," Justin drawled.

Sheltered on each side by her dark-haired,

suavely handsome older brothers, Julianna slipped dainty, lace-gloved hands into the crooks of their elbows. For twenty-three years Sebastian and Justin had protected her and sheltered her to the best of their ability—not that she had wanted it or needed it—but she loved them dearly for it.

Justin cocked a brow and addressed Sebastian. "While I realize it's normally a mother's duty to see that a young bride is adequately prepared for her wedding night, I trust you've seen to it that our sister has been apprised of all the . . . how may I put this delicately . . . the requisite information—"

"Actually, I asked that Sebastian save that duty for you, Justin. After all, you are a man of vast experience in that particular arena, are you not?"

It was a rare occasion to see Justin discomfited; Julianna savored it.

"Besides," she went on mildly, "there is no need. While I am not a woman of excessive skill, I do pride myself on my imagination—to say nothing of the fact that I became quite adept at listening at keyholes in my younger years when the two of you were in your cups. I garnered quite an education, shall we say. Therefore, I predict no shortcomings in that area."

Sebastian straightened himself to his full height. "The devil you say—"

"Julianna!" Justin was saying. "Now see here—"

"Stop looking so disapproving, both of you." They appeared so shocked that Julianna couldn't withhold a laugh.

Little did she know it would be the last time she laughed that day.

While her brothers were still glowering at her, her gaze shifted to the nave of the church. From the time she was a child, Julianna had cherished dreams of being married in St. George's in Hanover Square, built nearly a hundred years earlier—why, the marriage of the king's son, Prince Augustus, had taken place there in grand fashion! And thanks to Sebastian, the fanciful dreams of a child were about to become a reality—it was he who insisted her wedding take place at St. George's.

Julianna did not argue. It wasn't simply a child's fanciful dream; she knew, too, that for Sebastian, it was a symbol of prosperity and success.

They had come such a long, long way, the three of them, since the days when Society shunned the Sterlings. Upon their father's death, it was Sebastian who had restored respectability to their name.

The box pews on either side of the aisle were filled to overflowing. But Julianna noted several heads had begun to turn, traveling from the back of the church where they stood just to the side of the doors, to the front near the sanctuary . . .

Where Thomas should have awaited her.

An uneasy knot had begun to gather in the pit of her belly. "I daresay fully half the *ton* is here," she murmured.

"I do believe you'd have invited the whole of England had Sebastian allowed it," Justin said, with a faint smile. Sebastian made no comment.

The church was still. In the west gallery, the organist coughed while waiting for a signal from Reverend Hodgson, who had begun to shift from one foot to the other.

Several minutes later, Sebastian reached for his pocket watch and flipped it open, his expression grim. The ceremony was set for one o'clock.

It was nearly a quarter past the hour.

Julianna could not bear to look inside the church. The faces of the guests had turned from mild inquiry to pitying glances; the whispers had turned into an ominous hush.

Julianna looked up at Sebastian imploringly. "Something's wrong," she said, her voice low. "Thomas should have arrived by now."

Justin was not so generous. His features were tight-lipped. "He'd better have an explanation for this. My God, late for his own wedding—"

"Justin! Thomas is a good man, a compassionate man, the best of men. You know as well as I that he has a heart of gold!"

"Then where the devil is he?" growled Justin.

Julianna began to fret. "Oh, a dreadful accident has surely befallen him, for there is nothing that would keep him from this day! He is an honorable man. He—" her voice cracked "—otherwise he would be here. He *will* be here! There must be some reason . . ."

And so there was.

The side door opened. Three sets of eyes swiveled sharply when Samuel, Thomas's brother, suddenly appeared.

It was just like Justin not to bandy words. "Egad, man, where is Thomas?"

Sebastian stepped forward as well.

Samuel paused before Julianna. She could barely breathe. His bearing was such that it seemed he carried the weight of the universe on his shoulders.

Something was horribly, horribly wrong. She sensed it. She *knew* it. "Samuel. Samuel, tell me what's wrong!"

It was only later that she realized she should have known . . . He avoided her gaze. "I'm sorry, Julianna. But Thomas is gone."

Her heart gave a feeble thud. "Gone?" she said faintly.

"Yes. A note was delivered to me a short while ago. Oh, but I know not how to tell you this! Last night, you see—last night he left for Gretna Green . . . with Clarice Grey."

Samuel raised anxious eyes to her. "Julianna," he ventured tentatively, "did you hear me?"

Julianna stared. This couldn't be happening. It was a dream. Nay, a nightmare! Her heart was as cold as the stone beneath her slippers.

Behind her there was a collective gasp.

"Gretna Green!" someone was saying. "He's eloped to Gretna Green with another woman!"

And then it was spreading through the church, like a flame set to tinder, until her ears were roaring and she couldn't even think. Everyone was staring at her. She felt the touch of their eyes like shards of glass digging into her skin. She felt barren. Naked.

She had little memory of leaving the church. Sebastian and Justin hustled her outside and into the carriage, shielding her from the gaping stares of the guests, who had already begun to file from the nave.

When they rolled up in front of Sebastian's town house, she had yet to speak. Justin was still swearing, muttering something about a duel, when he leaped from the carriage.

Sebastian touched her shoulder. "Julianna?" he murmured. "Jules, are you all right?"

"I'm perfectly fine," she heard herself say in utterly precise tones. But she wasn't. Inside she was cringing. With utter calm she turned her head toward her brother.

"There will be a scandal, won't there?"

A ghost of a smile crept across Sebastian's lips.

"We're Sterlings, Jules. Perhaps it's inevitable. But we've weathered scandal before, haven't we?"

He meant to comfort, she knew. Yet how easy for him to say. After all, he was a man. It was easier for men. Men weren't branded as spinsters. As ape-leaders. Some old windbag wouldn't forever be whispering behind her fan about how *he* had been deserted on his wedding day . . .

She wanted to weep, to cry, to hurl herself into Sebastian's arms and sob out her heartache. As a child, he was the one who soothed her hurts and scrapes.

But this was a hurt he could not heal.

Through eyes so dry they hurt, she stared at him, pressing her lips together. She dared not blink, for she knew the tears would begin in earnest then. He searched her face endlessly, and she wondered if he could see the gash in her heart, the twist in her soul. She tried to be brave. She *would* be brave. She wouldn't cry. She wouldn't weep. Not yet. *Not yet.*

For that would come later.

Sebastian leaped out, then extended a hand. Julianna took it, alighting from the carriage. As she stepped toward the house, she felt the warming kiss of the sun upon her head. Mocking her, reviling her.

It was all gone, she thought wildly. All gone . . . her girlish hopes, her fanciful dreams.

She wanted to curl up into a ball and sob her heart out.

For something had happened that day. She was forever changed.

Forever shamed.

One

Spring 1818

$\mathcal{I}$t was a perfect night for thievery.

From beneath the crowning shelter of an aged oak tree, the figure on horseback surveyed the roadway. The hour was late, and with a sliver of moon slumbering behind a wisp of a cloud, the night was as dark and depthless as the yawning pits of hell. The faint rush of the wind sighed through the tree limbs to sing a plaintive, lonesome melody.

All the better to conceal his presence. All the better to aid his endeavor. All the better to await his opportunity.

Dressed wholly in black, from his hat to the soles of his boots, a dark mask obscured all but the glint of his eyes. He sat his mount—Percival—like a man accustomed to long hours on horseback, his posture straight as an arrow, betraying no hint of weariness . . . and with the silent stealth of a man who knew well and true that his presence must be concealed at all costs, until such time as he deemed the *right* time to strike.

Lest his very life be forfeit.

And the man known as the Magpie had no desire to meet his Maker.

Percival's ears pricked forward. Black-gloved fingers tightened on the reins. Squeezing his knees, he stilled the massive horse's movement. A fingertip pressed gently over his neck. "Wait," he cautioned.

The powerful animal quieted beneath his touch, but he could feel his muscles bunched and knotted, ready to spring into action.

With narrowed eyes, the man squinted into the encroaching darkness, directly to the east. This was not his first night masquerading as the Magpie. Nor would it be his last. Not until his purpose was accomplished to his satisfaction.

Beneath the black silk mask, a faint smile appeared. A familiar rush of excitement raced along his veins, an excitement he could not deny that he relished. His heartbeat quickened, for the pounding of hoofbeats had reached his ears as well as Percival's. The light from a dim yellow lantern had appeared as well, bobbing in the distance.

Quarry approached.

He waited until it was within sight, for he was

not a man to make mistakes. As if on cue— damn, but he had the devil's own luck!—the moon slid out from behind the cloud. The Magpie lifted his reins, broke free of the waist-high grasses beside the road, and stationed himself directly in the path of the lumbering coach.

When the coachman saw him, he stood on the box and hauled on the reins. With a jingle of the harness and a shout from the coachman, the vehicle rolled to a halt.

Coolly, the Magpie raised a pair of pistols dead center at the man.

"Stand and deliver!" came his cool demand.

Hours earlier, Julianna seized her skirt and ran across the courtyard at the inn, zigzagging to avoid the puddles left by yesterday's rain. "Wait!" she cried.

The driver clearly was not particularly disposed to patience. He glared at her. "Ye'd better hurry, mum," he grunted. "We're late already."

Late. Yes, that was certainly the word of the day. There was a *thump* as her trunk was loaded. And by Jove, she was determined to reach Bath, if not by tonight, then tomorrow.

Nothing about this journey had gone according to plan. Traveling by public coach had not been on the agenda. Unfortunately, she'd missed the speedy mail coach.

Breathless, Julianna hurtled herself inside.

She'd barely seated herself when the door closed and the contraption lurched forward.

There were three passengers besides her: an elderly woman; another woman with a huge, drooping bonnet; and a man next to her who Julianna guessed was her husband.

Julianna found herself next to the old woman. "Good day to all of you," she greeted pleasantly.

"Good day to ye," nodded the old woman.

The other woman eyed her gray-striped traveling gown curiously. "Are ye traveling alone then, madam?"

Madam? Mercy, but at twenty-seven, had she begun to age so dreadfully then?

"I am," Julianna returned evenly. "My maid and I were en route to Bath—I recently bought a house there, you see—when she became ill early in the afternoon. We stopped and spent the night at the inn. I'd hoped she would be quite recovered by today, but sadly that was not the case. By this afternoon, it was clear poor Peggy was in no condition to travel the remainder of the way to Bath, so I sent her back to London in my carriage." The fact that Julianna was unaccompanied didn't bother her in the least.

"That was most kind of ye, mum," said the other woman. "But we aren't traveling as far as Bath. And the roads aren't safe after dark."

Her husband sent her a censuring glance. "Leticia! 'Tis hardly your affair."

"Don't look at me like that, Charles. You know

it's true! There's that terrible highwayman, the Magpie. What will come next, I ask! Why, the wretched man may very well murder us in our beds, every one of us!" She cast an imploring glance at the elderly woman next to Julianna. "Mother, tell him!"

The old lady folded her hands and bobbed her head. "It's quite true, Charles," she said, her eyes round. "Oh, he's quite a horrid fellow, this Magpie."

"You see?" Leticia transferred her gaze to Julianna.

"I thank you for your concern, Mrs. . . ." Julianna paused meaningfully.

"Chadwick, Leticia and Charles," the woman said briskly. "And my mother is Mrs. Nelson. You've heard of him, haven't you? The Magpie?"

Julianna's mouth quirked. The London newspapers had been full of the Magpie's exploits—he was becoming quite the infamous brigand. Perhaps she was growing jaded, but it occurred to her that chance his reputation had been exaggerated, merely for the sake of selling more newspapers. Indeed, she would have almost welcomed an encounter with the Magpie, thus named for his cheekiness in robbing a coach carrying the private secretary of the Prime Minister himself, the Earl of Liverpool—a daring, if not foolhardy deed, to be sure.

But to think that they would be robbed by this notorious highwayman—she dismissed the notion out of hand. Such things did not happen to women such as herself. Had she been asked, she'd have described her life as rather mundane.

Three years ago, Sebastian had wed, and Julianna had taken it upon herself to move out of the family residence. The shame and scandal of being stranded at the altar had been difficult to bear. Julianna counted herself a realist, and she was aware the experience had not left her unscathed. But she liked to think she was at least somewhat wiser. She'd floundered for a time, spending months in Europe, dreading the day she must face the *ton* again.

What a shock it had been when she returned to London on the eve of Sebastian's wedding!

It was then that she'd realized it was time to face life head-on. There could be no more hiding away, for what would that accomplish? She and Justin and Sebastian would always be close—the circumstances of their childhood had seen to that. She lived quite comfortably on her allowance from Sebastian, but she had made some investments of her own that allowed her to purchase a modest town house in London, and her newest acquisition, a lovely little manor house in Bath.

Julianna was proud of her accomplishments, for she had discovered a courage and a dignity she hadn't known she possessed. It had begun that long-ago night when Thomas and Clarice had returned from Gretna Green. Apologetic and contrite, Thomas had come to her.

"I know my marriage to Clarice must have come as a shock," he'd said. "I can offer no excuse except one . . . Clarice is carrying my child, Julianna."

In stunned, muted silence, Julianna listened while Thomas relayed how Clarice had come to him in tears the night before they—Julianna and Thomas—were to wed.

"I cannot deny what I have done, Julianna. Clarice and I have been friends since we were children. We succumbed to a moment of weakness— a moment of abandon. It was wrong. I knew it. But I told myself you would never know. Indeed, both Clarice and I agreed that we could not continue to see each other. But when she came to me and confessed that she was with child, I could not deny her. Honor and duty compelled that I do the right thing and marry Clarice. And so I did. I will regret to the end of my days if I hurt you, Julianna. But it was the right thing to do."

If he had hurt her. He knew that he had. He knew that she'd loved him madly . . . And honor and duty. Well, those were things that Julianna understood, and so did her brothers. Indeed, it was all that had stopped Justin from calling him out. Oh, yes, she had understood . . .

But to forgive him his betrayal. That was not so easy.

And never would she forget. *Never*.

The pain and bitter hurt had faded. They were but a twinge in the region of her heart. But no man would ever turn her head again. Never again would she be so gullible, so trusting. She would rather grow old alone than marry simply for the sake of marrying.

For despite the abominable circumstances of their youth—their mother's abandonment, their father's disregard—Julianna had never lost faith in the sanctity of marriage. A nurturer, Sebastian had always called her, sweet and softhearted, always taking care of others.

It was true, she supposed. Oh, yes, it was in her nature to be a wife, a mother. She'd once speculated that it was the fact that their mother had run off with her lover that instilled in Julianna the desire to be everything their own mother was not. Indeed, Julianna had once been convinced that the whole sordid makeup of her parents' relationship had simply made her all the more determined that when she, Julianna, married—and as a child she had somehow never doubted that she *would*—it would be for love . . . and love alone. Ah, yes, the longing for a husband and children was something that only grew stronger as she grew older. Forever it seemed she had planned the day of her wedding.

Oddly, it no longer hurt to think of that day.

What hurt was knowing she would never have a child of her own. No, there would be no children. For there would be no husband.

And that particular heartache was one that had taken a long time to accept—and remained a secret locked tight in her breast for all eternity. She would never experience the joy of a child snug against her breasts . . . *her* child. For a husband was beyond her reach—perhaps more aptly, beyond her desire. And so she had buried the yearning for a child.

For it could never be.

No, she was no longer quite so carefree, seeing only the good in those around her. As for the Magpies of the world, well, in time this one would surely get his due.

"I daresay all the kingdom has heard of the Magpie," she returned lightly.

Mrs. Chadwick eyed her. "Are you not afraid?"

"Afraid of a man I cannot see, a man I've yet to meet?" Smiling, Julianna shook her head, mildly amused. Reports of such men and their misdeeds had fallen off in the last few years. The notion of a highwayman made her shiver, but not in dread. Why, if she were given to such fancies, the notion might be almost romantic!

"Now, if he were to leap through that

door"—she nodded—"I might be inclined to say otherwise."

"Oh, but you should be afraid. That's a pretty bauble at your throat. No doubt he would take great pleasure in relieving you of it. That and more." Mrs. Chadwick nodded knowingly.

Julianna raised her brows.

"Oh, indeed," put in her mother. "Why, the tales we've heard . . . they're not to be spoken of in polite company."

Mr. Chadwick finally spoke. "What nonsense is this?"

" 'Tis not nonsense, Charles!" His wife thrust her chin out. "A lady would not want to fall into his hands, for she would surely suffer a fate worse than death, and I think I need not expound on the matter! The man is a devil—'tis said he even has the devil's eyes—and everyone knows it!"

Her meaning was not lost on Julianna, whose smile froze. Until that moment, she'd actually found herself wishing for a little adventure . . . She chewed the inside of her cheek and reconsidered. For all the notoriety surrounding the Magpie, the papers in London had said nothing of his ravaging women.

Wringing her hands, Mrs. Chadwick glanced anxiously out the window. "Oh, but I do hope the driver hurries. I want to be home before dark. I won't feel safe until we're settled before the fire with a nice cuppa."

Charles Chadwick lifted his gaze heavenward. "For the love of God, missus, will you stop your whinin'! If the Magpie should waylay us, by God, I swear I shall put you on his horse myself and bid you good riddance!"

Mrs. Nelson gasped. "Well, I never!" Her mother glared daggers at her son-in-law.

Julianna directed her eyes to her lap, biting back a laugh. The four of them lapsed into silence.

They passed through several more villages but no more passengers joined them. It was late in the afternoon when the coach began to slow. Leticia Chadwick had scooted to the edge of the seat even before they came to a halt before a small tavern. "At last," she nearly sang out, then turned to Julianna. "May your journey be a safe one."

Julianna smiled her good-bye, welcoming the rush of clean air that swept in when the door opened. It was cool and fresh, with no stench of coal and smoke. It was good to be away from London, she decided. The decision to go to Bath had been an impetuous one, but she would so enjoy the chance to rest and catch her breath from the hectic pace of the Season, which was in full swing.

The trio disembarked. Julianna had wondered about their state of marital bliss—they were clearly not in the first blush of youth. She looked on when Charles Chadwick took his wife's arm protectively as they crossed the street. Leticia glanced up at him, a wisp of a smile on her lips. An odd ache filled Julianna's throat, an ache for what might have been . . .

Deliberately, she looked away.

No other passengers boarded. The coach did not linger. The driver shouted, and they were off. The wheels cracked and rumbled as they began to gain speed.

It wasn't long before the walls of darkness began to close in. She found herself peering out the window, anxiously searching the side of the road, trying to see behind every tree and bush until she began to grow dizzy. Oh, but this was silly, she chided herself, to be spooked by the Chadwicks' talk of highwaymen!

She forced herself to relax. Eventually, the roll and lurch of the coach lulled her into drowsiness. As she swayed with the rhythm of the coach, her eyes drifted shut.

The next thing, she felt herself tumbling to the floor. Jarred into wakefulness, she opened her eyes, rubbing her shoulder where she'd landed. What the deuce . . . ? Panic enveloped her; it was pitch-black inside the coach.

And outside as well.

She was just about to heave herself back onto the cushions when the sound of male voices punctuated the air outside. The coachman . . . and someone else.

"Put it down, I s-say!" the coachman stuttered. "There's nothing of value aboard, I swear! Mercy," the man blubbered. "I beg of you, have mercy!"

Even as a decidedly prickly unease slid down her spine, the door was wrenched open. She found herself staring at the gleaming barrels of twin pistols. In terror she lifted her gaze to the man who possessed them.

His eyes were all that was visible of his features. Even in the dark, there was no mistaking their color. They glimmered like clear, golden fire, pale and unearthly.

The devil's eyes.

"Nothing of value aboard, eh?"

A gust of chill night air funneled in. Yet it was like nothing compared to the chill she felt in hearing that voice . . . So softly querulous, like steel tearing through tightly stretched silk, she decided dazedly.

She had always despised silly, weak, helpless females. Yet when his gaze raked over her— *through* her, bold and ever so irreverent!—she felt stripped to the bone.

Goose bumps rose on her flesh. She couldn't move. She most certainly couldn't speak. She could not even swallow past the knot lodged deep in her throat. Fear numbed her mind. Her mouth was dry with a sickly dread such as she had never experienced. All she could think was that if Mrs. Chadwick were there, she might take great delight in knowing she'd been right to be so fearful. For somehow Julianna knew with a mind-chilling certainty that it was he . . .

The Magpie.

Two

$\mathcal{D}$ane Quincy Granville did not count on the coachman's reaction—nor his rashness. There was a crack of the whip, a frenzied shout. The horses bolted. Instinctively, Dane leaped back, very nearly knocked to the ground. The vehicle jolted forward, speeding toward a bend in the road.

The stupid fool! Christ, the coachman would never make the turn. The bend was too sharp. He was going too fast—

The night exploded. There was an excruciating crash, the sound of wood splintering and cracking . . . the high-pitched scream of the horses.

Then nothing.

Galvanized into action, Dane sprang for Percival. He raced ahead. Leaping from the stallion's back, he hurtled himself down the steep embankment where the coach had disappeared. Scrambling over the brush, he spied it. It was overturned, resting against the trunk of an ancient tree.

One wheel was still spinning as he reached it.

The horses were already gone. So was the driver. Their necks were broken, the driver's twisted at an odd angle from his body. Dane felt for a pulse, but he had seen enough of death to know it was too late.

Miraculously, the door to the main compartment had remained on its hinges. In fury and fear, Dane tore it off and lunged into the compartment.

The girl was still inside, coiled in a heap on the roof. His heart in his throat, he reached for her, easing her into his arms and outside.

His heart pounding, he knelt in the damp earth and stared down at her. "Wake up!" he commanded. As if because he willed it, it would be so . . . He gritted his teeth, seeking to instill his very will—his very life—inside her.

Her head fell limply over his arm.

"Dammit, girl, wake up!"

He was sick in the pit of his belly, in his very soul. If only the driver hadn't been so blasted skittish. So hasty! He wouldn't have harmed them, either of them. On a field near Brussels, he'd seen enough death and dying to last a lifetime. God knew it had changed him. Shaped him for all eternity. And for now, all he wanted was—

She moaned.

An odd little laugh broke from his chest, the sound almost brittle. After all his careful planning that *this* should occur . . . But he couldn't ascertain her injuries. Not here. Not in the dark. He must leave. Now. He couldn't afford to linger, else all might be for naught.

The girl did not wake as he rifled through the boot, retrieving a bulging sack and a valise. Seconds later, he whistled for Percival. Cradling the girl carefully against his chest, he lifted the reins and rode into the night.

As suddenly as he had appeared, the Magpie vanished into the shadows.

She was still unconscious a short time later, when he shouldered his way into a small hunting cottage. His stride as surefooted in the dark as in the light of day, he strode to the bed on the far wall and eased her down.

He made quick work of replenishing the fire, then returned to her. His manner briskly impersonal, his long-fingered hands slid over her, checking for broken bones.

She'd sustained a few cuts and bruises. The worst of the damage appeared to be a nasty crack on the back of her skull. It was swollen, the skin broken. When his fingers moved over it, she flinched. Rising, Dane fetched a basin of warm water and several strips of linen. Returning to the bedside, he cleaned the wound, his gaze roving over her as he worked.

Half a dozen thoughts washed through him. Quickly he revised his opinion. She was young, yet hardly in the first blush of youth. Her build was slight, her shoulders narrow; why, she'd hardly weighed much more than a child, he recalled absently. But delicately made though her body was, she was no girl, he decided with a black smile. She wore a traveling gown of striped watered silk buttoned up to her chin. Expensive fabric and expensive taste, he suspected. Both her clothing and fine-boned features declared her well breeched, a woman of wealth and privilege, a lady of quality. Impatiently, he loosened the buttons. How the devil could women even breathe in such clothing?

His gaze returned to her face. The point of her chin, delicate though it was, warned of a nature most purposeful. Nor had nature failed her, he decided. He suspected her eyes—had they been open—would be incredible. He could see each separate lash, thick and black and full, resting on the elegant sweep of her cheeks. Vaguely he wondered what color they were . . . Blue, he decided, for her skin was fairest ivory. There was a pixie quality about the narrow span of her face, the

slant of her brows. Her bonnet was gone; her hair
had come hopelessly undone, a wealth of rich,
chestnut strands that tumbled over the narrow set
of her shoulders.

His eyes narrowed, a silent speculation. What
the devil was a woman like this doing traveling
alone, without maid or companion to accompany
her? Even as the question simmered through his
mind, his regard settled on her hand.

She wore no ring, either wedding or betrothal.
So. No husband. No fiancé either.

Dane was well aware that had he been able to
glimpse his expression, it would have been im-
passive. His insides were not, however. A ripen-
ing awareness slipped over him, a subtle
tightening of his insides, yet his mind remained
curiously detached. While her body was hardly
lush, her mouth most certainly was . . . She was
not at all the kind of woman to whom he was
usually attracted. When he touched a woman, he
wanted to *know* she was a woman. He liked
warm, mature curves and lush womanhood filling his palms. This one—whoever she was!—was
too small, too slight. Indeed, he thought, uncon-
sciously measuring the slim length of her neck,
she was nearly given to scrawniness. So why this
strange, unsettling sensation curling low in his
belly?

It came as a shock to realize he gripped her
hand between his own—he hadn't even realized

he'd taken it! He dropped it as though he'd been burned, yet in the very next instant, he found himself tucking a blanket up over her shoulders.

Nor was it just his own behavior he found most perplexing.

A lean, furry body had leaped with effortless ease upon the bed. His brows shot high when the feline ignored him outright, stretched his long body against the chit's side, and proceeded to purr for all he was worth. Dane stared in amazement.

"Maximilian, you little traitor! This is most unlike you. I would remind you this chit is a stranger, and you take exception to strangers most vehemently. Indeed, I thought you disliked everyone but me most vehemently."

Huge, slanted yellow-green eyes blinked owlishly at him.

Dane sighed. "All right, all right, I admit it," he said aloud. "She is rather fetching, isn't she? In truth, she's *most* fetching."

The cat's purring grew louder. Reaching out, Dane ruffled the fur on his back, a faint smile on his lips.

But in the next instant, his mouth thinned. His expression turned grim. The lady was so still. So quiet. He'd seen head injuries before. It was possible she might never wake.

And if she did . . . well, then what? That was another matter entirely.

He did not wish her dead. He wished no one

dead! But Dane was not pleased that the fates chose to carry her into his path. Her presence was an unexpected—and most unwelcome—complication. He sighed. Yet it was beyond his power to change the fact that she was here. No, he could change nothing.

Maximilian looked up at him, stretched, and leaped lightly up to his shoulders.

Dane reached to scratch the creature's neck. "All we can do is wait, eh, my friend?"

Settling his length along the back of Dane's shoulders, Maximilian purred his agreement.

At almost the very same instant, Julianna stirred. Some innate sense she hadn't known she possessed sent prickles of alarm all along her skin. Something was wrong. Her head felt twice its size. She didn't want to move, for it was as if her limbs were weighted by lead. But there was softness beneath her. She was lying on a bed, she realized, smothered in warmth. Prying open first one eye, and then the other, she discovered her surroundings were laden in shadow. She stirred, only to have a knifelike pain shoot through her head. Gasping, she stilled into immobility. What on earth . . . ?

Little by little, she relived the scene on the roadway. Her thought processes were slow, almost tortuous, like slogging through wet sand. The gleam of pistols flashed in her mind's eye.

She recalled the jolting motion of the coach, flinging her hands up to catch herself . . .

Then nothing.

But now, she was here, in this strange place.

And so was he. The Magpie.

Watching her.

She could almost feel the hair stand up on the back of her neck, the bead of sweat pop out along her upper lip. Straining to see through the filmy shadows, for nary the light of even a single candle filled the void, only the eerie glow of dying embers from a fire, Julianna found herself in the grip of an unsettling awareness. Two things came to her in the space of a single heartbeat. There was something strange about his silhouette, she realized. His shoulders were odd and misshapen—sweet Lord, he was a hunchback!

That . . . and the fact that his mask was gone.

The sight gave rise to a stomach-churning fear. Still, she struggled to see him. Alas, she could discern nothing but the sharp blade of his nose, the broad sweep of his brow. There was a nightmarish cast to the room, to *him*. Her mind seemed capable of registering only darkness and shadows, shadows that seemed to undulate and shift from every corner, surrounding him, as if to shield him. Indeed, it was like a hazy mist clung to his form, dark and impenetrable. He turned then, facing her fully. Beneath thick black brows his eyes were aglow in the dark, golden and burning . . . the devil's eyes, a demon's eyes, just as Mrs. Chadwick predicted, Julianna thought vaguely.

He stepped close.

A chill went through her at the touch of those eyes. The pounding rhythm in her head matched the rampant rhythm of her heart. Her thoughts twisted and turned, like gnarled branches in the forest. He loomed above her like a black monster.

"So. You're awake then, mistress."

Mistress. It is not mistress, Julianna thought argumentatively. Her lips parted. She licked her lips, prepared to tell him exactly that, but her tongue felt weighted and clumsy.

"Don't try to talk," came his voice. Soft, low, even melodious. "It was quite a tumble you took. Indeed, you were pitched and rolled like a ball in a child's game."

Kindness? Advice? From a dreaded highwayman? "Go back to hell whence you came," she heard herself mutter.

And she paid for it. Oh, how she paid for it! Pain lanced from one side of her head to the other and back again. She bit back a moan. She felt cold, clammy, sick to the very essence of her being.

"Noble words, lady. But I suspect you know little of hell."

It was in her mind to argue, but suddenly Julianna had neither the strength nor the inclination. Her eyes squeezed shut, and she felt the world fading away. Darkness and confusion swirled all around. She felt herself sliding toward oblivion once more. She fought it, but it was no use. In some distant, faraway corner, she felt the bed dip.

"*No.*" The soft protest was hers.

"It's all right. I won't hurt you."

She tried to speak once more. She tried with every ounce of her being. But her body, her mind, refused to obey. And then the hard, heavy length of this great hulking man stretched out next to her. A part of her was appalled. She couldn't help but remember what Mrs. Chadwick had said. *He may well murder us in our beds.* This couldn't be happening, she decided vaguely. She—a very proper virtuous spinster—wasn't lying abed with a man next to her . . . and not just any man. A notorious highwayman.

A hunchback, she thought with a shudder.

It had to be a dream. Lud, a nightmare! When she woke, surely he would be gone.

But when next she woke, sunlight streamed all around her. The golden glow was surprisingly cozy, and the feeling gave her pause. Cautiously she moved her head. There was no answering pain this time, and she opened her eyes.

It was then she heard the splash of water. Her gaze followed the sound. The Magpie stood before a washbasin, clad only in boots and breeches. His head was down, the muscles of his arms knotted and keenly defined as he braced himself against the table.

Julianna's mouth went dry as she was given a heart-stopping view of his chest. She must surely have been dreaming last night, for there was nothing misshapen about his form, no hint of imperfection. No, she reiterated faintly, this was no hunchback to offend the eye or sensibility. Indeed, there was naught to be found in his form but a startling perfection. Every lean, solid inch of him was muscle and brawn. Amidst the dark, curly mat of hair on his chest, droplets of water sparkled like tiny jewels.

As if he sensed her regard, he slowly raised his head.

Their eyes caught.

It spun through Julianna's mind that his hair was dark and shaggy, too long for him to be considered a slave to fashion. And those eyes she had compared to the devil's were actually hazel, so light they were almost gold.

In that instant, Julianna's heart surely stood still. She wasn't sure which was more disconcerting— seeing him half-naked or knowing that this man had lain next to her the night through. Though it cost her pride mightily, she did not avert her eyes from his.

His voice, when he spoke, was like the Scotch

whisky her brother Sebastian favored—dry but laced with a touch of silky smoothness. "So," he murmured, arching one dark brow. "That was quite a nap you took. Indeed, for a time I was afraid you would not wake."

Julianna said nothing, merely watched him warily as she sat up. "I would have thought you'd rejoice if I hadn't woken."

"Why is that?"

"I've seen your face." The admission came without thought, without volition.

For the longest time he said nothing. When he spoke, his voice was almost deadly quiet. "So you have," he returned at last. "So you have."

Julianna looked at him sharply. Alas, she could gauge nothing of his meaning from his expression.

"I suppose you're nursing a bit of a headache. That's quite a lump you have there."

Julianna's hand went automatically to the back of her head. Indeed, there was a sizable knot there that made her wince.

His brows shot up. "What! Did you think I was a liar?"

Julianna sent him what she hoped was a suitably quelling glare.

"I'm not, you know."

"Oh? You are a highwayman, sir. I suspect you're many things, all of which are quite despicable."

"Ah, so you're feeling rather peevish again, are you?"

Julianna angled her chin high. "Where is the coachman?" she demanded. "Are you holding him here as well?"

Something flickered across his face, something that made her go cold inside. "He's gone," he said briefly.

"Gone," Julianna repeated. "What do you mean?"

He simply looked at her.

Her lips parted. "What," she said faintly. "You mean he's . . . dead?"

"Yes."

Julianna's eyes widened. For all that she couldn't decipher *him,* she was unaware her expression conveyed her every nuance of thought. "I . . . Mercy, you mean you . . . you . . ." She couldn't seem to complete the thought.

He took her meaning immediately. "I did not harm him," he said flatly, shrugging on his shirt. "He was dead when I reached him."

"Oh." Julianna averted her gaze. Tears filled her eyes. She blinked them back before he could see.

Beneath the covers, something brushed against her legs. Something she couldn't see. With a screech, she hurtled from the bed.

"You've rats in here!"

He caught her when she would have rushed past him. "It's only Maximilian."

"What, you've names for them?" She was aghast.

To her shock, he threw back his head and laughed, a low sound that was oddly pleasing— which left her *most* confused.

With a hitch of his chin, he indicated the bed she'd just vacated. "Look," was all he said.

Julianna glanced behind her, just as a shiny black head and two pointed ears popped out from beneath the coverlet. A long, fuzzy body followed. A *cat,* she realized in amazement, at first dumbfounded, then feeling profoundly like a fool. Huge yellow-green eyes regarded her in unblinking curiosity. The animal tipped its head to the side, as if in silent query.

"Meet Maximilian," said the robber. "He appears to have taken a liking to you, a fact that quite frankly surprises me to no end. Generally, Maximilian is a creature of most discerning taste."

"I can see that if he is attached to *you,*" Julianna retorted.

"Ah, a cheeky wench."

"Wench!" Julianna sizzled. Never in her life had she been called a wench. Why, no one would dare! That *he* had roused in her a seething rage. Drawing in a deep breath, Julianna prepared to heap upon him a most scathing denunciation.

Two things dawned on her in that instant, however. Rather belatedly she realized she was still clutching at him; indeed, she was wrapped around him in a most unseemly manner!

The second was the feel of him beneath her fingertips.

All at once she felt several degrees warmer. The bottom seemed to drop out of her belly, for he was as solid and unyielding as a rock, as hard as if he were fashioned of pure granite.

She attempted to step back; it appeared he had other intentions.

His hold on her tightened. He gave a slight shake of his head. His grip was not hurtful, but Julianna was acutely aware of those strong, masculine hands curled around her shoulders.

"You were alone in the coach," he said abruptly. "Why?"

Julianna looked him straight in the eye. "I am of an age, sir, where I am hardly in need of a chaperone."

"And do you always travel without a maid?"

"My maid was ill. I sent her back to London," she said levelly.

"And where were you going?"

Julianna lifted her chin. "To Bath," she told him evenly. "To my home."

"Who awaits you there?" He shot off questions, one after the other, like a firing squad.

"My husband," she said quickly.

His eyes narrowed. Before she could stop him, he snatched up her hand and held it high.

"You wear no ring nor have you ever," he stated flatly. "You, lady, are neither wed nor betrothed."

Dismay shot through her. And yet he was wrong, she decided wildly. She'd once worn Thomas's betrothal ring . . .

"I will ask you once more. Who awaits you there?"

Panic raced through her. Julianna tried to disguise it. "I told you, my husb—"

"My dear lady," he stated very deliberately, "I am a man of instinct. Why, my very life depends on it! Indeed, my very life depends on what I read in people's faces—and what I read in yours tells me that you are a liar. It tells me that no one is expecting you. So pray do not insult me by seeking to deceive me."

Julianna felt as if she'd been hit in the chest by a tremendous weight. By Jove, he was right. Peggy would surely think that she had already arrived in Bath. The servants in Bath did not know to expect her arrival. If either of her brothers called on her, or inquired as to her whereabouts, they would be told she was in Bath.

No one knew where she was. *No one.*

"What is your name?"

Her mouth opened. Her first instinct was to haughtily inform him her brother was the Marquess of Thurston; it was hastily revised. If he knew her real name, he might easily demand a ransom—it was altogether possible he could have her killed while collecting it!

Her mind was racing, yet she was amazingly calm, even brave, as she answered evenly. "I am Miss Julianna Clare." It was true; the omission of her surname was deliberate. Holding her breath, she forced her eyes to his. She was no fool. If she looked away, he would take it as a sign she was lying.

"And yours, sir? What is your name?"

Her response was much more swift than his. He had yet to release her hand, but rather gave a little bow over it. Manners from the Magpie! She wasn't sure if she was outraged or impressed.

"You may call me Dane."

Neither one of them fooled the other. Julianna was very certain the lack of *his* surname was just as calculated.

He straightened to his full height. Another calculated move, she suspected. Despite her determination not to be cowed, there was a sudden sharpness in his regard that gave her pause. There was something unrefined and unrestrained about this man, something that suddenly made her mouth go dry and her heart go all a-tumble.

She looked up—forever it seemed—until she felt as if her neck would surely crack! A man as big as her brothers was a rare man indeed. To struggle would prove futile. He was a large man, a strong man, a *bold* man. At such close range, he was even more imposing than he had appeared last night, wearing a mask and holding his pistols. His features were sharply arresting, his jaw squarely defined, his nose carved in perfect balance between the sculpted planes of his cheekbones. He was too masculine to be considered truly handsome—an artist would have tried to soften those uncompromising features. But somehow his hard face was the perfect setting for those lavish eyes, their clear gold brilliance enhanced by thick black lashes.

Her reaction to him was intense. *He* was intense. But suddenly his eyes were like thick fog, dark and impenetrable. They made her shiver inside.

She considered him with renewed caution, as well she should. He was, after all, a dangerous highwayman. A demon. For all she knew, a despoiler of women.

Even worse, as if he knew precisely the vein of her thoughts, he smiled slowly.

"What are your plans for me?" she asked stiffly.

A dark brow quirked high. "An excellent question," he appeared to muse. "I'm not, you see, in the habit of taking hostages."

Julianna couldn't help it. Though she'd told herself she would not shirk, she would not cower, she felt herself pale.

"Yes," he said softly. "I see you've grasped the crux of the situation. What *am* I to do with you? I can hardly let you go, now can I?" He shook his head. "Yet I dislike the word *hostage*."

Julianna held her spine stiff. "Would you prefer *prisoner*? Both are the same, are they not?"

"I suppose that's true." He stroked his jaw, as if to give the subject great thought. "Let us consider you . . . my guest. Yes, my guest."

"If I were your *guest*," Julianna observed coldly, "I could leave when I wish. And I cannot, can I?"

Something flickered across his features, something she couldn't decipher. Surely not guilt.

"No," he said after a moment. He spoke the word almost regretfully, yet there was the merest hint of a smile on his lips.

Oh! Was he feeling smug? Exactly what came over her then, Julianna could never say. She was suddenly fighting mad, angrier than she'd ever been in her life that he dared to trifle with her so.

Without hesitation she stepped around him, taking a direct path toward the door.

His smile was wiped clean. "Where the devil do you think you're going?" He reached for her. Julianna eluded him, swooping under his arm and darting for the portal. Quick as she was, he was quicker, grabbing her from behind and whirling her from her feet.

But Julianna was incensed. She fought for all she was worth, swinging her arms wildly. There was a *thunk!* as her elbow connected with something solid. Sensation zinged down her arm, but she paid no heed. The vile oath resounding above her head only made her all the more determined to land another blow.

It was impossible. The next thing she knew she was toppled back, the mattress beneath her. She gasped as a long, hard body followed hers down, and he was atop her. Sweet mercy!

Subdued but hardly beaten, held in place by the weight of his body and strong fingers curled around her wrists, she toyed with the notion of spitting in his face—a tactic never before employed in her life!

Above her the highwayman—Dane—gritted his teeth. "Do not dare!" he warned.

"You wretched beast!" she hissed, launching into a tirade the likes of which she hadn't even known she was capable. "You won't get away with this! You'll be caught and hung. Drawn and quartered. The authorities will take your body and—"

"Are you quite finished?" he demanded.

She regarded the cut just above his eye with a considerable amount of satisfaction. No doubt he wasn't feeling so smug, she decided. "I am not—"

"Oh, but you are. My God, you are a harridan. A shrew."

"How dare you!"

He continued as if she hadn't spoken. "Lord, but you're a bloodthirsty little thing, aren't you? And to think when I first saw you I deemed you a lady of remarkable gentility! But now I begin to see why you have no husband!"

"Must you insult me?"

Cool golden eyes stared directly into hers. "It is no insult but fact. And now that I have your undivided attention, I feel it only fair to inform you, my little kitten—"

"Don't call me that!"

He shook his head. "It's never wise to underestimate one's enemies, *kitten*, and I do believe you should heed my warning. I've more experience than you at this kind of thing."

"Meaning?"

He smiled, not a particularly nice smile. "I'm a thief. A brigand. A man wanted by the Crown. You can hardly predict what I might do now, can you?"

Julianna took a deep breath. Her blood was beginning to run cold. "You won't hurt me."

"What makes you so certain? You've seen my face, remember."

Julianna did not appreciate the reminder. "You wouldn't have brought me here," she said with far more certainty than she felt. "You'd have left me in the coach. And though I wish I could say otherwise, I've nothing of value with me, save the necklace I wear. No other jewelry, no—"

"Perhaps I brought you here for another purpose."

"What purpose?" Too late, she realized the foolishness of such a question. Stupidly, she realized she hadn't considered the possibility, not really.

But apparently he had. Or at least he *was*.

His gaze slid down her neck, unabashedly irreverent. Julianna drew a sharp breath, only to realize his attention was not riveted on the lace edge of her bodice. Glancing down, she was shocked to confront soft, pink flesh—the weight of his body had thrust up her breasts so that they were nearly half-exposed. She tried to wrench her arms down, but his fingers tightened ever so slightly.

"Perhaps I brought you here for my own"— there was a telling pause, a wicked arch of brow—"amusement. After all, we're alone in this cottage, kitten, just the two of us."

Julianna's throat closed off. She couldn't breathe. For the space of a heartbeat, she literally could not find a scrap of air in her lungs. She blanched, locking her lips to keep them from trembling.

What a fool she was! Had she really wished for a little adventure? Now she wished for all the world that she could take back her earlier words.

But if he expected her to cower, she wouldn't. Pride alone forbade it. She swallowed painfully. "Then do what you will. I won't fight you." It was a statement made with quiet dignity. "But you may as well know I'll find no pleasure in it."

Something flickered across his face. "Bravely spoken. But you may set your mind at ease. I will not force upon you a fate worse than death. Your virtue is safe . . . at least for the moment. Another time, perhaps. For now, I've other things to do."

He mocked her. He wounded her. But he let her go, and as he did, an icy tremor shot through her. The instant she was free, Julianna scrambled up against the wall, as far away from him as she could get.

He pulled a shirt over his head, then moved to retrieve a dark cloak from a hook on the wall, along with a black silk mask—his costume from the previous night, she realized. Folding them neatly, he put them into a small pouch and tugged the drawstring tight.

"You're leaving?" she asked. Drawing her knees against her chest, she regarded him.

"Oh, you need not fret," he said smoothly. "I'll be back, I promise."

"What? More coaches to rob? More women to kidnap?"

"I think not. The bed would be rather crowded

with three of us, don't you think? Though perhaps the idea does hold merit."

Did her tormentor see her blush? She had the disconcerting sensation he did, and that he delighted in it. "You're quite despicable." Her tone conveyed her disgust.

"So you've told me."

"And I have no intention of sleeping with you in this bed."

His smile was naught but a charade. "You slept with me last night, kitten." The silken undertone in his voice was decidedly seductive.

"And I won't be doing so again!" she told him heatedly.

He laughed, the rogue, he laughed! "What righteous indignation! Why, if your behavior is any indication, I could almost believe you've never shared a bed with a man before."

Julianna had no intention of dignifying such a comment. But she sucked in a breath when he approached again. It was all she could do not to launch herself from the bed. Miraculously, she held her ground.

Did he smile? Did he smirk? Still wearing that infuriating whatever-it-was expression, he leaned close. "You may as well know right now, we are in the middle of the forest, far from the nearest village. And no, I have no intention of telling you precisely *where* we are. So you can scream all you want, though it won't do any good. There's no

·

one to hear, you see." He ran a finger down her nose. "And now, *adieu*, my little kitten."

She slapped his hand away. "Stop calling me that!"

With a swagger he started toward the door. Ah, but somehow she'd known he would swagger, the arrogant oaf! Julianna was not yet finished. "Don't be surprised if I'm not here when you return!" she spouted.

That stopped him dead in his tracks. Slowly he turned, arching a brow in almost lazy amusement. "Perhaps the blow to your head has affected your hearing. So I will say again, there's no way you can escape. And I would hate to have to bind your hands and feet, though I will if that's what it takes to convince you. I fear it would be most unpleasant, however."

"You wouldn't dare," Julianna said with all the haughtiness she could muster.

His smile vanished, as quickly as if it had never been. "Wouldn't I? You won't be leaving here, kitten, and I will take whatever means I must to assure that you don't. The sooner you resign yourself to that fact, the better off you'll be. For you see, there is a limit to a man's patience—to *my* patience—so if you are wise, you will not tempt me. You will not test me, for you may well regret it."

His speech was delivered with matter-of-fact ease, yet his countenance was no less than forbidding, the bite in his tone unmistakable. Turning his back on her, he opened the door and disappeared outside, yanking the door tightly behind him. The next thing she heard was a key scraping in the lock.

Julianna gaped, sinking back against the wall, her spine like mush. Had she been standing, she would have surely collapsed, for her knees were still shaking! Unfamiliar though it was, she tasted fear in her mouth, and acrid and bitter it was!

Did he intend some darker purpose? Rape? Murder? Merciful Lord, had he just threatened her life?

Oh, if she only knew! For all her defiance—for all his lighthearted mockery—he frightened her.

For he had made his point well . . . and well indeed.

She could not forget. She was at the mercy of a treacherous brigand. A highwayman. The Magpie. For all she knew . . .

A most lethal killer.

Three

Dane had not lied. Miss Julianna Clare had been unconscious for so long he'd feared she might never awake. He was heartily glad her injury wasn't serious. For all the fragility of her appearance, it appeared she was a lively one—to say nothing of the fact that she was passing fair.

Gingerly, he fingered his eye. The skin beneath was puffy and broken. By God, the wench had drawn blood! He was amazed, outraged—and admiring, all at once.

Yet his mouth turned down as he whistled for Percival. Whom did he fool? No one but himself, it seemed. The chit was more than passing fair, far more.

She was a beauty, the likes of which stirred his blood in a way that hadn't happened in a long while. He'd watched her as she slept, the light from the morning sun spilling in through the window and lighting the hair that spilled on his pillow with sun-burnished gold. It had taken all his will to crawl from the bed this morning.

Saddling Percival, he pondered further. The lovely Julianna was clearly well-mannered, well-born, well fed, and well educated. Her clothing came from the very best shops on Bond Street, unless he was very much mistaken, and Dane was quite sure he wasn't. No twittering young debutante was the lady. Ah, yes, she was already past the first blush of youth. If he had to guess, he would put her age at somewhere just beyond her midtwenties.

But she was untried. Untouched, when it came to the ways of men. Dane would stake his life on that.

And the certainty aroused him undeniably.

Mounting Percival, he glanced back toward the hunting cottage in the woods; it belonged to his family, but it had recently been put to another use . . . Oh, but he wished with all his heart that Miss Julianna Clare was ugly, her charms nonexistent, her beauty wilted and faded. He recalled how she'd leaped from the bed—straight into his arms—when she'd felt Maximilian beneath the covers. Why, she'd been practically crawling up his leg! A most disturbing sensation, that, he decided almost irritably.

He shifted on Percival's back. Just thinking of her had a very physical effect. It made his blood swell heavy and thick between his thighs. Very odd, for Dane was a man who prided himself on being a master of his emotions. Considering his line of work, he had to be . . .

Yet his mind continued to stray.

He'd been right about her eyes. They were incredible. Not just blue, but sheer, brilliant cobalt. He had to remind himself that those brilliant eyes were not alight with passion, her mouth soft with yearning and seeking his. Instead they were glacial and cold, her tongue as icy as a blast of wind from the most dreary winter skies. Considering her position, she'd been remarkably defiant. It was, he admitted reluctantly, a fascinating mix—both strength and delicacy.

Yet, truth be told, he liked her spirit, her poise, the fact that her brain wasn't stuffed with muslin. Under other circumstances . . . He dismissed the notion almost immediately. The circumstances were what they were. There was no changing them. He was pragmatic, if nothing else, for Dane had learned long ago that wishful thinking was for fools. Yet patience was also his strongest virtue, for a less patient man could not do what he did. The waiting, thinking, trying to predict . . . He had a temper, too, one that was rarely quick to arise, but dangerous when it did.

He was also a man of action, and in this particular case, he would simply have to adapt. Certainly it wouldn't be the first time! He reminded himself he was a man who could charm and cajole and lie with ease, threaten and bully, capture and win . . . whatever he was called upon to do.

He sighed. Of course he'd seen the way she shrank against the headboard. If she glimpsed a beast in him, well, that was well and good. If she was convinced he was dangerous, so much the better. And much as he'd have liked to have done precisely the opposite—kissed the lovely Julianna's sweet, pink lips until she melted against him in yielding trust and ardor, he would not.

Nor did the lady need to know that his dastardly reputation as the Magpie far exceeded his deeds. He had a reputation to maintain. Not as a womanizer, but as a robber.

For if Dane had learned anything throughout his adult life, it was this . . . Fear could be a good thing. It kept one's senses sharp and alert. Ah, yes, fear was good as long as it did not develop into a malignancy that obliterated all else and kept one from living. . . .

Death—and dying—was the one inevitability in life. He had come to that realization on the battlefield at Waterloo, with bodies littered all around—a day that haunted him still. A day that would haunt him forever.

Dying was the one thing he was afraid of.

No one knew, of course. Dane defied it, decried it . . . denied it.

He was no hero. He was simply lucky.

Ah, yes, death and dying terrified him. But that was his own cross to bear. His own private demon.

His own private hell.

Julianna's heart was still slamming wildly against her ribs when the lock clicked. Her head had begun to throb as well. The urge to rest her aching head in her hands and succumb to a good cry was almost overwhelming. But when Thomas had deserted her at the altar, she'd cried until there were no more tears left, until she was empty and dry. Tears had accomplished nothing then. Nor would they now.

She had changed since then. She would not be weak. She must be strong. She would not feel sorry for herself or bemoan her predicament.

Better to make use of her time alone. Better to find a way *out* of it. Better to find a way out, period.

But first she had a most urgent need. Spying a chamber pot in the corner, she quickly made use of it. Replacing the lid, she turned and gazed around the cottage, taking note of her surroundings. It startled her to realize that the bed on which she reclined was quite comfortable. And now that she took the time to examine it, the cottage itself was actually quite good-sized, in excellent repair and—most surprising of all, clean as a whistle. A pair of wing chairs sat before the wide stone hearth. A small table and two chairs stood nearby; it was then she noticed the plate in the middle of it. Suddenly realizing she was ravenous, she crossed to the table and sat. Whatever the Magpie's intentions, it wasn't to starve her.

Unwrapping a wedge of cheese and bread, she broke off a hunk. It was simple fare, yet in Julianna's mind, she'd tasted no finer meal served from the most delicate china and finest crystal. There was even a small bottle of wine—and quite excellent wine, at that.

As she sated her hunger, her mind continued to race. With outrage. With possibilities. The Magpie was not like any robber she'd ever imagined—not that she had an intimate acquaintance with men of his ilk! But he was right, she decided, finishing the last bite of cheese almost angrily. It was not wise to underestimate one's enemies. And if he were wise, he would not underestimate *her*.

Wiping her mouth, she eyed the massive cupboard across from her. A search revealed that it was well stocked. It also held the portmanteau she'd packed for the journey to Bath.

Julianna couldn't help it. She made a small sound of pleasure. So. Her captor had had the foresight to retrieve her belongings.

Careful, warned a voice. *Remember, there's a price on his head.*

It was a sobering thought. No doubt he'd only taken it believing there were jewels or such inside! Again her gaze roamed the room. There was something odd about it. It came to her slowly; and then she called herself every sort of bloody idiot. This was not, she realized, the cottage of a man of meager means. The furniture was sturdy and well crafted, no pallet on the floor but a proper bed; the bedding, even the wine, all spoke of comfort.

So. He was not just a robber, but a successful one.

Dusting off her hands, she got to her feet. The ache in her head had begun to subside, but she was still smarting inside that he'd locked her in, the wretch! Moving to the door, she tugged and pulled and rattled the latch, all to no avail.

Calmly, she assessed the windows. There were four in all, two on either side of the door. Discouragement shot through her, for they were tiny and set high in the wall. Even if she stood on a chair, she would never be able to climb through; it was too high.

Rubbish! He was right. His absence afforded no opportunity for escape.

It was then she spied a burlap sack in the corner next to the cupboard. Her hands on the ties, she paused, aware of a sliver of guilt. It was almost as if she were snooping in someone else's home without permission . . . which you are, chided a voice in her mind.

But certainly the circumstances were out of the ordinary. With that, she loosened the ties and peeked inside.

The bag was stuffed with banknotes! The thief!

Beside her, Maximilian rubbed up against her. "You should tell your master there are safer ways to make a living than stealing."

In answer, Maximilian thrust his head beneath her palm, seeking her touch.

With a sigh, Julianna moved to sit in the chair before the fire. Maximilian leaped lightly in her lap, kneaded her belly several times, then settled against her and closed his eyes.

Julianna stroked her fingers through his fur, glad for Maximilian's company, such as it was. Perhaps she should be ashamed, but if this was to be her temporary prison, she was glad it was at least a comfortable one. For it *would* be temporary, she promised herself. Clearly she wasn't going anywhere, not yet anyway. And since it appeared she had all the time in the world to ponder her method of escape, that was exactly what she would do.

*   *   *

Julianna spent the remainder of the day quietly.
By evening, her headache had subsided, and she
was feeling much better. She had no idea of the
time, other than to gauge it by the color of the sky
through the windows and the shadows seeping
into the cottage. The night aged, and for a time
she could see the moon shining high in the sky.

Still the Magpie did not return.

Her mind turned, refusing to be still. What if
he'd been caught? Captured? What if he'd been
strung up on the spot? No one would even know
she was here, wherever the devil that was!

The thought persisted. However much she disliked the wretch, she certainly had no wish to
see his neck stretched by a noose. Oddly, when
she finally crawled into bed, it was this thought
that kept her from sleep. Finally, she lit the bedside candle and lay back, staring at the ceiling.
Maximilian had nosed his way beneath the covers and warmed her side. Miraculously, she had
just begun to doze when she heard the key grate
in the lock.

The door swung wide. A rush of cool moist air
accompanied his entrance.

Julianna was instantly wide-awake.

There was a bag slung over his shoulder. He
handled it as though it weighed no more than a
bag of feathers, depositing it across the room beside the other.

He turned. His brows shot high. "So you're awake! I trust you had a pleasant day?"

Julianna leveled upon him a gaze of utter disdain. Her newfound friend, Maximilian, had already deserted her. He'd bounded from the bed at the sound of the key in the lock. Leaping onto the table, he jumped to his master's back and lay curled across his shoulders like a fur. In the back of her mind, it came to her that's what she had seen when she first awoke—and to think she'd thought her captor a hunchback!

Now two pairs of golden eyes surveyed her. He wore his arrogance like a medal of honor; it was there in the incline of his chin, the curl of his lips in that ever-so-confident smile.

Clad in black from head to toe, the very sight of him made a shiver run through her. He filled every corner of the room in a way that was utterly foreign to her, in a way that had naught to do with size, though his height and breadth and brawn proved impossible to ignore! For it was more than that, much more. Had the cottage been a hundred times larger, it would have made no difference. There was something about him that set her insides to quivering like pudding. Like it or not, his was a presence all-powerful, all-consuming. He commanded the eye . . . nay, he *demanded* it!

No fop here. No dandified Corinthian. She could smell the wind in his hair, the earth on his skin. He was quite handsome—he, a highway-man! She was stung by the acknowledgment, then struck by the strangest notion that despite the wildness she sensed in him, here was a man who would have been at home in the most elegant drawing rooms of the *haut ton*. It was a notion that left her puzzled. Confused.

Most shocking of all, consumed by utter fascination.

Oh, the deuce take him! Whatever was wrong with her? The blow to her head must have addled her senses!

"My dearest Julianna, you surprise me." He tossed his mask aside and removed his cloak, hanging it over the hook.

"My dearest *Dane*," she emphasized sweetly, "how so?" If he thought he could get the best of her, he was mistaken.

He approached, sending prickles of awareness over her skin.

"Under the circumstances, I might easily have had an hysterical female on my hands. But you do not call for your Maker. You do not call for help. Instead you seem quite calm."

Julianna glared. "What, do you have someone outside spying on me?"

He threw back his head and laughed as if she'd said something immensely amusing, a rich deep sound that might have been pleasing had it not been directed at *her*.

"You did make a point of warning me that screaming would serve no purpose," she reminded him.

"So I did. Nonetheless, as composed as you are, one could almost believe you are accustomed to being—" He paused.

"What? You think I've been kidnapped before? Hardly. Besides, what point is there in expending useless energy in melodramatics?"

"Precisely." He smiled. "But that you think so ill of me wounds me."

A chestnut brow arched in query.

"Oh, come," he said lightly. "I have yet to hear of your gratitude for my gallantry in rescuing you."

Julianna snorted, a most unladylike sound. Come to think of it, she was saying a lot of unladylike things. More strange behavior to dissect . . . or was it?

The rogue stood before her, strong hands propped on his hips, his stance straight as an arrow. And to think she'd been worried for his safety!

"A rescuer does not imprison his charge," she snapped, "or advise her that screaming will accomplish nothing."

"We could argue the point until dawn, but then we wouldn't get any sleep now, would we? And while I regret being such an inhospitable host and leaving you alone for so long, I suddenly find I am excessively weary."

He advanced toward the bed. Her guard went up as he nudged Maximilian from his shoulders, then stripped off his shirt. Confronted with the sight of his naked, hairy chest, her heart began to pound in thick, uneven strokes.

Julianna wet her lips. "I suggest a simpler solution. Let me go, and there will be no need for argument."

He said nothing, but bent to remove his boots.

Julianna had already scooted to the far side of the bed. "Please," she said again, a touch of ragged pleading to her tone now, "let me go."

"No."

His bluntness stung. He didn't even have the courtesy to look at her!

"Why not?"

He gave no answer.

She took a deep breath. "I can pay you. My father—he was a wealthy man. I have money enough—"

"I don't want your money."

He was growing impatient. She gestured to the two sacks in the corner. "Pray forgive me if I am skeptical!"

His eyes narrowed. "Ah," he said silkily. "Snooping, were we, kitten?"

Kitten again. Drat the man! "Snooping is not a criminal offense. Theft is!"

"I begin to think I should have bound you *and* gagged you. So now, if you don't mind, I should like to go to sleep." He lifted a corner of the coverlet.

Julianna glared. "Aren't you afraid I'll escape while you sleep?"

His slow-growing smile should have served as a warning. He paused, reached for the key he'd laid on the bedside table, and dropped it deep into the pocket of his breeches. Still wearing that smug smile, he climbed into bed beside her.

The pompous ass! Julianna fumed and turned her back on him, putting as much space as possible between them. With the key inside his breeches there was little she could do. She longed to flee while she had the chance, but she needed the key! How the devil was she to get it?

She was totally unaware that she tossed and turned until his voice split the night.

"For pity's sake, can you not be still!"

Julianna froze. Peering up through the shadows, she saw him glaring over at her, his scrutiny like the prick of a knife. "A few hours of rest is all I crave. Can you not oblige me?"

Julianna spoke not a word. A sense of helplessness assailed her. Releasing a long, uneven breath, she tore her eyes away from his accusing gaze.

Beside her, he raised up on an elbow. "What is this?" he demanded. "You've not decided to turn weepy on me now, have you?"

Her fingers clutched at the blanket. She stared

at the rafters on the ceiling. Stupidly, foolishly, she *did* want to cry.

Time stretched endlessly.

"I'm sorry," he said rather stiffly. "I neglected to ask you how you feel tonight."

Manners again! Who would have expected such from a highwayman? She jerked when a hand came down to rest on her shoulder.

"I'm fine," she said raggedly.

"Are you?" Lean fingers came up to graze her temple. "You're looking rather pale, my dear. Are you sure you're all right?"

"Yes," she said wildly. "No."

"Ah, I do so like a woman who knows her own mind."

Julianna wet her lips. "Well," she said in a tiny, quavering voice, "my head does ache a bit."

"You'll feel better in the morning. Try to sleep."

His manner was gruff, but there was a subtle softening in his tone. And his hands on her face . . . his touch was unexpectedly gentle. But now he turned his back and laid his head down.

Damn! The key was farther away than ever. There was no way she could retrieve it without waking him. Why, no doubt he slept with one eye open.

Julianna's mind was churning. Arguing had done no good. Pleading fared no better. She was clearly going to have to come up with another way to extricate herself from this dilemma, for she refused to spend another night lying next to this oaf! Oddly, she'd thought a man like him would be impervious to tears. Yet she had the strangest sensation he was discomfited at the thought of her weeping . . . What would he do if she burst into sobs? Would he let her go? Or would it merely make him angry?

Julianna was not quite willing to test the supposition . . . or him.

Time. She needed time to think. Time to plan her escape. She thought of her brother Sebastian, ever a great one for planning. There had to be a way out . . .

Somehow . . . some *way*.

Four

Dane was puzzled. He was also worried. He could not help it. From the moment the chit woke that morning, she had been unaccountably quiet. Wan and subdued throughout the day. And so weak she could barely stand! Why, he'd had to help her to the table to eat. Naturally, he'd insisted she remain in bed the rest of the day.

Surprisingly, she hadn't argued.

He couldn't help it. Her sudden frailty worried him. She'd sustained some lumps and bruises during the accident. But was it possible the bump on her head was worse than he'd thought?

Riding away from the cottage that evening, he paused and looked back. Damnation! He couldn't help but feel guilty over locking her in.

Tomorrow, he decided cautiously. If she wasn't

better tomorrow, he would simply have to fetch a physician.

Phillip wouldn't be pleased at the turn of events. Alas, it couldn't be helped.

Ten o'clock the next evening found him miles away, riding into a deserted clearing. His lovely guest was still very much on his mind.

Behind him, a twig snapped. Dane whirled.

"Phillip!"

His friend Phillip Talbot materialized from the shadows. "Either you're growing careless," he said, "or my skills are improving."

Dane merely raised a brow. He'd met Phillip shortly after returning from the battlefield, and it wasn't long before friendship sprung up between them. Beneath Phillip's affable manner and kindly features was a man of lightning-quick intellect. Dane greatly admired his attention to detail, his ability to foresee the unforeseeable.

Most of all, he trusted him implicitly . . . it was the same with Phillip.

A most necessary commodity in the affairs they conducted.

Phillip stared at his face. "What the devil happened to you?" he asked in astonishment.

Dane cursed the moon, which chose to slide out from beneath a cloud a moment before. He'd forgotten his black eye. Devoid of his mask, no doubt he was quite a sight.

"A slight accident," he said lightly.

Phillip wasn't fooled.

"Someone tried to darken your daylights. Who?"

With an economy of words, Dane told him about the carriage accident two nights earlier. Phillip was quiet for a moment when he finished.

"This is most unfortunate," he said. "I'd hoped there would be no more forfeiture of life."

"You of all people know that sometimes things happen we cannot predict."

Phillip nodded. "The lady's involvement complicates matters. What the devil are you going to do with her?"

"I'm not sure yet," Dane admitted, "but I'll think of something. She knows nothing, nor is she suspicious, and I intend for it to stay that way. Someday the chit will tell her grandchildren how she was kidnapped by a highwayman and lived to tell the tale. For now, I can't have her running to the authorities."

"Perhaps we could have her spirited away to the north. By the time she made her way back to civilization, perhaps this will be over."

Dane was shaking his head. "It would not be wise to involve anyone else. That, I fear, would increase the chances of being discovered." He paused. "But what of you? What of our quarry?"

"Covering his tracks well. What else can we expect when he's one of our own—and managed to murder two unsuspecting souls while making it appear an accident?"

"Yes, it was clever. A wet, rainy night and a runaway carriage . . . I doubt the pair of them even saw it coming. The poor woman's only crime was in overhearing her husband and that *rat*," Dane stated grimly. "All she wanted was to keep her husband from going back to prison. And the bastard is brazen enough to continue his plan."

"Brazen. Yes, the culprit is that, isn't he?" Phillip paused, then studied his friend. "As for you, my friend, the Magpie is garnering quite a reputation as well," he observed quietly. "You should hear what's being said about you, Dane. The people may soon be clamoring for your head."

"It can't be helped. We cannot openly conduct an inquiry. That would put the blackguard on alert, to say nothing of how it would embarrass the Home Office." Dane shrugged and offered a faint smile. "The Magpie shall ride until this bastard is caught."

Phillip's gaze sharpened. "This is not a game, Dane. What will you do if someone decides to shoot?"

"I'd best be quick and duck then, eh?" He gave a wink.

Phillip sighed. "Be serious! Barring that, what

will happen if you're caught? If that should occur, there's a good chance you'd be strung up before the Home Office could intervene."

"What, do you have so little confidence in
me?" Dane clapped a hand on Phillip's shoulder.
"I knew the risks at the outset, Phillip. There's a
reason you do what you do and I do what I do."

Phillip sighed. "You relish it, don't you? The
adventure, the danger?"

He had, once. But now . . . now Dane wasn't
sure. He was a man of action, not a man who
could sit back and bide his time. He hadn't
Phillip's patience. But the excitement was no
longer as satisfactory as it had once been . . .
why, he wasn't quite sure.

The smile he gave Phillip was inscrutable.

A breeze ruffled Phillip's light brown hair. "Do
you know," he said slowly, "I should love to be in
your place for just one night."

"You? A highwayman? An adventurer?"

"I admit, I envy you. I have for quite some
time."

Dane couldn't help it. He grinned and touched
the puffiness of his eye. "This is not to be envied,
my friend."

"Nonetheless, I think I should like the thrill,
the rush of the blood through my veins, the anticipation of never being quite sure what the next
moment will bring, yet being ready and willing

to face it unafraid. I daresay it would never be boring."

Dane lifted his brows. Unafraid? Ah, if he only knew . . . And, though keen of mind and sharp of wit, Dane had never considered that Phillip the strategist might long for something else.

"Is that not life?" he murmured. "The challenge of each new day?"

"I daresay my life is infinitely less exciting than yours, Dane."

Dane eyed him curiously.

"Ah, well," Phillip said. "Perhaps someday. For now there is work to be done."

"So there is," Dane agreed. He whistled for Percival.

"I should be off as well." Phillip brushed an insect from his coat, then looked over at Dane. "When shall we meet again?"

"Let us see how the game plays out for a time, eh? I shall contact you in London."

Phillip watched as Dane swung up onto Percival's back. "To success," Phillip said with a faint smile.

Dane inclined his head. "Indeed," he murmured.

With a brief salute he rode into the night.

Miles away in London, the streets of Westminster were nearly deserted. Within a small, brick-fronted house, Nigel Roxbury strode into a tiny study and picked up a sheaf of papers from the middle of his desk. In the corner, a tall pendulum clock ticked loudly.

Dressed in a worn black jacket, his was a face undistinguished by any particularly remarkable features—except for the patch that covered one eye. Shrewd, calculating, and tough were among the traits attributed to him by his colleagues. Still, he considered himself a relatively simple man. He did not aspire to wealth. God knew he was in the wrong profession for that. He did not whore or gamble or drink to excess. But he was a great admirer of all things ancient, the graceful simplicity and line.

He glanced at the clock. Almost midnight. Where the devil was she—

A knock sounded.

He strode to the door and threw it open. With a swish of her skirts, a woman entered, pulling back the veil that covered her face.

Though some ten years his senior, she was, he admitted, a woman who had aged most gracefully. Her skin was still ivory and smooth, her features elegantly refined, but there a glint of silver here and there streaked in her hair. Clad in a gown of the latest Parisian fashion, her petite form remained as slim as many a girl's.

"Greetings, *madame*!" He led her into the study. "Ah, you have something for me!"

She handed him a small box. Impatiently, he pulled off the lid and thrust aside the coarse yellow straw. His eyes gleamed as he lifted out a gleaning statuette. The light from the lamp glinted off the smooth gold surface.

"Glorious! Absolutely glorious!"

Taking a seat across from him, his visitor arranged her skirts over her knees.

"That piece is worth a fortune."

"And I am paying a small fortune for this and the other pieces you will bring."

"Yes," she said archly. "And I can only wonder how a man such as you can afford such pieces."

"Oh, come!" he admonished. "Must you look at me so? Why should only the rich indulge their passions? For twenty years I've longed for such treasures. Your late husband Armand and I shared a fascination for the splendors of Egypt. Oh, but he was a generous man to allow others to view them at their leisure! He chose to donate his collection to a museum. I find, however, that I am not so magnanimous."

"It is not your passion to which I object," the woman said coldly, "it is how you go about it."

"Ah, you mean *your* involvement. Come, a few pilfered pieces from the tombs of the ancients, otherwise destined for the art market! I can hardly compete with private collectors or museum buyers, can I? How fortuitous for me, though, that you remained acquainted with the curator's assistant François."

"Yes," she said shortly, "and I must pay him."

His eyes flickered. "I fear there has been a slight problem."

Her eyes flashed. "We had an agreement!"

"And it will be honored," he said irritably. "There has simply been a delay in the transfer of funds."

"The transfer of funds," she repeated.

Roxbury's expression hardened. "That damned highwayman the Magpie has seen fit to rob me," he said brusquely. "And François did insist on gold."

"I see. Perhaps there will be some delay, then, in the next transfer of your goods."

"It would not be wise to threaten me, *madame*. You know who you deal with. Neither of us wants to lose what we have, do we?" With a finger he traced the headdress of the statuette, admiring it once more before glancing at her. "We both have a great deal to gain. As you say, it is a mutually advantageous agreement, is it not?"

Her pointed chin came up. "I do not stand to profit from this."

"Oh, but you do," he contradicted. "And you know what will happen if you try to trick me. One word from me, and you won't be able to show your face anywhere in Europe. Your secret will be out. The estate you inherited will be lost. Your marriage to Armand Lemieux will be exposed as the sham it was should I choose to reveal you already had a husband! You will lose all you gained at Lemieux's death. Your life, as you know it, will end."

"I loved Armand!"

"And you certainly loved what he gave you, didn't you? But I find I'm curious. What of my brother? What of James? Did you love him too? He died, *madame*. He drowned, and you lived. I knew of your plan, you know. I always wondered that you took a fancy to a Roxbury, a man who was not upper-crust. James did always fancy himself a man about town, though, didn't he? I confess, it was he who taught me to appreciate the finer things in life." With his fingertips he caressed the statue. "Oh, but James was always a *bon vivant*, wasn't he? He pledged me to secrecy, you know, for I guessed about the two of you. What a man will not do," he mocked, "for love of a woman! Ah, but you did quite well without him, didn't you? I daresay, as Armand Lemieux's wife, you fared much better!"

"You are a cunning, crafty man. And quite ruthless."

"Thank you, *madame*."

"It was not meant as a compliment."

"Nonetheless, I take it as such." He caressed

the statuette once more, then set it aside. "When will the next piece arrive?"

She moved stiffly to the door. "I will send word."

His eyes glinted. "I anticipate our next encounter then with the utmost pleasure."

To his amusement, she did not echo the sentiment.

Dawn streaked the horizon when Dane let himself into the cottage. It had proved a fruitless night. He'd spent hours waiting for the coach, but his wait had been in vain. Frustrated, he finally departed for the cottage.

His mood was thoughtful as he unsaddled Percival and led him beneath a shelter that had been built next to the cottage. Was the culprit onto him? he wondered. He was reminded of Phillip. So it was excitement he craved, did he? For all that Phillip claimed he wished to be in his place for the night, he had the feeling Phillip would not have relished lying in wait on such a miserable evening.

The fire had burned down to embers. Dane threw a chunk of wood onto the grate. He stood a moment, watching the flames leap high. Finally, he walked over to stand above his captive.

She was sleeping soundly, her face turned away from him on the pillow. Dane released a breath of relief. Thank God. No doubt she would be back to plaguing him tomorrow, fiery and tart, which posed the question . . . What *was* he to do with her?

Sighing, he sat and removed his boots. He was too tired to search for answers. For the moment, he possessed neither the will nor the wit to do battle with a tongue such as hers. He was exhausted. Sitting, he removed his boots and his shirt. A few hours' rest was all he needed. Then he would be ready for a new day—and his unexpected charge.

Raising a corner of the blanket, he slid into the narrow space, taking care not to disturb her. She gave no sign of waking, but continued to slumber on. Dane closed his eyes.

Sleep claimed him. And in his sleep, he dreamed. Of *her*. Of the lovely Julianna. Dimly, he felt her slide above him. Oh, but she was fair and sweet, her beautiful hair swirling over his chest as she bent over him. He fancied he could see her, poised above him as one small hand daringly explored, skimming the grid of his belly.

He felt himself smile. It would be good with her, he decided. Indeed, it would be exquisite. Her hand was sliding down . . . down. Lower, he thought, willing her to cup his rod, to touch and explore. To feel him grow hard beneath her fingertips.

In some faraway part of his mind, he regretted the barrier of his breeches. Out of consideration for her sensibilities, he hadn't discarded them these last few nights. Her fingertips extended, a tentative venture. With dainty hesitance, almost stealthily . . .

With an oath, he vaulted from the bed.

The lovely lady was already on her feet. She was backing away. Her eyes were sizzling, pure, bright, and filled with blue fire.

She stopped. In her hands she held one of his pistols, aimed directly at the middle of his chest.

"Don't move!" she cried. "Stop right there."

Dane froze. Bloody hell! He'd been careless. He'd been foolish, and both might well come back to haunt him. Oh, but he should have known! He'd sensed her willfulness in the tilt of her chin.

"Give me the key," she said, her voice very low.

A dawning awareness slipped over him. Damn! he thought. She was neither meek nor weak, and quite insistent.

Bloody hell, this was what happened by letting down his guard. He should have known better. He *did* know better! Never again would he be so gullible.

"Well," he said. "It appears I underestimated you. You weren't ill, were you?"

Her lips pressed together.

"It was a ruse. A way to disarm me, I suppose." He paused. "I suppose you think you're very clever."

"Cleverness has nothing to do with it. You wouldn't let me go!" Her tone was accusing.

Their eyes met. Softly he said, "I was worried about you, kitten."

"Worried! You left me alone for hours on end."

"Not because I wanted to," he said immediately. And indeed, he hadn't. But if he hadn't shown up for his meeting with Phillip, it would have thrown everything into chaos. All would have been ruined.

"Why should I believe anything you say? From your own lips, you're a thief. A brigand!"

A logical assumption, he thought.

". . . and now I want that key!"

Dane shook his head. "And where would you go? I told you, we're in the middle of the forest, far from the nearest village. Would you rather be lost than here with me? I won't harm you." His tone was cajoling. "If that was my intention, I would have done so by now."

Dane eyed her, silently calculating the distance between them. She stood perhaps ten paces away. She was a well-bred young woman, clearly of privileged upbringing. It was a miracle she knew one end of a pistol from the other.

"If you want the key, you'll have to take it

from me. You'll have to get close. And who will have the advantage then, I wonder?"

Her eyes flickered.

"You won't shoot," he predicted.

"I will! Do you think you know me so well? You do not know me at all, sir! Now put your hands up!"

Damn! His hands inched up, while he eyed the barrel, which was level with his chest. "Yes. But have you ever seen a dead man?"

"I have. My father."

"Perhaps I should rephrase. Have you ever seen a man die? Have you ever seen a man shot?"

"Stop it!" she said wildly. "I know what you're doing!"

"It's not a pretty sight," he continued. "Frankly, it's damned messy. Granted, that depends on where a man is shot. A head wound—"

"Cease!"

"You're sweating, kitten. I can see it from here. I think if you were to shoot me, you'd probably faint dead away." Her resolve was weakening. The tables were about to turn. Perhaps it was stubborn pride, but he was reasonably certain his instincts hadn't deserted him entirely.

His eyes bored into hers. "I thought you were going to shoot."

"I am. I will!" She swallowed hard. She was faltering, the barrel of the pistol wavering.

"Then do it," he dared.

She retreated a step. "Stay there!" she said shakily.

Smug now, Dane took a step forward.

Julianna squeezed her eyes shut, turned her head aside . . . and fired.

Five

*I*t was most odd how it happened . . . It was not pain, but shock that filled his mind. His heart seemed to sputter, then resumed with hard, thudding strokes. A sensation of blinding heat was spreading through his chest. He couldn't breathe. Was this how it would happen then . . . ? God rot it, this scrap of a woman had managed what Napoleon's army could not do. His knees weakened. Damnation! He would not swoon like a woman—by God, he would not! Yet fear washed through him—the secret fear that no one knew of. A hundred things passed through his mind in that instant.

Still stunned, he raised incredulous eyes to hers. But she wasn't there . . . Sweet Christ, he might die . . . and the chit was rifling through his pockets.

After that blasted key.

The sound was deafening. Hearing it, Julianna dropped the pistol; she was dimly aware of it clattering across the floor. For the space of a heartbeat, she couldn't see. The acrid smell of smoke filled the air before her and burned her throat. When it cleared, she saw him.

The shot had brought him to his knees.

A curious haze seemed to surround her; she saw herself as if through a dark mist. Almost before she knew what she was about, she was at his side, thrusting her hand into the pockets of his breeches.

She emerged with the key to the door.

It glinted in her palm, catching the light from the window. She stared at it dumbly for an instant, then scrambled to her feet, nearly tripping in her haste. Bolting toward the door, she thrust the key in the lock; it clattered to the floor. With a cry she bent to retrieve it. Straightening, she looked from the key in her palm, back to his face.

Little did she realize it was a moment that would change her life forever.

Dane was wavering, his expression one of sheer disbelief. Julianna stood motionless, paralyzed by what she glimpsed there. Something naked. Something vulnerable. Something almost pleading.

She wasn't quite sure what she'd intended. Her thoughts were a wild scramble in her brain. She'd closed her eyes . . . she had no conscious recollection of pulling the trigger. The next thing she knew there was that dreadful explosion, and her ears were ringing.

She, who had always thought herself a tender-hearted soul . . . had just shot a man.

A sickening sense of shame spilled through her. What had she done? She was appalled. Horrified at her own behavior. She'd only meant to frighten him . . . a silly notion, that! As if a highwayman would be afraid of *her*!

But at least he wasn't dead. At least not yet anyway. She darted back toward him.

He was looking up at her. Gritting his teeth, he fought to stay upright. "Go," he said tightly. "Just go, damn you!"

But she couldn't. She knew then she couldn't leave him.

The effort seemed to expend all his strength. He pitched forward on the floor.

Kneeling beside him, Julianna shook his good shoulder, as if to jar him awake. "No!" she cried desperately. "No!"

Wrapping her arms around him, she tried to turn him over.

His eyes flickered open. He stared at her, almost as if he was angry. She knew it when his brows drew together fiercely over his nose. "Why the devil are you still here?"

"I shot you," she said grimly. "Now I'm going to save you."

He was right. There was blood. A good deal of it.

He had turned to his back. A bright red stain was blooming on the front of his shirt. Frantically, Julianna dug her fingers into the opening and ripped it away. Blood welled, pooling above his heart, thick and dark and crimson. Looking at it, the bitter taste of bile burned her throat.

"Julianna. Julianna."

The sound of her name wrenched her gaze to his.

Dane had pushed himself to a sitting position. "You're going to have to help me, kitten."

Julianna took a deep breath. Steadying her nerves, she slid her shoulder beneath his and slid an arm around his back. In truth she wasn't much help; his frame was too large. He'd have pinned her cold if he'd fallen. It was his own strength that got him to the bed. But as he lay back, she noticed how pale he was, his skin shades whiter than before. Beads of sweat dotted his upper lip.

"The bleeding must be staunched. There's a basket of cloths in the cupboard. Will you fetch them?"

Julianna scurried to obey, wadding up a clean white cloth and holding it to his shoulder.

"Press hard," he said. "I realize you're just a puny little thing, but try, will you, kitten?"

"Don't call me that!" Her breath was sawing in and out of her throat. It was half sob, half angry protest. Almost defiantly she leaned into him, using the heel of her hand to increase the pressure. Dane sucked in a scraping, labored breath.

It seemed to take hours before, at last, the bleeding slowed to a trickle. She could see the hole where the bullet had gone in. The flesh around it was black with gunpowder. Somehow she hadn't expected that, and it shook her to the core.

Dane released the air from his lungs and looked at her. He regretted what he had to tell her, but it had to be done. "I'm afraid your work isn't done yet, kitten. You're going to have to remove the bullet."

"What!" she said faintly.

"The ball is still in my shoulder."

She stared at him dumbly. Was he suggesting . . . "Maybe you're wrong. Maybe it—"

He was shaking his head. "If it had gone clean through, it would have gone out through my back. It didn't."

Julianna stared at him in horror. She shook her head wildly. "No. I can't—"

"Who else? You're the only one who can. I certainly can't. Besides, you said you were going to save me."

What had she been thinking, to say such a thing? Julianna's heart began to pound against her ribs. Hard, so very, very hard . . .

"You can do it, I know you can."

She wished she had as much faith in her abilities as he did. "How could you know that? You don't even know me."

"I think you are a woman with a remarkable will. And you have a steady hand, don't you?"

Julianna swallowed hard. "Tell me what to do."

"In the cupboard, you'll find a basin. In it you'll find everything you need. And bring the bottle of brandy that's there, too." His voice was beginning to show signs of pain.

Julianna did as he said. "My word, I could almost believe you were expecting this." Julianna unfolded a small leather case. In the pockets were a sharp-edged knife, another with a hook on the end, and a pair of tweezers. Another held needle and thread.

She sent him an incredulous look. "Surgeon's tools?" she asked in amazement.

One corner of his mouth crooked up, the tiniest smile. "Let us just say I believe in being prepared." In the aftermath, Dane felt a sheer and utter fool. He hadn't been prepared for *her* shooting him. Perhaps the wound had addled his senses, but he couldn't be angry with her. What she had done had taken a great deal of mettle.

Nor was Julianna surprised, once she paused to consider. It was a dangerous life he'd chosen.

She listened intently to his instructions. After dousing the knife with brandy, she gathered her courage and took it up. Her heart thundered so loud she could scarcely think.

Dane held up a hand. "Wait!"

Julianna stopped, the point of the knife poised over his chest. He grabbed the bottle and took several long swallows. He started to set it down, then paused.

"Perhaps you'd like some, too."

That she even considered it spoke to her state! She glanced pointedly at the knife in her hand. "I think not, sir. If I do, I won't have a steady hand, now will I?"

Her prim tone nearly set him off. A dull haze had settled over him. Whether it was pain or the effects of the brandy, he didn't know.

He leaned back. Quietly he spoke. "I'm ready," was all he said.

Uttering a fervent prayer, Julianna went to work.

Only once did Julianna brave a glance at his face; it was a mistake, for she nearly dropped the knife. He was as pale as winter's snow, his eyes squeezed shut. She wondered wildly if he'd passed out—indeed, she hoped he had. But then he swallowed, the cords in his neck standing taut.

Tears stood high and bright in her eyes. Tears she refused to allow to fall.

Perspiration gathered on her brow. How he could stand the probe of the instruments in his chest, she had no idea. She encountered flesh, muscle—cringed at the hardness of bone. But he was being incredibly brave, and the knowledge made her ache inside.

Minutes later, the ball dropped into the basin. But he'd begun to bleed again, and her probing had widened the opening where the ball had first torn into his shoulder. She had no choice but to stitch it closed as best she was able. She was breathing hard by the time she sat back.

A tremor went through him. His eyes opened. "There. That wasn't so bad, was it?" His tone was hoarse, but a whisper of sound. And he was trying valiantly to smile.

Julianna couldn't. Her throat was clogged tight. She could barely breathe. His blood was warm. Sticky on her fingertips.

The walls of the cottage tilted crazily. Her stomach began to heave. Lunging outside, she lost the contents of her stomach.

Her arms clamped tight to her breast, she rocked back and forth, over and over. She felt like the world was going crazy, and *she* along with it.

All she'd wanted was a few days away from

London. Perhaps a trifling bit of excitement to liven her humdrum life!

But not this. Never this.

Hot, blinding tears streamed from her eyes. Finally, she wiped her cheeks with the backs of her hands, dabbed at her mouth with the end of her gown, and walked back inside.

Dane's eyes never left her pale face. "Better?" he murmured.

Standing above him, she nodded, still unable to speak, trying desperately to calm her wayward emotions. And he seemed to know it, for his gaze sharpened intently.

"You'll be all right, won't you?"

She raised her head. "Why wouldn't I?" she said with all the dignity she could muster.

He gave a faint smile. "Why indeed?" The smile faded. "You're a puzzling little creature, aren't you? First you shoot me, then you cry."

Julianna didn't know what to say, and so she said nothing.

His mouth opened. He was about to say something more, but all at once he stopped. His eyes were glazed and unfocused. He gave a tiny shake of his head. She sensed him struggling to remain aware. But it was no use. His eyes closed. He succumbed to exhaustion and pain.

Or so she thought.

All at once his eyelids snapped open.

"Percival. I forgot about Percival." He was quite agitated. "He must be looked after."

Julianna frowned. "Percival? Is he your friend?"

He looked at her as if she'd gone daft. "Percival is the finest mount a man could ever have," he declared. "But . . . he must be fed."

Groaning, he sought to rise. Julianna pressed him back to the bed. "You needn't worry! I'll do it."

"You will?"

"I will," she said firmly. "I promise."

Her assurance appeared to satisfy him. Within seconds he was asleep.

Pulling the covers up, Julianna shook her head. The unexpected makings of a smile tugged at her lips. Here he was, hurt and wounded, and he was concerned about his *horse*.

How very like a man.

Six

Dane lay still and quiet throughout the day. Julianna could have sworn he moved not a single whit. Anxious, she surveyed him. Countless times she bent her head to his lips, as if to reassure herself that he still lived.

While he slept, she tidied the cottage. Her gown was quite ruined, the bodice filthy and stained with crimson splotches from tending Dane. She tossed it into the fire, along with the bloody rags, and quickly donned another.

Toward evening, she let herself out of the cottage. Dane had not been lying when he'd told her they were in the midst of the forest. Overhead the sky was a serene, dusky blue. There was a stream nearby; the muted gurgle of water reached her ears.

It was going to be up to her, she realized, to attend to their needs—their essentials were food, water, and warmth. It was spring, and while the days were warm, the nights were cold. She'd have to keep the fire going, she decided. If she let it die out, she was half-afraid she'd never get another started. She was rather ashamed to admit that never in her life had she started one herself, from tinder and kindling.

There was a stack of wood just outside the door, so she carried in enough wood to last through the night and into the next morning. She found Percival in a small building attached to the cottage. Half of it had been transformed into several stalls. Her eyes widened as she laid eyes on the towering black stallion. She approached cautiously, stopping a few feet away.

He was a beautiful animal. He watched her with attentive scrutiny, his eyes large and expressive, his ears pricked forward. His coat was like black gloss, shiny and sleek, gleaming in the evening light. He stood with quivering skin, his sleek, powerful muscles bunched.

Julianna had the sensation of being weighed and measured, and hoped she passed judgment. Slowly lifting a hand, she ran her nails gently down the sleek lines of his neck. His skin quivered beneath her hand. Julianna could feel his power beneath her touch, but he displayed no hint of aggression.

"My, but you're a big fellow, aren't you? Just like your master." He snorted and gave a proud shake of his head. She continued to stroke him, talking to him in low, soothing tones, letting him acquaint himself with her scent and presence.

Before long, the animal bumped his nose beneath her free hand. Soon he did it again.

Julianna chuckled. "What, are you looking for a lump of sugar? I'm sorry, Percival, but I'm afraid I've nothing for you today."

Looking over, she saw a door near the outside wall. In the small room within, she found what she was looking for—a bag of feed. Seizing the bucket next to it, she filled it to the brim. With no more hesitation, she let herself inside the stall, for she sensed that the mighty animal had accepted her—at least she hoped he had!

He nickered as she poured the feed into a bucket. Patting his neck, she withdrew, picking up another that was half-full of water. Across the clearing, she discovered what she was after— a well.

Filling the pail from Percival's stall with cool, clear water, she saw that Maximilian had wandered outside as well. He and Percival stood nose to nose, huge black beast to tiny black beast. The sight made her smile. Clearly the pair were already well acquainted with each other.

Her smile slipped. An odd little ache speared

her heart. She was perilously near to tears . . . again! Memory surfaced, unbidden. She felt horrible about pretending to be ill. Deceit was not in her nature. What was it Dane had said before she shot him?

I was worried about you, kitten.

Had he been? Had he really? And afterward, when she had returned inside . . . A piercing shaft of guilt rent her breast. It wasn't himself he'd been concerned about, but her. What kind of man was he? she wondered. And why did she even care? What little she knew of him had little to commend him. He was an outlaw, a robber.

Yet everything inside told her he was not a man without heart, a man without a soul.

As she was not a woman without conscience.

Biting her lip, she glanced at Percival, slurping thirstily from the bucket. She could leave. She *should* leave. She now had the *means* to leave. She had only to ride away, to leave him and be free.

But she no longer had the will. She could not abandon Dane. She simply could not.

Maximilian was sidling around her feet. Suddenly he bounded toward the door of the cottage, which stood ajar. He stopped, gazing back at her with huge, slanted eyes. As if he were waiting . . .

Julianna sighed. "Yes, Maximilian. I'm coming."

*   *   *

Throughout the night Dane alternated between burning hot and shaking chills. Once he woke and stared at her through searing, golden eyes. Julianna had the unsettling sensation he saw right through her, as if she weren't even there. She chafed at her helplessness, their isolation. She had no medicine. All she could do was keep the wound clean, and wait.

She was exhausted, but afraid to sleep, afraid he might need her. By noon the following day, her mind was made up. If he was not better by the next morning, she would ride out. There had to be a village somewhere. A road. A farm nearby. There had to be *something* she could do.

But what if someone realizes he's the Magpie? chided a voice in her mind. *What then? How will you feel then?*

Like a traitor, she admitted. It made no sense, for she owed him nothing. She had taken care of him as best she was able. Yet she couldn't explain her strange feelings toward him. It was almost akin to . . . loyalty. Oh, but it made no sense! And that, too, she didn't understand.

Yet one thing was abundantly clear. She couldn't let him die either.

Stirring the fire, her mind made up, she resumed her vigil at the bedside. She had drawn a chair close so she could watch him. His brows and the lock of hair on his forehead were very dark against his skin, which was bleached of color. She brushed at the hair that persisted in springing forward on his forehead, the gesture oddly tender.

"You have to be all right, Dane. You *have* to."

Almost before she knew what she was about, her hand crept within his where it rested on the blanket; his fingers curled around hers. He seemed to like that—indeed, she could have sworn he rested easier when she touched him. More than once her head drooped, and she jerked herself awake.

It was Maximilian who knew even before she did . . . he leaped up onto the bed and stretched out beside his master.

It gave her a start to discover Dane's eyes open wide and focused directly upon her. But this time his regard was clear and steady.

"You're still here. I thought I dreamed it."

His voice was hoarse and rusty.

"How do you feel?" she asked.

He shot her a telling look. The golden brown of his eyes was a stark contrast to the bristly shadow of his beard. He looked rather dangerous, his jaw rough and dark with stubble, but his features were rimmed with fatigue.

His eyes closed. She both saw and heard the uneven breath he took. "How long?" he rasped.

"I beg your pardon?"

His eyes opened. He wet his lips with his tongue. "How long have I been unconscious?"

"Since yesterday morning."

His gaze traveled to the windows, where daylight cast a mellow glow within the cottage. "The entire day?" He shook his head. "That's not possible."

Julianna smiled slightly. "I'm afraid it is."

Dane said nothing. His gaze had fallen to their hands. Julianna snapped hers back to her lap. She could feel the heat of a blush creeping beneath her skin.

A dark brow hiked upward, but he chose to make no comment. Julianna was heartily grateful. Her heart gave an odd little flutter. Vaguely, she wondered what it would be like to feel the hardness of his lips moving over hers . . . Blast the man! What was it about him that affected her so? She was not in the habit of thinking thusly about any man. And why it should be *this* man, she had no idea . . .

The thought was abruptly cut off when he sat up and pushed the blanket aside.

"What the devil are you doing?"

"What the devil does it look like?" he retorted.

Julianna surged upright. The chair hurtled backward, hitting the planked flooring with a bang. She paid no heed. "You are not to get up," she admonished sternly. "Do you hear me, sir?"

He was frowning as ferociously as she. "My

dearest Julianna, it's impossible not to." With a grimace he swung his feet to the floor. "And under the circumstances, don't you think it's utterly ridiculous that you persist in calling me 'sir'? My name is Dane."

"Very well then. Dane. Now tell me, Dane, where do you think you're going?"

He muttered an explosive curse.

Her eyes flashed. "There is no need to swear!"

"My dear, there is every need. It is not my intention to offend your sensibilities. However, I do not know quite how to say this, other than . . . given the situation, I'm finding that a man has certain needs." He paused, gauging her reaction.

"Needs?" Her mouth popped open. Her blue eyes blazed and her spine went stiff. "How can you even be thinking of such things—"

"Not," he interrupted, "*those* kinds of needs." He slanted her what he hoped was a suitably meaningful gaze. "I don't suppose you would be kind enough to leave me alone for a few minutes?"

Julianna stood stock still. "Oh," she gasped. "Oh!" She gulped, her face burning as she practically flew out the door. She was tempted to tell him to call if he needed her, yet how would that have sounded?

She allowed what was surely a suitably appropriate amount of time for him to use the chamber pot, then knocked on the door, still feeling rather foolish.

There was no answer. She listened intently, then knocked again, more loudly this time.

"Dane?" she called.

He made no reply. Worried, she opened the door and peeked inside. He was standing near the table, a marked consternation on his features as he braced himself with one hand. Her embarrassment fled, for he was pale as a sheet. He appeared ready to crash to the floor. She thrust a chair behind him just as his knees gave way.

"Everything is spinning."

"Put your head on the table." Gently she pushed his head down.

Long moments passed before he finally raised his head. She was relieved to note some of the color had seeped back into his face. "Christ," he muttered.

"How do you feel?"

"Weak as a babe," he admitted.

"You lost a goodly amount of blood," Julianna said quietly. "It may take some time before you feel quite like yourself again."

He sighed. "Well," he murmured dryly, "it appears the tables have been turned. I am wholly in your hands then. Dare I trust you?"

Julianna couldn't withhold the smile that was creeping across her lips. "You can indeed," she said briskly. "Now back to bed with you, si—"

She broke off when his brows shot high, and he began shaking his head in reproof.

She slipped an arm through his. "Back to bed with you, Dane."

This time she received no argument in return.

It was later that she found herself reflecting . . . The tables had been turned indeed. The Magpie was totally in her hands. It was a strange thought to consider. Well, not completely in her hands, she decided. Weakness or not, there was an aura of leashed strength about him that nothing or no one could hide. His hard frame dominated most of the bed. She was not fooled by the way he lay still, quietly dozing. The sight of his naked chest was disconcerting, and she couldn't prevent her eyes from straying to it again and again throughout the day. More than once she felt her face grow hot, and she had to divert her attention elsewhere.

In rummaging through the cupboard, she'd found some dried beef. He would never regain his strength if he didn't eat, she reasoned. But she didn't think it would be wise for him to eat too heavily.

Several black iron kettles of varying sizes hung near the fireplace. Reaching up, she plucked the smallest from its berth. Filling it with fresh water from the well, she placed it on a hook suspended over the fire, threw in a handful of beef and a measure of salt. Dusting off her hands, she stepped back to wait. After feeding Percival, carrying in more wood and filling a bucket with water, she returned to the fire. Raising the lid, she sniffed and peered warily within. The liquid was dark and murky; it didn't look particularly palatable. Oh, what she wouldn't have given for a pastry and pot of chocolate!

Nighttime shadows crept into the cabin. She lit several candles and walked back to the pot. It was then that Dane awoke. "What is that?" he asked.

"Broth. I thought it would be good for you. Would you like some?"

He nodded.

Julianna carefully ladled it into a wooden bowl and carried it to the bed. Dane was pushing himself to a sitting position, his back against the wall. As he did, icy-hot needles shot through his chest, all the way down his left arm. The movement arrested, he cradled his arm with his good hand.

"God rot it—" he gave an explosive curse "—I don't think I can hold the damned bowl!"

"It's all right." She hastened forward. "I can feed you, if you like—"

He was scowling, his mouth tight. "It is not all right! I won't have you feeding me like a child!"

Julianna froze. She was caught squarely between the desire to dump the broth over his head and an elusive hurt. And it was that which Dane saw.

Yet before he could say a word, she said carefully, "Perhaps tomorrow you'll feel well enough to sit at the table. For now, I have an idea."

Seconds later, she stepped to the bedside, handing him a cup with the hot broth.

Wordlessly he accepted it. Unthinkingly he took a sip. His eyes watered. He choked back a cough. God above, had she emptied the entire tin of salt in the kettle? Over the rim of the cup, her features flashed before him, the brilliance of her eyes wide and wary, yet he read in them an eagerness to please.

And here he was, he thought grimly, acting the beast.

Wretched though it was, he drained the broth, every last drop.

He set the cup aside and leaned back. "I'm sorry," he said quietly. "I shouldn't have lost my temper. It's not your fault."

Oh, but it was. And they both knew it. Julianna battled a rush of stupid, foolish tears. She would have stepped back lest he see, but he caught her fingers.

She gave a tiny shake of her head. "I . . . It's all right," she said awkwardly.

He frowned suddenly. His gaze roved over her face. "You look tired," he observed.

"I'm fine." She flashed a smile. "Truly."

But Dane saw beneath the façade. "You're exhausted, aren't you?"

"Now why would you say such a thing!"

So. The lady was stubborn and persistent. He tried another tack.

"When was the last time you slept?"

"I cannot remember."

He cocked a brow. "*Have* you slept?"

"A little," she lied.

"You haven't," he pronounced flatly.

"I did!" she insisted. "I slept there!" She pointed to the chair next to her.

His eyes narrowed. He made a disapproving sound low in his throat.

"Well, you won't be sleeping there tonight."

She yanked her hand away and propped them on her hips. "You're certainly in no condition to stop me," she pointed out.

"No?" Dane allowed a smile to curl his lips, nodding at the empty cup. "Your sustenance has given me renewed strength."

She blinked. She wasn't looking quite so sure of herself.

Holding her gaze, he reached for the coverlet, his intention clear.

"Don't you dare!" It was an ardent, vehement protest.

Dane paused, raising a brow in silent query.

"Oh, bother!" she cried.

Dane sighed. "Need I remind you I am hardly in any condition to accost you? And what would people think of me if they knew I let a woman sit in a chair all night while I occupied the bed?"

Her eyes met his rather unwillingly, he decided. But she was softening; he sensed it.

"They would, no doubt, say you are a rogue, which you are."

He lifted a corner of the blanket. "You won't do either of us any good without rest."

"It would be highly improper for me to sleep with you in that bed."

He scowled. "Lady," he growled, "you already have."

"It is most ungentlemanly of you to remind me of that." It was true. But she hadn't had a choice then, with him the Magpie and she his captive. But now—now, she did.

She was weakening. This was madness, she told herself. She did not know this man. What she did know of his character was thoroughly reprehensible!

Her fingers were imprisoned within his once more. She felt him tugging, inexorably pulling her toward him.

"Come," he invited. "Come lie with me, kitten."

Her eyes widened. "If you weren't hurt," she stated, "I do believe I'd slap you."

Dane made a sound that was part laugh, part

groan as she slid in beside him. A man would have to be dead not to be aware of this woman's loveliness. "Ah, kitten! If I wasn't hurt, I do believe I'd deserve it."

Seven

*J*ulianna was up when Dane woke the next morning. She was just pinning her hair before the small oval mirror on the wall next to the door. She turned when she saw that he was awake.

"Good morning," she murmured, with a tentative smile.

"Good morning," he returned.

A shaft of hungry desire shot through him as he watched her approach. She'd changed into a simple gown of white muslin. Dane's eyes followed the delicate blue lace that edged the rounded bodice. Beneath the cloth her breasts swelled round and high, her skin milky white and smooth. He wanted to touch it—touch *her*, to see if she was as soft as she looked. And when she sat and bent slightly to peer at his shoulder, it was all he could do to tear his gaze from the cleft between. Even the sharp knifelike pain that sizzled through him as he flexed his shoulder couldn't banish the sharp, sudden stab of longing that shot through him. The scent of roses drifted to his nostrils. God, but she was fresh and sweet, and he was suddenly achingly aware of his own disheveled appearance.

Little did he realize that while he was indulging in his perusal, Julianna was taking stock of him as well. In all her days, she didn't know when she'd encountered such stark, bold masculinity. It was most vexing, she decided irritably. Why the devil did he affect her so?

She sat, trying to keep her gaze trained on the bandage—impossible! With his throat and chest bare, he seemed bigger than ever. The sheer size of the man was overwhelming. His forearms were long and corded with muscle, covered with silky-looking dark hair. Even his wrists were big, his fingers lean and strong-looking. When hers brushed his hair-roughened flesh, her stomach dropped like a brick.

The muscles in her belly contracted. A tingle of some strange, unnamed emotion curled her insides. Almost desperately, she sought to quiet her leaping pulse. There should have been layers and layers of clothing between them. Shirt, vest, jacket, cravat. She wasn't used to it. She wasn't used to touching a man, period. Instead, there was nothing between them, nothing but a rather daunting expanse of brazenly male skin. . . .

She strove for a breezy, even tone. "Let's have a look at this, shall we?"

"Must we?" He was grim, wincing as she began to unwind the bandage from around his shoulder.

She inhaled sharply when at last it was revealed. Her stomach lurched at the sight of the raised, swollen flesh, bracketed by her stitches.

"That bad, eh?"

Julianna examined it more closely. It was raw and jagged and crusted with blood. "Actually, no," she ventured cautiously. "It's bruised and red, but I think that's to be expected. Frankly, it looks better than I thought it would."

She had already placed a basin of hot water and a stack of clean cloths on the table. Dane steeled himself when she began to clean it, but she was very gentle. He watched her fingers as she worked. They were slender and small, like the rest of her. He vaguely recalled her hands on his body. Smoothing his brow, a voice speaking in dulcet, soothing tones. But her tongue was tart—an intriguing contradiction, he mused!

He surveyed her as she very efficiently folded a

clean pad into a square. "You're very capable. Have you worked in a hospital?"

Julianna blinked. "Heavens, no."

"Are you laughing?" he demanded.

"A little."

"Why?"

"Well, to be sure, the only experience I have is with animals."

Even when she was very young, she was always taking in some poor creature or other—an orphaned rabbit, a dog whose leg had been caught in some kind of trap . . . Oh, how she'd wanted to keep him once he was well! She'd begged and begged.

Papa had refused.

From her brother Justin she'd inherited a hint of stubborn defiance, for she had nursed the animal back to health without her father's knowledge, keeping him hidden in the boathouse away from sight. Sebastian and Justin had helped as well, sneaking her juicy tidbits of food for the mongrel. And when he was well, Prudence from the village near Thurston Hall had given him a home and shelter.

Papa would have been furious if he'd known. Not that any of them had cared, however . . .

"What kind of animals?" he asked.

Julianna shrugged. "Several rabbits. A bird with a broken wing once." She couldn't quite hide the tiny little smile that flirted at the corners of her mouth. "But I daresay, you are the most beastly of all."

"Thank you. I'm glad I know what you really think of me."

"You weren't complaining a few days ago," she reminded him.

"True." He watched as she held the square, easing his arm up as she began to wrap another strip around it to hold it in place. "But it would appear someone has taught you well."

Julianna was intent on her task, her tone rather absentminded. "Actually, Sebastian tended my bumps and bruises when I was young."

"You call your father by his given name?"

"No, of course not. Sebastian is my brother."

Dane gave her an odd look. "Your brother tended your scrapes?"

"You would have to know my brother. He's a very protective sort."

"Where was your mother?"

Her smile slowly faded. It was a logical question, she supposed. "I don't even remember my mother."

"I'm sorry." He paused. "She died when you were young?"

"Yes. She—she ran off with another man." The admission came out all in a rush. "Across the Channel. The two of them were killed."

He was staring at her. "Good God."

"Yes, it was all quite disgraceful."

"What about your father?"

"He died a number of years ago, too." Her fingers plucked at her gown. Her laugh was a little forced as she raised her head. "I don't know why I told you that. It's rare that I even think of it."

Dane didn't say anything for a few seconds. Then he asked, "How old are you, Julianna?"

Her eyes narrowed. "That, sir, is none of your affair."

"Oh, come," he said brashly. "How old are you?"

She glared at him, the soft line of her lips compressed into a tight seam.

"Very well then. I shall hazard a guess. Are you eight-and-twenty?"

"I am not!" she said through her teeth.

He'd offended her. Younger then. Dane hastily revised his guess.

"Seven-and-twenty?"

She neither denied nor confirmed it. Ah, so he was right. She was seven-and-twenty.

"Why aren't you wed?"

"That's not a question one should ask a lady!"

He persisted. "Are you a bluestocking?"

Julianna could feel her face growing hot. "Must you persist in insulting me?"

"I mean no insult. Someone should have married a beauty like you long ago. You should have had at least three babes at your breast already."

Babes. She was reminded of her brothers' little

ones—Sebastian's twins, Geoffrey and Sophie, Justin's new daughter Lizzie. She loved them dearly, but they weren't *hers*. And all at once she felt the loss keenly.

And his gibe hurt. Julianna couldn't help it. She'd thought herself well beyond it, but it did.

Her mind veered straight to Thomas. A rending ache tore through her, but she was determined not to show it. *If only*, she thought. *If only*. Deep in her soul, she knew Thomas was not the man for her—would never have been the man for her—but there were times that she longed for what might have been . . .

"You ask questions you have no business asking," she told him bluntly.

"Perhaps. But what if I said I am a man who values truth and honesty?"

"You? An outlaw?" She took a deep breath. "Tell me then. Why aren't *you* wed? Or are you?"

"I am not."

She gave him a withering stare. "Perhaps no one would have you."

"That may be true. But I have never asked anyone to be my wife."

"I cannot imagine that anyone would say yes," she shot back. "Being a highwayman can hardly be a stable livelihood."

Little wonder that she scoffed. He deserved that, he realized. He had been teasing, but he was also curious. Yet he sensed her defensiveness, an elusive hurt, but he would not press. Since the lovely Julianna was clearly sensitive about her age and her marital state, and since it seemed the conversation was taking a turn neither of them were prepared to discuss, Dane decided a change of subject was in order.

He ran a hand over his raspy chin. "Have you ever shaved a man?"

Her stunned expression was all the answer he needed. But he discovered she was up to any challenge he presented.

Her eyes took on a gleam. "You would trust me with a razor at your throat?"

The question took him aback. Dane couldn't help it. His gaze slid up and down her form. All of a sudden he wasn't so sure . . .

"You may not be an honest man," she said sweetly, "but it seems you are a brave one."

As it happened, she held the mirror while he scraped the stubble from his face and neck. Wiping the last of the soap from his chin, he glanced at her.

"Is that better?"

She nodded her approval. "A vast improvement," she pronounced. She replaced his shaving supplies in the cupboard and turned back, pursing her lips. "I suppose you're hungry."

"I am. But I don't want any of that damned broth."

Her mouth opened, then closed with a snap. She was clearly affronted. "I'll have you know I went to a great deal of trouble to fix that broth."

"And I appreciate your efforts. Truly. But I'm ravenous, kitten."

"Yes, I imagine you are." Her ire faded. She looked suddenly worried. "But I ate the last of the bread yesterday. And . . ."

She was chewing on her lip. "What?" he prompted.

She met his gaze reluctantly. "I think it only fair to tell you I've never cooked a meal in my life," she confided in a small voice.

"Really?" He feigned great shock. "Why, I should never have guessed."

Her eyes narrowed. "Are you making light of me?"

"Not in the slightest. I have every faith in you. Now, if you will only listen, I have a suggestion. Outside on the north corner of the cottage, there is a small storeroom . . ."

An hour later the cottage was filled with the aroma of meat and vegetables. Julianna stirred the stew, humming a little as she crushed some herbs in her fingers and sprinkled them over the top.

But when she reached for the salt, Dane reared up. "Easy on the salt, kitten!" he called.

By the time night draped its shadow over the forest, Julianna was nearly dropping with exhaustion. She swiped at the hair falling into her eyes. What would Sebastian and Justin think if they could see her now? she wondered, hauling water and wood. She was dirty, disheveled, and they would surely never believe their eyes!

But she was certainly feeling rather proud of herself.

Dane looked on as she dropped onto the side of the bed. "Tired?" he asked.

"A little," she admitted.

"I'm sorry. I've given you a merry chase today, haven't I?"

There was no disputing that her charge was a trying patient. He fretted, grumbled, stewed, and complained about his inactivity—and the fact that she wouldn't allow him up. Yet it flitted through her mind that not once today had she thought of London. Not once had she wished to be elsewhere. Granted, there hadn't been time! Still, she enjoyed being busy. And—she had liked being needed.

Even if it was by an outlaw!

She shrugged, tugging one foot onto her knee and pulling off her slipper. Oh, but her feet did ache! She was quite certain she hadn't sat down even once throughout the day.

Dane adjusted his arm on the pillow. "My dear Julianna, if it eases your mind, removing your stockings will hardly send me into fits of lust."

Julianna frowned at him. His habit of discerning her thoughts was rather vexing, his suggestion quite improper. Yet what about their acquaintance had been proper anyway?

Tugging off her slippers, she rubbed her feet, blew out the candles, and slipped beneath the sheet.

They lay together, shoulder to shoulder. The only sound was the crackle and hiss of the fire.

It was Dane who broke the silence. "I suppose this is quite a change from your life of leisure. You do lead a life of leisure, I take it?"

"Yes, but I am not a laggard."

His eyes flickered. "I didn't mean to imply that you were." He paused. "What would you be doing if you weren't here?"

She considered. "Well," she said thoughtfully, "if I were at my home in Bath, I would probably be out for an evening walk in the countryside. If I were in London, I would likely be dancing at a ball—" there was no mistaking the smile beneath the words "—I suppose in either case, my feet would surely be aching anyway."

He laughed. "Thank you. That eases my mind considerably." Silence drifted between them, yet it was an oddly intimate silence.

"Julianna?"

"Yes?"

"Why did you stay, Miss Julianna Clare?" He stopped. Something flickered across his face. "I didn't think you would."

Miss Julianna Clare. Guilt lodged in her breast. Her smile froze. A faint distress crept into her eyes, for she'd forgotten that particular untruth. "Why are you asking me this?"

"I should think it would be obvious. Because I wish to know." He turned to the side, leaning on his good shoulder.

"Dane!" she protested. "You shouldn't—"

"I want to see you when you answer." Heedless of the fire that burned in his shoulder, he snared her chin. A thumb beneath her jaw, he brought her gaze to his.

"Why did you stay?" Quietly, he posed the question once more. "You didn't have to. You could have left me."

Sudden, startling tears brimmed in her eyes. "No," she stated haltingly. "I couldn't. I looked back, and I saw you, the way you looked at me . . . and I couldn't leave you like that. I just couldn't! And—I'm so sorry I shot you. You cannot know how sorry I am!"

He nearly groaned. "You're a tenderhearted soul, aren't you, kitten?"

She shook her head. "Dane, I—"

A finger slid along the line of her jaw. "Hush," he commanded. "*Hush*."

Their eyes collided.

The words she'd been about to utter evaporated.

He didn't plan it, though God knew he'd imagined it. It simply . . . happened. Dane didn't know why—he didn't care. His gaze lowered slowly on her lips. Leaning over, he saw the way her eyes widened—a flash of realization—as she discerned his intent.

His mouth closed slowly over hers.

She didn't stop him.

No, she didn't stop him—and the earth could have been splintering to pieces all around them— and Dane wouldn't have cared. Nothing could have stopped *him* from kissing her. Her lashes fluttered shut. Her lips parted beneath his. The scent of lemon that clung to her skin teased his nostrils . . . The whisper of a sigh echoed in his mouth.

He took his time, acquainting himself with the essence of her mouth. Tasting her, the way the center of her lower lip pouted out ever so slightly, there where the color bloomed to a ripe shade of pink . . . the heat of her breath mingling with his, the way her breathing quickened.

The ache in his shoulder was forgotten. She was so slight and delicate, he was half-afraid to lean over her, afraid she could not bear his weight.

A shudder ran through him. He wanted her. Closer. Close as a man and woman could be. He wanted to stretch out beside her, pull her clothes off, and chart every sweet, creamy inch of her, then drive deep inside her and satisfy the ache in his gut. He could feel the muslin covering her breasts scratching against his chest. A part of him wanted to tear it away—she persisted in wearing her gown to bed, dammit! But the rational part of him prevailed. This was not a time for lust. Indeed, he'd promised her. She was untried. Untested. He knew it instinctively, and he didn't want to frighten her.

When at last he raised his head, his heart was drumming. Julianna's eyes climbed slowly to his, searching his face, her breath coming in little pants that drove him half-wild. Within the depths of her eyes he glimpsed a soft confusion, the same shattering tumult he was feeling.

Her lips parted.

A finger pressed to the center of her lips, Dane shook his head. He didn't understand it, but he wanted nothing to ruin the spell of this moment.

He managed a glimmer of a smile. "Don't, kitten. Not a word. Just . . . just go to sleep."

With a fingertip he brushed her eyes closed.

And sleep she did, clear through till morn.

Eight

For the second day in a row, Julianna arose before Dane. He woke late, but his condition was much improved over the day before, enough that he rose and walked about the cottage. But she knew he was frustrated with being limited to the use of one arm. At her suggestion, they fashioned a sling for his arm, and he seemed pleased with it.

Neither of them spoke of what had transpired the night before.

Julianna was heartily glad. Indeed, she was still having trouble believing it. She went hot all over whenever she thought of it—and she could not *stop* thinking of it!

Why had he kissed her?

Moreover, why had she *let* him?

She had no answer. She knew only that Dane was a man who drew her gaze again and again, and there was no help for it.

Why? her mind screamed.

It was sheer madness. After Thomas's betrayal, she had retreated for months. She despised scandal as much as Sebastian. When she'd finally emerged, the gentlemen of the *ton* had tried to rally her attentions. She had firmly rebuffed any attempts to court her. Deep in her heart, she had told herself she would never again allow herself to be hurt the way Thomas had hurt her. That way she wouldn't miss what she would never have.

And so she had schooled herself well. She hadn't allowed herself to wonder what it would be like to lie naked with a man, to feel his mouth running over her skin, his touch burning into her body. Her breasts. Her belly. Even there between her thighs . . .

But last night she had. In the wee hours before dawn, she had dreamed. She had seen herself lying nude with Dane. Beneath him. And he had been naked, too. Gloriously naked . . .

It was a dream that was wild. Torrid. So vividly erotic she had quite shocked herself. No wonder she had practically leaped out of bed this morning!

Why should this . . . this . . . this *rogue* affect her so?

He'd put on a shirt, for which she was eternally

grateful. But the material clung to the shape of him; the muscles of his shoulders were clearly visible, curved and hard. The shirt was open at the throat, revealing a pie-shaped wedge of hair-matted skin that brought a surge of heat to her cheeks. Oh, yes, even with that impressive chest covered, it rendered her no less aware of him!

Her eyes followed him as he rose to poke at the fire. She couldn't deny that his profile was intriguingly arresting. She traced the bold slash of black brows, the blade of his nose—there was a slight bump she hadn't noticed before—the squareness of his jaw. He needed to shave, she thought vaguely. His cheeks and chin were again shadowed with his beard. God rot it, his raw masculinity scrambled her senses and made her pulse skid wildly—she was appalled at herself for even thinking in such a way!

It did not help that she caught him staring at her more than once. Replacing the poker, he turned.

He was staring once more.

Julianna had had enough. "Why do you look at me like that?"

Something flickered across his features. "I was thinking I've seen you before."

"I think not," she said coolly.

He raised a brow. "And what if I said I think you're wrong?"

She gave him a quelling look. "And where

might that have been? I daresay we do not travel in the same circles. Or have you robbed me before?"

His brow remained cocked high. "I've robbed you of nothing, kitten. Nothing but a kiss. And indeed, I think it was freely given."

So much for her earlier relief. Julianna did not appreciate the reminder. "Must you mock me?" she asked stiffly.

The flash of humor disappeared. He was suddenly intent. "I do not mock you, Julianna." He studied her, his head tilted to one side. "Tell me," he said suddenly. "Are you angry that I kissed you?"

All at once there was an unfamiliar dryness in her throat. A hot tide of color surged into her cheeks. She averted her eyes.

"That's none of your affair." Drat! Her tone wasn't at all steady.

"Of course it's my affair. If I am the perpetrator, don't I deserve to know?"

Julianna had no wish to debate on either count.

She tried to step by him. He stopped her, lean fingers winding around the fragile span of her wrist, a gentle entrapment.

"Kitten? Won't you tell me?"

Julianna avoided his gaze. She looked at the opening of his shirt. No salvation there. She could look no higher.

"Yes," she said shakily. "I mean no." She was

floundering, and there was no help for it. "Oh, I don't know what I mean!"

"Well, that certainly clarifies the matter. Perhaps"—his eyes took on a gleam—"another kiss might help you decide."

Julianna's heart was beating high in her throat. He was tugging her inexorably closer.

"What the devil are you doing?" she heard herself ask.

"It is but a kiss, kitten. Will you not grant a dying man his last wish?"

Her eyes jerked up. "You are not dying!"

"I could," he stated brashly. "Infection might set in. It's been known to happen."

Lord, he was right . . . But then she saw laughter surface in his eyes.

She stiffened. "You are a womanizer, aren't you?" she accused.

"Not true." He defended himself staunchly.

"Isn't it? There was a woman on the coach— her name was Mrs. Chadwick. She said that the Magpie . . . that you . . . that you have a liking for the ladies."

"Only *this* particular lady," he countered.

Her heart lurched. His arm was curling around her waist now. Suddenly it was impossible to swallow, difficult even to breathe.

She placed her fingertips on his chest, mindful of his wound. "Dane—"

His gaze pinned hers. "Be still, kitten," he whispered, "and let me kiss you."

Those words should have brought the scene to a sizzling halt . . . her hand to his cheek—and hard! Whatever objection she might have made dried up in her breast. In all honesty, she wasn't sure she wanted to object. Everything inside her stood still as his mouth came down on hers. Locked fast against his chest, she let it happen . . . she *wanted* it to happen. And it was just like before, she decided fuzzily. No, it was better.

Sensation surrounded her. She could feel his strength, his sheer length against hers, the heat emanating from his body. His mouth on hers was meltingly sweet, sliding to the corner of hers.

"Open your mouth for me, kitten . . ." The plea was no less urgent for its softness. "Ah, God. Yes. *Yes*. Just like that." He gave an odd little laugh. "You're very responsive, aren't you, kitten?"

Her lips parted. There was no thought of refusal. Of denial. Not even when he tasted her. *Tasted* her with his tongue, sliding along hers with no hesitation, the texture of his pleasurably rough, a slow, almost leisurely journey that explored the dark interior of her mouth. The contact sent a jolt through her, but she didn't move. She couldn't. She was—God help her—she was curious.

She had always left the sensual journeys to others. It certainly wasn't something she could discuss with her brothers! She had been brought up to be a lady, and the dictates of a lifetime were hard to abandon. Thomas had been the only man ever to kiss her, and that but a chaste brush on the lips. It was nothing like this wild, lingering contact that went on and on. There had been no secret adventures in the garden, no tentative explorations in the dark. And, while she had wondered what it might actually be like to *experience* such things, her wistful imaginings had always been rather vague and nebulous.

Except for that dream last night. That hot, wicked dream.

And now it was finally happening. To her. *To her.*

And God above, it was more than curiosity. There was nothing vague about her response either. A jolt of sheer pleasure shot through her. The muscles in her belly contracted. Tiny needles of excitement centered in her breasts. She wanted to feel Dane's hands—his mouth, sweet Lord, his delightfully wicked *tongue*—curling around her nipples in the same way he explored the depths of her mouth, painting them wet and dark. It had been like that in her dream, she realized. . . . She felt wanton. Wicked, but deliciously so. At seven-and-twenty, she was not a naïve young girl. She might be innocent, but regardless of her lack of firsthand knowledge, she was not ignorant.

She felt bereft when he finally released her mouth. Clutching at the front of his shirt, she blinked, her breathing shallow.

"Oh, my," she heard herself say.

His laugh was husky. He sounded as short of breath as she. "My thoughts precisely."

Julianna blushed fiercely.

"I won't apologize." He smiled crookedly. "You're very lovely. But I expect you know that."

Something within her cried out. Had Thomas ever told her that? she wondered with a pang. Had he ever made her feel the way that Dane did? The burning, all-consuming way she felt at the touch of Dane's mouth hot upon hers blazed through her like wildfire.

"And now, kitten, my head is buzzing. I fear I had better sit down before I fall down."

The next afternoon Dane sat on the bed. Cautiously he removed the sling. He flexed the left side of his torso, only to wince as a sharp twinge cut through his shoulder. It was damned stiff and sore, and he had to remind himself that only time would heal it.

Julianna had just entered the cottage, carrying a small bowl full of apples. On seeing his grimace, she stopped short and glared her displeasure. "What the devil do you think you're doing?"

Dane smiled sheepishly. "What you think I shouldn't, apparently."

"Indeed." She bent to retrieve an apple that had rolled onto the floor.

His smile widened. She wore the same muslin gown she'd worn yesterday. The material of her gown was rather thin, and with the sunlight pouring through the window as it was, it offered him a rather tantalizing view of her round little backside.

When she straightened he was trying to replace the sling—with little success. "Julianna? I seem to require a bit of assistance."

Julianna set aside the basket and came to his aid. The material had become rather twisted, though, and it necessitated refolding it and tying it again. The first attempt failed, and Julianna bent forward to adjust the length of the sling, intent on the undertaking. She sighed in vexation.

Dane offered no complaints. In truth, he was rather enjoying himself. Seated as he was, it put his head at a level with her bosom. The bodice of her gown gaped. Dane stared straight into the valley between what appeared to be delectably round, firm breasts.

Oh, yes, he thought. This was better still . . .

"Ahem!"

Reluctantly, he lifted his gaze. Her eyes were snapping.

"I do believe you're enjoying this!"

He quirked a brow. "I do believe I am."

"I suppose you will offer no apology this time either, will you?"

"My dear Julianna, in my defense, I can only say that I am a man. And you are truly a vision the likes of which I've never seen before."

She flipped her plait over her shoulder. "Do you think you can turn my head with such talk, sir?"

"Well, you've certainly turned mine."

"I beg your pardon?"

He accorded her a lazily rakish smile, his gaze drifting briefly to her breasts. "Clearly I was mistaken when I called you a puny little thing."

She sputtered. "You—you!"

He chuckled at the tide of color that turned her cheeks the color of a new spring dawn. "Oh, come. You are hardly clumsily made."

"I should leave you to fend for yourself!"

"No doubt you should," he agreed. His gaze captured hers. Softly he said, "But if I had the chance to choose my nurse, it would only be you, kitten. And I meant what I said. You are truly a most enchanting vision." His gaze roved slowly over her features. Her lips were softly parted, pink and moist. "Are you aware your eyes change color with the sway of your mood? I never knew there were so many lovely shades of blue."

She blushed again—but this time with pleasure, he noted.

Her gaze skidded away. Her hands clasped together before her, a nervous gesture. "I . . . ah, I believe it's time to see to Percival." She darted outside.

And indeed Julianna was nervous. Oh, it wasn't that she was afraid of him. Perhaps she should have been, she realized. She was alone with a stranger. She knew nothing of his past. What she knew of his present circumstances was most reprehensible! Had another woman recounted the events of these past few days, she would have expected her to be reeling with fear.

What she felt was far different. What she felt was something she'd felt with no man, not even Thomas. When Dane was close, she was seized with a near-painful awareness. She couldn't seem to think straight. She should never have allowed him to kiss her. She most certainly shouldn't have kissed him back! But she had . . . and she didn't understand it.

Any more than she understood why she was still here.

Outside the day was warm and bright, the sun a rich buttercup yellow as it poured through the treetops. In truth, she needed a moment to collect herself. To no avail, for he followed her outside.

Julianna did not speak as she fed Percival; it was Dane who hefted the bucket of water from the well and carried it to Percival's stall.

"He likes you," Dane commented, when Percival thrust his nose beneath her hand.

Julianna glanced at him. "You sound surprised."

"He can be a monster," he admitted. He watched her for a moment. "I must thank you for taking such good care of him for me."

Julianna glanced at him sharply. Was he chiding her? Judging from his expression, it appeared not.

She rubbed the animal's velvet nose. "Percival," she said casually. "A noble name for a noble animal. Did you name him?"

"I did."

"Why Percival?" she asked.

"It's said that Percival was so quick he could spear a bird in the wing with his javelin. I thought it a fitting name, for he's truly as fleet as the wind."

"You must be well-read if you are so familiar with King Arthur and his knights. But I daresay, it is an odd choice of name for a highwayman, is it not?"

Dane's smile froze. He went very still.

"And indeed, I am given to wonder where you acquired your education."

He went silent, turning and walking back inside the cottage.

Julianna was right behind him. "Did you not hear me, sir?"

"There is nothing wrong with my hearing, lady." His tone was cool, his expression equally so as he faced her.

"Then why do you not answer?"

"You are remarkably persistent, aren't you?"

"Sometimes annoying, according to my brothers."

"Brothers? You have more than one?"

"I have two, Sebastian and Justin. But we weren't talking about me, Dane. We were talking about you."

Standing near the rough wooden table, he eyed her. "Your point, Julianna? I trust there is one?"

Taking a deep breath, she faced him squarely. "Only this, sir." She picked up his free hand, turning it over in hers, running her fingers over the tips of his. "I do not believe you are a man of humble origins. These are not the hands of an ordinary laborer. You are neither uncouth nor uncivilized. Therefore, I must deduce that you are anything but common. Perhaps you are even a gentleman."

Nor was she done. She gestured to his boots. "Those, I would venture to say, are made of the finest leather."

"Clearly my efforts are not without fail then."

"Indeed," she challenged. "Nonetheless, I think you are an educated robber."

"But of course. If I were not intelligent," he retorted, "I'd have been caught by now. Besides, what can I say? Being a highwayman can be a lucrative trade." He pointed to the two bulging bags sitting in the corner. "There's a great deal of money in those."

"Yes, so I've seen." Mercy, he was boasting!

He gave her an assessing gaze. "Ah, yes. I'd forgotten you liking to snoop in things that are not yours."

Julianna glared. By Jove, she would feel no remorse!

But in the next second, everything changed. He walked over to the fireplace mantel and picked up one of his pistols. She couldn't look away as lean, dark fingers slid almost caressingly along the smooth metal of the barrel.

Her stomach did a peculiar flip-flop. "What are you doing?"

"I have a proposition for you, kitten. Would you like to learn how to shoot?"

Julianna's gaze jerked upward. He was watching her closely. "What?"

"Perhaps then, the next time you take aim at my heart, you won't miss."

An angry hurt welled inside her. "Oh!" she cried, "must you taunt me? You know very well that's a perfectly horrid thing to say!"

"Come. What do you say? I'll show you how to shoot." His gaze drifted deliberately down. A faint smile curled his lips. "Unless," he offered casually, "you can think of something better to do." His gaze lingered on the thrust of her breasts beneath her gown before coming back up to tangle with hers.

She caught her breath, suddenly steaming inside. "I take that back!" she told him heatedly. "You, sir, are clearly no gentleman."

Nine

The sharp blast of a pistol reverberated through the clearing.

"Kitten"—he laughed—"you are abominably bad."

Julianna muttered under her breath, glancing in vexation at the piece of paper he'd nailed to a tree trunk. She was not particularly comfortable handling the weapon, but it no longer felt so alien in her hand. And after the first few shots, she was no longer closing her eyes—but that was probably due to Dane's prodding.

As for him, his nearness was distracting. Disturbing. And he was coming deliberately close, brushing his fingers against her bare arm, curling his fingers around hers for far longer than necessary. She was quite certain of it. And once again he eased close, pressing his chest against her back as he helped her sight the weapon.

"Ready?" he asked.

She nodded, even as she struggled to regain control of her senses. Her attention constantly wandered when he was near—no wonder she found it difficult to concentrate!

Yet another shot went far wide of the trunk of the oak tree.

He gave an exaggerated sigh. "I begin to fear this is hopeless. You did not tell me you were in need of spectacles."

Julianna shot him a supremely glacial look.

"If I hit the target—" She posed the question quite sweetly as he primed the pistol. "—will you answer my question?"

"I will."

"And if I hit it twice, will you answer two?"

He smiled and handed the pistol back. "Most assuredly."

"And three?" she challenged. "Will you answer three questions?"

He chuckled. "I will," he declared. "Though such a feat would surely be deemed a miracle."

Oh, but he was confident. Cocky even! Clearly he had little faith in her abilities, which made Julianna all the more determined to prove him wrong.

He nodded for her to proceed.

Julianna squinted at the target . . . and hit it dead center.

He cocked his head. A black brow climbed high. "Impressive. But can you do it again?"

Julianna fired once more. It was a much easier task when she focused on the target and not his presence!

"Sheer luck," was all he said when the next shot followed the same path as the first. A third followed, but the fourth missed its mark.

Still, Julianna had every intention of holding him to his bargain. "You are a man who can be haughty of brow and haughty of manner," she stated, handing the pistol back to him. "I daresay, a man accustomed to command. Therefore, I am given to wonder if you served in the war." She watched him closely. "Did you?"

Something flickered in his eyes. At last he nodded.

"I knew it! Were you a hero?"

He appeared to hesitate. "Some say so," he admitted reluctantly, "though I call it loyalty to my country and my fellow soldiers."

Julianna's mind was off and running. So why, she asked herself, would such a man resort to being a highwayman?

"I've told you about my family, my brothers. Even how my mother ran off. But what of you?

You've said you do not have a wife. Do you have other family?" She held her breath.

For the longest time she thought he would refuse to answer. Finally, he said gruffly, "My parents are dead. But I have two older sisters."

"Ah," she said lightly. "And what do your sisters think of their brother being the Magpie?"

His expression grew stormy.

Julianna sucked in a breath. "They don't know, do they?"

"That's four, kitten. More than your allotment." He began to walk back toward the cottage.

"Wait! Is this cottage your home the year through?"

That brought him back around. "Now why would you ask that? I suppose you intend to lead the authorities back here when you leave!"

"How could I do that when I don't know where we are?"

"How indeed?" He eyed her, a glance of little patience. "Are you coming?" he asked shortly.

"Yes. But I should like to know—"

He whirled, scowling blackly. "No more questions, Julianna."

Julianna. Those occasions he had called her by her given name were rare. This was serious, she decided.

Her mind was troubled, her thoughts whirling, as she fell into step behind him. Something wasn't quite right about this man. Everything in-side told her he was not a man without principle. Without morals. Without conviction.

Yet that very same sense warned he was not what he pretended to be. He harbored secrets . . .

Of that, she was suddenly very, very certain.

Nigel Roxbury was pleased. He was *exceedingly* pleased that the Magpie had not made an appear-ance of late. Perhaps the fool had been caught in the act, and word of his demise had not yet reached London. Faith, but he prayed it was so!

He had been furious when several of his ship-ments had been stolen. And that wretched high-wayman the Magpie was responsible.

Leaning back in his chair, Roxbury adjusted the patch over his eye. He'd thought his plan quite ingenious. After all, he could hardly steal from the Royal Mint itself, and Boswell had been a skilled artisan! The currency looked remark-ably real. Most likely, the Magpie believed it *was* real, the fool!

Once the currency was produced, the distribu-tion was already in place. That was the beauty of it—the fact that *he* was privy to such informa-tion, by virtue of his position. No one was harmed, and the fruits of his labor afforded him the opportunity to buy what he could not other-wise afford—his pretty baubles from the sands of Egypt. Bogus currency in exchange for gold . . .

Of course there had been that messy affair with Boswell's wife . . . he was still amazed the Boswell bitch had possessed the effrontery to try to turn him in! A pity about the two of them.

But now he had gained their share as well.

At last there was a knock. He couldn't quite hide his satisfaction as he opened the door to his visitor.

"*Madame*, I've been expecting you. What have you for me?" He delved through the box she carried, lifting out a jar that had once housed the organs of the dead; it was topped with the head of a falcon. Turning it upside down, he shook it, his eyes glinting when she pressed a handkerchief to her mouth in distaste.

"Another splendid piece," Roxbury praised, setting it on the table behind his desk.

She said nothing, merely regarded him through the silk of her veil.

"For pity's sake, there's no need to hide from me."

She tossed her head but slid back the veil. "You lack your brother's charm," she informed him. "I must confess, I have been wondering how the devil you found me."

"I did not go looking for you, my dear. Imagine my surprise when I saw that sketch of you in the Paris newspaper. It really was quite remarkable. How lucky that my memory did not fail me.

And how lucky I was that you continued your social proclivities after your husband's death!"

She held out her hand. "Is our business concluded?"

He retrieved a small pouch from his desk and dropped it into her palm. "For tonight it is," he murmured lightly. "Pleasant dreams, *madame*."

One week after she'd shot him, Julianna removed the stitches from Dane's shoulder. But where the two of them were concerned—Dane and Julianna—tensions were mounting.

Lying next to her each night, it was impossible not to be aware of her beauty. Her voice was sweeter than the sun shining through the blackest night. Pure, bright, and untarnished. If it were up to him, he'd have said to hell with Phillip and Nigel. To hell with the world at large. He wanted to make slow, lingering love to her, take his time about it, bury himself deep and hear her moan— and make it last for hours. Hell, all night, if that's what it took to satisfy his craving for her.

But something inside warned that just once would not do with the lovely Julianna. Just once would only sharpen his desire to feel her softness beneath him again and again and again.

Christ, this was madness. He had a job to do. An enemy to trap.

And the lovely Julianna was not a ninnyhammer. She was smart and intelligent, compassionate and tenderhearted. He remembered her crying as she'd removed the bullet. He liked her hands on his body. But much to his vexation, she noticed everything.

He had to watch what he said around her. That much was clear. Damn, but it was growing harder and harder. Yet he couldn't risk having her find out the truth about him. He couldn't take the chance . . .

It had been a mistake to bring her here. He'd been a fool. Yet how could he have left her, knowing she might be hurt?

Her presence complicated things greatly—and in ways he could never have foreseen! She twisted him in knots, inside and out. And he would soon be well. What then?

He didn't know. God above, but he didn't.

Julianna was no less aware of Dane. She was drawn to him, drawn to him in a way that had never happened before. One day, her gaze returned to him, again and again. He sat before the fire, Maximilian in his lap. She watched, as if in fascination, as he idly brushed his long fingers through Maximilian's silky fur. And she wondered what it would be like to feel those lean-fingered hands stroking along *her* spine. Why, she might easily purr in sated contentment as Maximilian was purring. . . .

No matter that he was stirringly handsome, he was a highwayman, destined for the hangman's noose. But that seemed not to matter when he'd kissed her.

He made no move to kiss her again, and . . . oh, though it made no sense, she wanted him to. She wanted it with every fiber of her soul, for when his lips touched hers, nothing else seemed to matter. Several times she caught him watching her, a brooding air about him that was unsettling. What was in his mind? If only she knew. But alas, she would not ask—not after the way he'd snapped at her when she had deigned to question him.

Late one afternoon, she held the door wide as he carried a load of firewood in his good arm. He muttered a brusque thank-you as he passed by, but he did not return her regard. Julianna sensed his refusal to meet her gaze was deliberate. But his task was not an easy one. Carrying the wood with one arm proved awkward, and the topmost chunk tumbled from its perch and clattered across the floor.

Julianna was immediately on her feet. "I'll get—"

"Leave it!" His tone was razor-sharp. Dumping the wood near the hearth, he tore off the sling and flung it to the floor.

Julianna was shaking her head in reproof. "Dane," she scolded, "I don't think you're—"

"I believe I'm fully capable of judging what's best for me, Julianna."

Julianna clamped back a sizzling retort. Inside she was seething. Lord, but he was in a mood! Ignoring him, she presented him with her back and straightened the bedclothes, determinedly ignoring him. She could hear him rummaging through the cupboard behind her.

When she turned back, Dane was tossing a length of linen over his shoulder.

"Going somewhere?" she inquired when he stepped toward the door.

"I'm going to take a bath in the stream." It was almost a growl. He paused, his eyes glinting as he turned and paused, resting his uninjured shoulder against the doorjamb. One corner of his mouth curled upward in a smile that was almost lazy. His gaze traveled her form from head to toe. "Does the idea appeal to you, kitten? Perhaps you'll join me then."

Oh, how she longed to slap his cheek! "Do not flatter yourself," she snapped. "I would dearly love a bath. But you, sir, would hardly be my first choice of companion!"

In shock she heard her own words. In the aftermath, she very nearly choked. What the devil had come over her? Sweet Lord, had she really just said what she had? She was appalled at her own daring.

And Dane was amused. "Kitten! I confess, I am intrigued. I should dearly love to know who your first choice would be. What a lucky, lucky man!"

Julianna shot him a withering glance. His smile widened. Apparently she'd managed to restore his good humor. And it was just like him to tease her about her own folly! "A scant quarter hour, kitten, and the stream is yours. Simply follow the path between the oak trees. You can't miss it."

Long after he'd left her alone, Julianna was certain her face was still flaming. She picked up his pocket watch, sitting on the table where he'd left it. Twenty minutes had passed. Where was he? she thought impatiently.

Fifteen minutes later she was pacing around the table. Panic struck a chord in her. He should have been back by now. Why wasn't he? Perhaps he'd underestimated his strength. Perhaps he was unconscious. Maybe even hurt.

Grabbing a length of linen, clean clothing, and a small cake of soap, she almost bolted out the door.

High above, birds sang from the treetops as she scurried down the path. It was a warm, beautiful day, but she was too agitated to enjoy it. Rounding a bend, through a stand of trees, the stream came into view. Beyond was a flower-clad hillside. Julianna lifted her skirt and stepped over a gnarled root. The sight of a pile of clothing made her stop short. A flutter of movement caught her eye.

Slowly she raised her gaze. Unaware of her presence, Dane was floating lazily on his back. Movement was impossible. Her throat constricted. He was naked. *Naked*. Her mind grappled, but logic prevailed. *Dolt!* chided a silent voice. *How else is he to bathe?*

There was a splash, then he was on his feet. Tossing the water from his hair, he started toward the bank. Looking up, he caught sight of her.

It was too late to run. Too late to hide. She'd been caught, as surely as a hare in a trap.

"This is an unexpected pleasure, kitten. Did you come to join me after all?"

Julianna couldn't have moved to save her soul. Her pulse was clamoring. Her heart was thudding in her ears, thick and heavy.

She swallowed the dryness in her throat. "You were so long, I-I thought something was wrong. I thought something had happened." By God, she wouldn't act like a child, either embarrassed or silly or flighty. She would neither gape nor gasp. She had no intention of giving herself away. No, she would not reveal that he was the first naked male she'd confronted in her life—and to be sure, it was a sight she knew would remain burned in her memory for a long time to come.

The water was placid and serene. She wished he hadn't stopped where it was so deep. Daring as the thought was, she didn't care. She would have loved the chance to study his form at leisure, to indulge what was surely a wanton curiosity. Not that she cared, surprisingly enough. As it was, all she could do was stare.

He was overwhelmingly masculine, his skin sleek and shiny wet. An angry, fiery red scar marred his shoulder. Seeing it, a surge of regret shot through her. Julianna found herself possessed of the urge to run her fingers over it, to press her lips upon it and kiss away the hurt and pain.

Her gaze slipped lower. Droplets of water trapped in the hair on his chest glittered in the sunlight. A quiver tore through her, and she licked her lips. His belly was taut and defined by hard bands of muscle. Below, the water lapped at the ridge of his hips, hiding his—

"Kitten," he said softly.

She dragged her gaze up at the sound of her name. It gave her a start to realize he'd been watching her all the while.

Their eyes caught—and held. "Kitten," he said softly, "are you certain you won't change your mind?"

Her cheeks burned. Wordlessly, she shook her head.

"As you wish then." Bold as you please, he began to wade from the stream.

Julianna sucked in a breath and hastily turned her back. If it was of no consequence to him that she saw him naked, why should it matter to her? Oh, but she longed to give in to temptation! For in her mind's eye, she could still see the outline of a shockingly brazen masculinity. Little wonder that her newfound courage was nowhere to be found. Nay, she wasn't quite so bold as she would have liked.

A few steps behind her she could hear the rustle of clothing. Nonetheless, she actually jumped when he laid a hand on her shoulder. "It's quite safe now." His voice was laden with amusement.

When she turned, a maddening smile lurked on his lips.

"A pity you didn't take me up on the offer, kitten. I venture to say that we should do very well together, you and I."

Oh, the insufferable wretch! His high-handedness provoked a rebellious response.

"I didn't come to see you," she said tartly. "I only came for—for a bath!"

And now it seemed she had no choice but to follow through.

"In that case, I shall be happy to stay and scrub your back."

Julianna's eyes flashed. She bestowed on him a haughty stare.

"No?" He remained where he was, his boots planted firmly. It appeared he was undaunted, the rogue!

"No," she informed him flatly. "And I trust you will not spy on me when you think I'm not looking."

"Kitten, you wound me, that you think so little of me," he said lightly. He executed a smart bow and dropped a cake of soap into her palm. "But should you change your mind, you have only to call my name."

"I will not," she responded tartly.

"Ah, but a man can hope, can he not?"

Oh, but he was infuriating . . . infuriatingly disarming! Julianna watched him as he ambled toward the forest. Any fool would know better than to accept the word of a highwayman. Why should she believe he would honor his word? *Why indeed?* asked a voice in her mind. *Because you know he will*, answered another. *Whatever else he was, he was a gentleman* . . . Ach, but it made no sense! Why did she persist in regarding such a man in a such a way?

Odd, how her heart blustered and squalled, like a storm at sea.

Quickly she disrobed and waded into the stream. The water was freezing; she gasped in shock. Certainly she would not linger, as Dane had been wont to do. Sinking down, she washed hastily, dunking her head beneath the surface to wet her hair. Chilly as it was, it was wonderfully refreshing to be clean.

She dried hurriedly with the length of linen, shivering a little as she drew on her gown. Seating herself on a flat-topped boulder, she pulled her hair over her shoulder, wrung it out, and tugged her comb through the wet strands. As she unrolled her stockings up over the arch of one foot, a sound behind her snared her attention. She turned sharply.

Confound it! Had she been wrong about Dane? She scanned the forest, her lips pressed together. Overhead, a bird dipped and wheeled and turned in a vibrant blue sky. A leaf floated lazily down to the forest floor.

There was nothing.

It was silly, to think that someone was watching her. Pushing aside her uneasiness, she quickly gathered up her clothing and the wet toweling, then left the stream. When she reached the cottage, she crossed the clearing. Maximilian was sitting at the base of a stout oak. He rose and snaked between her feet, rubbing himself against her ankles. Reaching up on tiptoe, she draped her gown across a low-hanging branch so that it could air out. She'd just finished hanging the wet linen when Maximilian yowled and bounded toward the cottage.

She glanced down in surprise. "Maximilian!" she said with a laugh. "Whatever has gotten into you?"

When she looked up, she realized they weren't alone. A large dog stood on the other side of the clearing.

Her smile froze. The fine hairs on the back of her neck prickled, as if in warning. She had never been afraid of strange animals. Growing up at

Thurston Hall, she'd encountered many. But this one was filthy, his long hair matted with brambles. Chills ran up and down her spine.

A low growl vibrated deep in the animal's throat. His lips pulled back, baring his fangs. Saliva dripped from his mouth. Snarling viciously, he crouched back on his haunches, his eyes wild, as if preparing to spring.

Julianna had already begun to move toward the cottage. Her steps quickened, but she was afraid to move too suddenly. The door was ajar. She gauged the distance. Could she make it before—

The animal lunged.

Her slipper caught on an exposed root. She went down hard, jarring the breath from her lungs. Instinctively, she tried to lurch upright. Her hem snagged on the jagged root. She tugged frantically, dimly aware of the cloth tearing. But she was still caught, and she came down hard yet again.

A jagged cry caught in her throat. "Dane!" she heard herself cry. "*Dane!*"

It all happened in a haze. Dane appeared in the doorway. From the corner of her eye she saw the dog barreling toward her.

A deafening explosion seared the air.

In midleap, the mongrel dropped to the ground scant inches from her face.

"Julianna! Christ, are you all right?"

Julianna blinked, struggling to focus. Her head

swam giddily as she was hauled to her feet. Slowly, she turned her head and looked down. The mongrel lay at her feet, sprawled limply on his side. His eyes were still open, his teeth bared. A sticky stream of blood was still spreading, mingling with the dust.

Her stomach heaved.

"Julianna!"

Her gaze shifted back to Dane. Stricken, she regarded him. "You killed him," she said faintly. And then again: "You killed him."

Dane reached for her. "Kitten—"

The word sparked something inside her. Her eyes seemed to blaze. She wrenched away.

"Julianna! What the devil?" Strong hands closed over her shoulders.

Julianna turned on him. Her fists rained against his chest. "You didn't have to kill him!" she cried, over and over and over. "You didn't have to kill him!"

"Julianna! He was mad. He would have attacked you! My God, if he'd bitten you . . . I had to!"

Her expression was wild. She was in a frenzy, pummeling him for all she was worth.

Uttering an explosive curse, Dane caught her wrists. "Kitten!"

"Don't!" she screamed, a cry torn from deep in her vitals. "Don't call me that!"

Hard arms closed around her, capturing her

flailing arms and pinning them to her sides. "Julianna!" His tone was razor-sharp. "Stop this!" She didn't even hear him. "*Julianna!*"

Dazed, her head fell back. She looked at him as he scoured her features.

"What is it? What the devil is wrong?"

As quickly as they had erupted, her struggles ceased. All the fire went out of her.

Her eyes squeezed shut. She slumped against him. "Oh, God," she whispered.

And then she began to cry.

Ten

*D*ane would not soon forget the terrified scream that brought him crashing out the door of the cottage, nor the sight that met his eyes. Christ, if he hadn't had the presence of mind to grab a pistol . . . In the weeks before Waterloo, one of his men had been bitten by a mad dog. His death had been horrifying, sad, tragic— and excruciatingly painful. To think that Julianna might have suffered the same end . . . But he dare not think of that.

His features grim, he picked her up and carried her into the cottage, ignoring the ache in his shoulder.

He kicked the door shut with the heel of his boot. He was bewildered, alarmed, stunned by the way she'd lashed out at him. The shock of nearly being attacked was understandable. Even her near hysteria was understandable. What the devil was wrong?

Her face had gone pasty white. One look in her beautiful blue eyes, and he had the eerie sense she had retreated to another time, another place, where the remnants of something horrible battered her mind and heart.

Kitten, he had said. Lord, but it seemed so innocent! Indeed, he'd grown so used to it, it emerged unwittingly. But then he remembered that once before her temper had flared high. Why, he wondered. *Why?*

Now, in the aftermath, it was as if she'd been bled of every drop of strength. Dane sat in the chair before the fire, cradling her on his lap. Turning her face into his neck, she sobbed quietly, pitiful, heart-wrenching sobs that turned him inside out. Something caught at his chest—at his very soul.

He let her cry until at last she was spent. She lay with her head on his chest, her hand curled beside it. One hand drifted up and down her spine.

With the other he guided a damp chestnut curl behind her ear. "Julianna," he said softly. "What were you thinking of? What happened to you?" He paused uncertainly, his gaze mutely questioning.

She shivered. She shivered as if she were caught

in the midst of a freezing storm from the north. Dane covered her hands in his. Her skin was ice-cold. He weaved his fingers through hers, seeking to warm her.

"Tell me, sweet."

She regarded him with tear-bright eyes. "He killed them," she said woodenly.

"Who?" he prompted gently. "What?"

She swallowed hard. "My father," she said jerkily. "He killed my kittens." There was a heartrending pause. "He drowned them, Dane. He *drowned* them."

Dane sucked in a breath. "What happened?" he asked quietly.

"I was perhaps eight or so. I . . . we were at Thurston Hall, in the country. My brothers were away at school. The tabby in the stable gave birth to kittens. They were darling, so soft. So sweet. Two were white as snow, the other a spotted tabby like his mother. When they were born, I asked my father if I could have one for my very own. I—I was rather lonely, you see. But he said he wouldn't have such creatures in his house, that they were dirty and filthy and belonged in the stable with the mice. But I didn't care. They were so darling. So when they were old enough to be away from their mother, I took them.

"They made me laugh, Dane. I can still see them chasing each other's tails. I named them— Alfred, Rebecca, and Irwin. I—I pretended they were my babies. I wrapped them in blankets and cuddled them. I played with them and scolded them and sang to them . . . they even slept with me in my bed." A wisp of a smile crossed her lips.

It waned all too soon, though.

She continued. "But my father . . . he found them in my room one day. He was furious. He shouted and raged. I had disobeyed him. And he wasn't a man to stand for that, not from any of his children. So I had to be punished."

"Good God! He punished you by drowning your kittens?"

She nodded.

Dane swore silently. No wonder she hated being called *kitten*.

But there was more.

He could only listen while she went on. "He dumped them in a sack and grabbed my hand. I remember crying, all the way to the stream." There was a tiny little break in her voice. "He . . . he made me watch. He made me *listen*." Tears slid unchecked down her cheeks. She cringed, clamping her hands over her ears and curling into a tight little ball against him.

His heart stood still. "Oh, Jesus," he whispered, feeling himself pale . . . and feeling her pain like the stab of a knife.

Dane's lips compressed to a thin, harsh line. Inside he was seething. A black rage blistered his gut, darker than any he'd ever known. Damn the bastard who had been her father! If the wretch had been before him now, he'd have taken great pleasure in throttling the man. How could any man do such a thing to his own child?

"I suppose you think it's silly." Her voice was muffled against his shoulder.

He stroked the groove of her spine, a soothing, monotonous movement. "No. Lord, no." Tenderhearted Julianna, always looking after her animals . . . and now him. So sweet. So nurturing. He could see how it battered her—how it still hurt her. He was stunned by her revelation. It was so different from his own childhood.

Something nagged at his brain. Seeing her like this, he was more puzzled than ever that no man had wed her—that she had never married. It wasn't just her beauty. She possessed a sweetness of nature that shone from within. She was meant to be a wife, a mother, to hold her children close to her breast as she had once held her kittens.

He should have known. Perhaps he *had* known. There was strength behind her softness. Darkness behind the screen of fragile beauty. Secrets behind the lightness of her smile.

"It was the blood that did it," she said suddenly. "When my kittens drowned, there wasn't any blood . . ." Graceful fingers plucked at the front of his shirt. She raised her head and stared at him, her eyes huge and wounded. "Dane . . . the dog . . . will you—"

"I'll bury him," he finished gently, so she wouldn't have to.

"Thank you." She whispered her gratitude.

"You're quite welcome." His expression solemn, he watched her. All of a sudden her gaze shied away.

He frowned. "What is it?"

"I've done it again. I don't know why I'm telling you this," she confided, her voice very low. "It was something I never even told my brothers."

"Why not?" He was more curious than anything else. From the way she spoke of her brothers, he'd already guessed that they were close.

"It wouldn't have changed what happened. There was nothing they could have done. But mostly—I couldn't bear to think of it again."

"Little wonder." Dane's lips were thin. "Julianna, forgive me for being blunt, but I wouldn't have liked your father."

"I'm not sure anyone did," she said after a moment. "He was a harsh, rigid man, very stern." She seemed to hesitate. When she spoke again, her voice was barely audible. "I was almost fourteen when he died. And—I cried when my kittens died. But I didn't cry when *he* died. May God forgive me, but—I wasn't sad. The truth is . . . I was almost relieved. I felt . . . like perhaps we could finally be happy, Sebastian, Justin, and I." Shadows invaded her eyes. "Do you think that's terribly wrong of me?"

"Not," he stated grimly, "under the circumstances."

She bit her lip. "And that, too, is something I've never told anyone."

Dane couldn't help it. He was rather uncomfortable. He liked that she trusted him enough to confide in him so. Yet a sliver of guilt cut through him. He hadn't earned her trust. He didn't deserve it, not really. For he had not been totally open with her . . .

But he couldn't tell her the truth. There was too much at stake. He couldn't risk involving her.

His mind drifted. After a moment he said, "We all have our demons, Julianna. For I, too, have something I've never told a living soul."

"You do? Truly?"

He nodded, steeling himself. "I'm afraid," he admitted at last.

"You? Of what?"

"Of dying." He released a long breath. "I wasn't, until Waterloo. When one is young, it's not something one worries about, is it? Like you, it was . . . something I prefer not to think about. It was—a battle unlike any other. Volleys of musket and cannon fire all around. Smoke so thick we nearly choked. We certainly couldn't see. I thought it would never end! I remember, men were falling all around me. Like sticks being felled by a hand from above. And when it was over, thousands were dead all around me, and I was alive. And all I could feel was a mind-numbing relief that it was them, and not me. I was hailed as a hero, when in truth I was, in a word, or rather two, quite terrified. And that made me feel like a coward. And so"—he shook his head—"so very ashamed."

"Ashamed! Why?"

"Because I was glad—glad!—that I was alive. That I had not been the one to die. That someone else had fallen—and not me." He hesitated. "It seems wrong somehow."

"I don't think it's wrong to feel that way. I should imagine anyone would feel like that. It's simply that not everyone would admit to it."

"Perhaps. Perhaps not. But either way, since that day, I"—Christ, he could barely stand to say it—"I cannot bear to think of death and dying."

He lapsed into silence, then tipped his head to the side and regarded her. "Any more secrets you wish to share?"

To his surprise, a look of utter surprise flitted across her features. The breath she drew was deep and ragged. Her lips parted.

With his thumb he wiped the glistening dampness from her cheek. "Here now! I'm only teasing."

"Dane—"

His arms encircled her. "You don't have to say any more, sweet, I swear." He drew her tight against him—tight!—sliding his arms around her back and bringing her against him. It seemed she clung to him forever. The damp heat of her tears against his shirt twisted him into knots.

And then it happened.

Slowly she raised her head.

Their eyes locked. *They* were locked fast in an intimate embrace. A *scorchingly* intimate embrace, the air between them heated and close. At some point her arms had twined around his neck. She was so slight he could barely feel her weight in his lap. But he could feel the press of soft, ripe breasts resting against his chest. One slim leg was wedged between the steely strength of his; her thigh pressed against his rod. Heat rose in his body—he couldn't stop it.

He swelled hard and full.

She swallowed.

Silence thundered all around them.

He stared down at her, sensing she was caught in the same shattering void as he. A current of awareness streaked through him. Her eyes were riveted to his, her arms wound tight around his neck. Everything inside him had gone taut.

He sucked in a harsh breath. God, she smelled like lemons, crisp and light, a scent that was uniquely hers. Holding her against him like this . . . it was part joy, part pain. His gaze traced the contours of her face, the delicate molding of her cheeks and chin.

A voice in his head clamored for him to release her. His mind urged one course, while his body willed otherwise. He didn't trust himself to touch her. He *shouldn't* trust himself to touch her. But the afternoon sunlight was shining through her hair, making it shimmer like honey. Her mouth was dewy and tremulous and vulnerable, hovering but a breath beneath his.

His hands clenched on her waist, whether to lift her away, or draw her nearer still, he didn't know.

It was she who broke the stalemate.

Her eyes were still awash with tears, blue and shimmering. He couldn't look away as her fingertips came to rest directly on the center of his lips. "Dane," she whispered. "*Dane.*" And within that sound was immersed the same fierce yearning, a sound that eroded what little shred of will he possessed.

The moment was young, the time ripe, and a dozen different emotions were roiling inside him . . .

And then there was no turning back.

His mouth captured hers, a kiss of deep, rousing exploration. There was no withholding it. He succumbed to a desire that had been building for days. And knowing she was not indifferent to him set him afire like flame to tinder.

In one swift surge of power he was on his feet, bearing her to the bed.

He eased down beside her. Her gaze never left his as she trailed her fingers over his jaw. Her eyes searched his face. "I'm sorry. Did I hurt you?"

A half smile curled his lips. "A puny little thing like you? I think not." He caught her hand and pressed a kiss into her palm.

Her fingertips extended, the merest caress. She looked up at him, as if to gauge his reaction.

His smile faded. His eyes darkened.

Slowly, he lowered his head. His kiss was languid and unhurried. Her eyelids fluttered shut. Her lips parted. She offered her mouth with a breathless little sound of pleasure. The tip of her tongue touched his, her response sweetly unbridled. She tasted delicious, and he pictured the delicate pink tip of her tongue lapping against his naked skin. Venturing across his chest, swirling around his navel, down his belly until she reached his—

The vision shook him to his very bones. It was like a fist ramming hard into his gut, driving the air from his lungs. Sweet Christ, *that* didn't bear thinking about. His mouth opened wider as he caught her to him, his kiss turning almost ferocious. Her hands slipped beneath his shirt, sliding along his ribs, creeping upward, a tentative exploration until finally her palms splayed wide on the bare skin of his back. She arched against him, the entire sweet length of her body against his. A shudder tore through him, and he nearly groaned.

His fingers fumbled with the ribbon that laced the neck of her gown. He plunged his fingers inside the cloth, tugging it aside and revealing the sleekness of her shoulder . . . revealing her breast.

Perfection. Sheer perfection, he marveled. Her skin was pale and gleaming, the color of cream. Her breasts were small but sweetly formed, her nipples plump and pink, the same pale rose as a new dawn.

His head descended. He blew across the tip of one breast, watching it tighten. His tongue curled wetly around first one, then the other, feeling those dusky crowns peak hard in his mouth.

"Dane . . . oh, Dane." He reveled in her tiny little gasp, the bite of her nails on his back. The fingers of one slim hand came up to tangle in the hair on his nape, as if to hold him there.

She was untried. A virgin, surely. Oh, God, but he was sorely tempted to put the theory to the test . . . but he was not a despoiler of innocent females, though indeed she tested his restraint to the utmost!

He was quite, quite certain no man had ever kissed her as he had. Touched her as he had. Yet something inside compelled him to know. He *had* to.

His mouth returned to hers. "Are you a virgin?" he muttered.

Beneath him, she went very still.

"Julianna, sweet . . . tell me. You've never done this before, have you?"

"I—I've been kissed. I have," she cried, when he raised a brow.

"So you're a virgin?"

She turned her face blindly into his shoulder. "Why do you ask?"

Dane made a sound low in his throat. Slipping his knuckles beneath her chin, he brought her eyes to his.

The silence dangled.

He rested his forehead against hers. "Julianna," he said softly. "You are, aren't you?"

Her gaze returned to his. Her cheeks were flaming. "Yes," she said weakly. "Yes!" The jagged little cry broke from her lips. Her head dipped low, but not before he glimpsed the sheen of tears that turned her eyes to pure sapphire.

Her vulnerability sped straight to his heart. Dane was a man who disliked vulnerability—not because he viewed it as weakness. Nay, instead it made him long to put it to rights.

"Hush, Julianna. *Hush*. It's all right. It's nothing to be ashamed of."

"I am not ashamed!" she cried.

Only then did he realize he'd clamped her buttocks against him, tugging her into the notch between his thighs.

He was still iron-hard and erect. Pulsing, pulsing, pulsing against the hollow of her belly. . . . A part of him wanted to roll her to her back and let desire rule.

He wanted her. He wanted her with a pounding, driving force that made his blood boil. He wanted to taste every pale inch of her skin, proclaim her captivating innocence for his own. He longed to hear her moan her need into his mouth as he buried himself deep, feeling her hot and wet and tight around him as they both hurtled to climax.

He could have seduced her. Cajoled her into warm, sweet compliance until she was writhing and fevered and panting against him. And she wouldn't have stopped him. Some strange inner sense told him she would have allowed him to do whatever he wished.

And somehow that shriveled his ardor as nothing else could have.

Leaning back on the pillow, his features drawn into a grimace, he loosed his grip on her.

Julianna drew a sharp breath. "Dane—" A silent question hovered between them.

He expelled a long, pent-up sigh, then wrapped her in a loose embrace. Tucking her head against his shoulder, he rested his chin against shining chestnut waves, seeking to quiet the tumult in his veins.

"Just let me hold you for a while," he said very quietly. "Just let me hold you."

Eleven

The last faint rays of evening trickled in through the high windows when Julianna awoke. She lay there for a long time, aware that she was alone. She dimly recalled Dane leaving the bed sometime earlier.

Pushing aside the blanket—she didn't remember his covering her—she swung her feet to the floor. The sight of her naked breasts was jarring. She started to tug the gown up over her shoulders, then abruptly changed her mind when she spied the mongrel's blood spattered on the side of the skirt. Her stomach started to churn, but she willed it away.

Shucking the gown, she stood before the washbasin in her linen chemise. Her eyes were puffy and swollen and gritty from tears; she soaked a cloth and pressed it to her eyes. The cold felt wonderfully refreshing, and she laid it aside reluctantly.

The reminder was inevitable, perhaps. She winced as she recalled her outburst. Uncertainty and regret whirled in her chest, a veritable tempest. She was reminded of all she'd told Dane. Such frailty was unlike her. She prided herself on her independence. She was most assuredly *not* a namby-pamby miss.

But no doubt Dane was convinced otherwise. She'd come completely undone. What had he thought of her? Did he think her weak? Childish?

Yet he'd been remarkably understanding. Comforting, even. And . . . God, but it felt so good to lie against his length. To absorb his heat and feel safe and secure in a way she'd never felt before.

A burning ache seared her heart. What would it be like, she wondered wistfully, to lie beside a man night after night—to feel the strength of a man's arms tight about her back and know it meant forever? To know his warmth. His tenderness. Pain crowded her breast, for that was something she would never experience.

And she felt the loss to the marrow of her bones!

For Dane's arms had been warm. Strong and tender, his embrace a haven of shelter and safety.

And when he'd kissed her . . . ah, when he'd

kissed her! Thomas's cool lips had been nothing compared to what Dane had done. Nothing that resounded in the fiber of her soul, in the depths of her heart. And when his fingers skimmed her bare skin. Her bare breast . . .

Heaven help her, but that was something she could not regret.

Nor would she soon forget. Indeed, she could not banish the terrifying feeling she might *never* forget . . .

She was still standing before the washbasin when the door swung open. There was dirt on his shirt; she knew what it signified.

Her gaze didn't waver from his. "It's done?"

He nodded.

She swallowed. "Thank you."

His gaze flickered over her, and she flushed. Her gown lay over the back of the chair. Modesty compelled that she reach for it. Clutching it against her chest, she turned back to him.

She could not move.

Caught in the last fading light of the day, the very sight of him made her throat constrict. He was so handsome he stole her breath. His shirt was open at the throat, revealing a masculine tangle of hair. She could almost feel his skin beneath her fingertips once more, sleek and smooth. She jerked her gaze upward to his features, but that was no better. His mouth was unsmiling, but not severe. She recalled that hot, molten way he'd kissed her, the hot, moist cave of his mouth on her nipples. Her face began to heat. And now he was staring at her, hard, at the color high and bright upon her cheekbones.

Disconcerted, she turned toward the fire. Her heart began to pound as she felt him walk up behind her. Oh, but he was close. So very close . . .

She started when he pulled her back against his chest. His forearm pressed snug against the sides of her breast.

"You don't have to hide yourself from me, Julianna."

Julianna caught her lower lip between her teeth. Rarely was she at a loss for words, but this was one of those rare situations when she was.

She could feel the rush of his breath against her ear.

"You're angry," he said after a moment.

"No," she managed, with a shake of her head.

"Then why won't you look at me?"

Within his tone lay a soft rebuke. Lean hands cupped her shoulders. He turned her around, retaining possession of her shoulders.

Julianna licked her lips and summoned her courage. "I am not angry," she emphasized. "Why would I be angry?"

To that he merely raised a brow. His gaze drifted down to her breasts.

She chose her words carefully. "This is a situation that is not familiar to me. Frankly, I'm not sure precisely how to act."

Something lit in his eyes. "Love," he remarked, "I think that is a certainty."

His amusement pricked her temper. "Do not make light of me!"

Dane sighed. "For pity's sake, would you stop clutching your gown to yourself that way? Contrary to what you appear to believe, I am still capable of a modicum of restraint."

"Yes, I do believe that is quite apparent!"

His eyes narrowed. "What the devil is that supposed to mean?"

Too late, Julianna regretted her outburst.

He stared at her. "Wait," he said slowly. "Surely you cannot think I don't want you."

Her mind was churning so that she could scarcely think. "I told you," she admitted, her voice very low. "I don't know what to think."

His regard sharpened. Something flickered across his features. To her surprise, he tugged her gown from her grasp and tossed it aside. Then he proceeded to look the length of her, his regard unhurried. Standing before him clad only in the frail thinness of her chemise, she blushed, but didn't hide herself.

He weaved his fingers through her hair. "Do you know what I want?" he asked softly.

Julianna stared up at him. His eyes were beautiful, like crystal in his bronzed face, a shimmer of gold. They reflected the light and shadow . . . and the flaming heat of desire.

Caught fast in the hold of those beautiful golden eyes, her heart knocked wildly. She shook her head.

"You've slept beside me all these nights, Julianna. And I've lain awake wondering what you would look like naked. I've wondered what it would be like to feel your thighs warm against mine. *Between* mine. I want to lay you down. Here. Now. I want to touch you. Feel you warm and damp against my fingers. Kiss you. Taste you with my tongue. Everywhere, Julianna. *Everywhere.*"

A little shock went through her. Her mind went hazy. The words were hot. Molten. She could almost believe he meant . . . But no. Surely he didn't. Surely he *couldn't.*

He gazed directly into her eyes, as if he sought to see clear inside her. "Does that shock you, sweet?"

Her throat closed. For the span of a moment, speech was impossible. Oh, sweet Lord, he *did* . . .

Her tongue came out to wet her lips. "You meant it to, didn't you?" she asked faintly.

"Perhaps." He caught her hand. "I burn inside," he whispered. "All over. But especially here." His fingers trapped hers. He brought them down . . . down . . . until they rested on the swelling ridge of his erection. "I burn for you, Julianna. My body burns. My *heart* burns."

Julianna stared. He was solemnly intent. And now it seemed her heart surely ceased to beat. She could feel him, the thickening swell of his rod against her fingertips, the measure of a need that made her eyes widen and her heart throb. "So does mine," she said faintly.

Dane exhaled, a sharp expulsion of breath. Her eyes were brilliant and blue and unfaltering. He squeezed his own shut. Pulling her hand away, he swore, a long, vividly explicit curse. It was damned difficult seeing her like this, half-naked, the sheen of her body clearly visible through the thin cloth.

"God, Julianna, you shouldn't say that."

Her heart gave a little thump. "Why not?" she whispered.

His laugh was rather brittle. "You are not making this easy for me. I am trying to do the honorable thing."

A hot ache crowded her throat.

"Only an honorable man would have lain beside me these many nights and not . . ." Her voice trailed away. Her gaze conveyed the words that she could not.

His gaze bored into hers. "Julianna," he said, gritting. "Oh, Christ."

His mouth came down on hers, dark and urgent and ravenous. When he kissed her the very earth crumpled beneath her feet. It made no sense that he should know her as he did, the way that he did. Yet this man understood her as no one else ever had. And yes, he seemed to know precisely what she wanted. What she needed. To be held and sheltered. To be *wanted*.

Who she was didn't seem to matter. Who *he* was, she cared not.

All that mattered was the hungry need she tasted in his kiss, in the fierce way he held her riveted against him. With effortless ease he swung her up in his arms and carried her to the bed, she clung to him. There was no thought of denial. In that moment, she wanted to be needed. She needed for him to need her.

Impatiently he peeled off his own clothing, kicked aside his breeches, and stretched out beside her. The width of his shoulders blotted out the light from the fire. Divested of clothing, he seemed even bigger.

Unable to stop herself, Julianna reached for him. Then her hands were on his chest. His *naked* chest. She registered heat and strength. His skin was hot. Fiery hot, reminding her of what he'd said . . .

I burn for you. My body burns. My heart burns.

An odd dryness filled her throat. Their lips touched. Clinging. His mouth opened wider, and he took from her a deep, urgent kiss that branded her insides. Her heart was knocking so hard she could scarcely breathe. A lean brown hand slipped beneath her chemise, his fingers closing one by one around her buttocks. Her heart stood still as he pulled her tight against his thighs . . . into them. One mind-stealing glimpse of his erection sent her eyes skidding to his face. She was afraid to look at him, yet she could feel him. Held full and tight against him by the muscled arm around her back, she was achingly aware of all that lay beneath the steely strength of his thighs. . . . Especially there. Hard and thick and so supremely male.

A tiny little gasp escaped her throat.

Dane's head came up. His fingers threaded in her hair, cleaving her eyes to his. "Are you afraid?" His voice was low and taut.

She shook her head, her eyes liquid. "Not of you," she confided.

Something flashed in his eyes, some hint of satisfaction. He barely brushed her lips. "I want to see you," he whispered against the corner of her mouth. "All of you, sweet. *All of you.*"

She knew what he was doing. This was her journey—this sojourn into the world of passion—and he would lead her down the path. But this first step must belong to her.

Sitting up, her heart lodged high in her throat,

she reached for the hem of her chemise. There was a rustle of fabric as she bared her body.

And perhaps she bared her soul.

Holding herself utterly still, she felt his gaze pour over her skin, a slow, scorching appraisal that set her pulse all a-clamor. Beneath his unbending regard, her breasts grew heavy and achy. There was fire in her blood, she decided hazily. A blaze in her heart.

There were reasons this shouldn't be happening, but none of them seemed to matter. She was offering herself to him. In some far-distant part of her, perhaps she was amazed. Stunned at her own daring. She didn't care. This wasn't London. They were alone. There was no one but the two of them. No one to please but themselves. No one to see. No one to care. No one to gossip in snide, hurtful ways. No one to whisper behind their hands and eye her in that sad, pitying way she had always detested. Here there was no one to *please* but herself.

No, the strictures of society had no place here. The rules were her own. The rules were *theirs.* Here with Dane, it was different. *She* was different. She trembled with a yearning unfulfilled. She wanted to know what she would never know otherwise. He made her feel strange. Daring. She almost felt as if she didn't recognize herself.

And she wanted to be bold. She longed to be

adventurous and uncaring, to give in to her desire, to be all those things she had never allowed herself to be.

And so she allowed herself no time to think. Indeed, thought suddenly seemed . . . superfluous, here in this cottage. Here with Dane. For when he touched her—when he kissed her!— time and space and the world itself eroded to nothingness. She felt . . . so many things she'd never felt before! Alive as never before. Free as never before.

Dane had pushed himself to a sitting position as well. A lone fingertip traced a nerve-shattering path around the border of one nipple; almost ere she drew a tremulous breath, it was joined by the other. A tremor shot through her as the heat of his palms slid over her breasts, replacing his fingers. He played with the tips, the wispiest caress.

"Lovely, my sweet Julianna. Absolutely lovely."

He murmured his praise, his voice exquisitely low and rich, almost as mesmerizing as the sight of his hands on her breasts, so lean and brown, intensely masculine. She was tingling, especially there at the tips of her breasts.

Suddenly he shifted. She couldn't look away as he leaned forward and trapped her nipple in his mouth; his tongue circled an avid pattern, and he sucked hard like a babe hungry for milk. The sensation was unbearably sweet . . . nay, nigh unbearable. Feeling giddy, with a gasp she caught at the hardness of his shoulders. Everything inside went weak and utterly boneless. She was melting, she decided dimly, both inside and out. Of their own volition her hands fitted to the contours of his shoulders.

He caught her in his arms as she slid down, snaring her close. Her eyes were soft and dewy and dazed, as blue as a sunlit sky after a morning rain, an expression that only ignited the fires with him. His features twisted in a grimace that was part pain, part pleasure, he gritted his teeth, squarely in the middle between the throes of heaven and the blackest pits of hell. Her mouth hovered just beneath his, tempting . . . ah, so tempting! Her body, slim and lithe and naked, aroused him almost past bearing.

He should have let her be. He should never have touched her. Held her. For where the lovely Julianna was concerned, it seemed his self-control was almost nonexistent. Almost . . . but not quite.

He wanted her. He wanted her so badly he was shaking. Not with fever. But with need. Want. Like an untried boy. A lad. A screaming desire clamored throughout every part of him. But especially, there in the part of him he could not hide. He ached for her. More than anything, he wanted to curl her small hand around his burning flesh, feel her stroking, seeking. In his mind's eye he conjured up vivid, sensual images. Of Julianna above him. Astride him. Of him above her, her legs spread wide to receive him as he drove himself home. The very thought made sweat pop out on his brow; his pulse raced apace with the throbbing of his staff. Yet if she touched him— sweet Lord, if she touched him, he would surely spill himself on the spot!

He could not contain the rampant desire that seized hold of his body, his every sense. Nor could he yield to it. Reason urged retreat. No, warned an insistent voice in his mind, he could not have her. He longed to plant himself deep. He ground away the thought. Nothing should hurt her. Nothing would, he concluded, including himself. But by God, he could please her. Pleasure her without breaching her.

Almost desperately his mouth closed over hers. His kiss was half-wild, only barely under control, but she knew what he wanted. Her lips parted, open and avid beneath his. With a tiny little moan, her tongue sparred with his, a wantonly evocative rhythm. Both the sound and her warm, welcoming response spurred him over the edge.

A shudder ripped through him. His fingers skimmed the plane of her belly, pursuing a relentless path downward. For one stark, breathless moment he paused, the heel of his hand resting possessively on the hollow of her belly, his fingertips poised directly above her nest of chestnut fleece. With unerring boldness he claimed her as his own, intent on seeing to her gratification.

She jerked when his first encompassing pass grazed pink, dewy folds, but she did not shrink; the second explored with unerring precision, parting each side of her silken pocket to search out the secret nub hidden deep within, so achingly sensitive she nearly cried out.

"Such soft, lovely curls," he breathed against the corner of her mouth. "Part your legs, yes, that's the way. Open to me, sweet, open *for* me. Oh, Julianna, sweet Julianna, you're damp and so ready, aren't you?"

With the very tips of his fingers he taunted and teased, his fingers toying with the gateway to her body, discovering plump, pliant flesh. It swelled to a delicious fullness; the glistening evidence of her passion bedewed his fingertips. Elation soared. Her shiver nearly obliterated his control. And then he dared still more.

His middle finger slid inside her.

In shock, her mouth opened against his.

"Shhh. My finger. That's all."

By slow, insidious degrees, it worked deeper. Higher, a sweeping invasion of her channel. Her inner walls clenched around his finger, even as her nails bit deep into his shoulders.

"Another," he whispered.

And it was done.

She gasped, a sound of need. She was twisting

around it . . . against him. Her flesh was tight. Wet. Both the realization and the feel of her tested his control to the utmost. Gently he plied her. Stroking. Seeking. Again and again, a tormentingly wicked rhythm, deeper and deeper, high and deep. And all the while his thumb continued to ply its magic, circling the delicate nub, indulging in a wild, wanton rhythm of its own.

It was heated. Shattering. Almost frightening, for there was an explosive storm building inside her. Gathering strength until she felt she would fly apart inside. She could feel herself twisting. Writhing. Desperately searching, but for what . . . *what*? Shaken, she tore her mouth from his.

His hot whisper rushed past her cheek. "It's all right, sweet. It's supposed to happen. Just *let* it happen. Don't fight it."

She didn't. She couldn't. And then it did . . . Her eyes squeezed shut. Her body convulsed, again and again, as molten waves of pleasure shot through her.

Her eyes opened, dazed and smoky. Dane's mouth was on the arch of her neck. A featherlight kiss was pressed upon the peak of each breast. And then his body slid down . . . ever downward. His mouth mapped a flaming trail across the hollow of her belly.

Warm fingertips grazed the back of her legs,

lifting—adjusting—until her knees were upright. Warm breath drizzled through her nether fleece; her own grew painfully shallow. His thumbs brushed across curls already damp from the wanton play of his fingers.

A stab of dark sensation shot through her. His promise echoed in her mind. *I want to touch you . . . Kiss you. Taste you with my tongue. Everywhere . . .* Everywhere.

Her mind balked. Her eyes widened. Her entire body went hot.

Oh, no, she thought vaguely. *No.*

"Dane—" His name was a half-choked sound. Her fingers curled tightly around his where one hand splayed on the hollow of her belly. "You cannot. I . . . it cannot be proper!"

Slowly he raised his head, lifting burning eyes to hers. "Do you trust me, Julianna?" His voice was strangely thick.

She shouldn't, she thought wildly. Yet she did. Every sense within her—all she knew of him— signaled that he was not a man without principles. Without morals. Without conviction. And the feelings coursing through her . . . they couldn't be shameful, could they?

"You know I do," she said weakly.

"Then let me please you. Let me . . ." Turning his head, he kissed the inside of one slim white thigh.

She inhaled raggedly. "Dane," she whispered helplessly. "You shouldn't. Oh, God, you can't. Not . . . there. Not *there*."

The words dissolved into a moan. Her hands fluttered to the sheets. Her heart was pounding. She still could not believe that he would—

He did.

Her mind faltered. Her senses swarmed. Her throat locked. With the bulk of his shoulders he spread wide her trembling limbs.

A white-hot jolt went through her at his first brazenly intimate caress—a kiss so daringly explicit her eyes squeezed shut. Her thighs weakened. Her knees drifted apart. She lay open to him, open and vulnerable, open to whatever he sought. Whatever he willed.

It came again, and again, the surge of his tongue nudging, delving full and high within her curls. Blistering heat shot through her. Oh, God, she was melting. Melting inside and out. Against him . . . his mouth.

The lapping velvet of his tongue was blazingly erotic. A divine, lazy torment. Retreating. Advancing, circling around and around the nugget of sensation centered deep within weeping pink folds.

Her breath emerged in a rush. She thrust her hips against him in a wanton frenzy.

"Please," she moaned. "Oh, please." She was

begging, seeking that exquisite pleasure once more. She was close. Tantalizingly close.

Her breathless cries pushed Dane nearer the edge. He savored each ragged breath, each desperate gasp. Half-mad himself, at last he laid his tongue full against her cleft, her swollen core. It came then, all that he sought . . . all that she wanted. A sound that was half sob, half moan, and sheer bliss tore from her throat.

Spurred on by her scalding release, burying his head against her, he shuddered his own.

Twelve

*J*ulianna was still trembling when he settled her into his arms and covered them both with the blanket. Long, blessed moments passed before she was able to speak.

"My word," she said faintly. "That was quite . . . quite . . ."

He levered himself up and to her side. His laugh was low and husky as he propped himself on an elbow. "Yes, it was quite that, wasn't it?" he teased.

Vivid images still fluttered through her mind, starkly erotic. The brazen possession of his hand, dark and lean, straying down her belly, sliding over her thighs. Clamped between. The way she lay open to him. To his fingers. His mouth.

Later she would ask herself how she dared. For

now, she gathered every ounce of her courage. "Dane"—her tone was scarcely more than a breath—"why didn't you—" Her gaze shied away. She stopped short.

"What? Come, out with it now, love."

"Oh!" she cried, raising her head to glare at him. "You did not . . . *we* did not . . ."

He picked up a chestnut curl that streamed across his chest. "I find the prospect of you blushing all over an interesting one."

What maddening audacity! Still, the need to know quested restlessly inside her. "Dane! You know very well what I mean!"

His brows shot high. He chuckled. "After what just passed between us," he said almost lazily, "you should have no qualms about saying it."

"Very well then! Why didn't you make love to me?"

His smile waned. He gave her a long, slow look. "Oh, but I did," he said very quietly. He tilted his head to the side and gazed down at her. "There is more than one way for a man and woman to make love, little one."

"Yes, yes, but—"

"Ah." He nodded sagely. "You are divining to tell me you know the how and why and *where* all the proper male and female body parts should connect, eh?"

"Yes, precisely so! And I'm quite aware that—"

He gave her a cool, thoughtful look. "Did I not please you?"

Her cheeks were flaming. "You know you did," she blurted. "But what about you? You did not find—completion."

He arched a brow. "Didn't I?" he murmured.

Her eyes widened. She hid her face against his shoulder. In a way, Julianna realized, what he had done had been more intimate than if he'd been *inside* her. And yet . . . "Dane," she said, her voice half-stifled, "I thought that you would make love to me in—in the customary way."

A smile lit his eyes. "The customary way?" he repeated, amused. "Oh, my, but you've a lot to learn."

"Do not mock me! You didn't . . . and you could have—" She floundered. "—you could have, and I know you're quite aware of it!"

His eyes flickered. He laid his fingers against the fiery heat of her cheek. "I wanted to. I wanted to more than anything." He cast a rueful glance down his body. "I do believe the evidence was without question. God knows I could not hide it, could I?" He traced the line of her jaw. "You tempted me, Julianna. You tempted me almost past bearing. You tempt me still."

Confusion roiled within her. "Then why—"

With his thumb and forefinger, he turned her face up to his. His expression was utterly grave.

"Listen to me, sweet. I care for you. I care for you more than is good for the both of us. And that is why I will not take what should belong to your husband."

She stared. "What?"

"You don't understand, do you?"

Her eyes clung to his. She shook her head.

Softly he spoke. "You, my lovely Julianna, are very much a lady. And I am not without scruples. Your virginity doesn't belong to me. And however much I am tempted—however much my body urges otherwise—I am not so selfish that I will take it." He paused. "It should be given on your wedding night . . . to the man who will be your husband."

Julianna's breath caught. Deliberately, she turned her face aside. "It's you who doesn't understand." She paused, trying to ignore the sudden pinch in her heart. "I'll never marry. Never."

Dane made a sound. "Of course you will—"

"No," she said tonelessly. "I won't."

His eyes narrowed. "You're fetching beyond measure. You're young. Why the devil would you believe such a thing? Why would you even say it?"

The wisp of a smile crossed her lips, yet it seemed to hold a wealth of sadness.

"I will soon be eight-and-twenty. In Society's eyes, I am on the shelf. I have accepted that I will have no husband. That I will bear no children."

"Julianna," he started to chide.

Her voice cut across his. "It is not by chance, but by choice." Her gaze slipped away.

Dane wasn't so sure. In the instant before she turned her face aside, her expression betrayed a far-different emotion in her eyes.

"That is not what you want," he said immediately.

"That is what must be."

He frowned, watching in puzzlement as she dragged the sheet up over her nakedness. Why was she so adamant? he wondered. So certain? And what madness was this that she would resign herself to a life of solitude?

She looked no higher than his chin. "Do you remember when you asked why I wasn't married?"

He nodded.

Her voice, when at last it came, was so low he had to strain to hear. "I almost was—once."

"When?"

"Four years ago."

"You ended the engagement?"

An expression that might have been pain flitted across her features. "No," she said in an odd voice. "He ended the wedding. Or more precisely, he never appeared."

Dane looked at her sharply. "What?"

She shrugged. Her attempt at a smile was valiant but an abysmal failure. Sensing how she'd been hurt, he caught her hand in his; her fingers looked small and pale trapped within his. "What happened?"

"I had known Thomas for nearly three years. He asked me to marry him several times, but I wanted to wait. After the wretchedness of my parents' marriage, I wanted both of us to be sure it was *right*, that it was what both of us wanted. I was ecstatic. I wanted everything to be perfect. I'd always dreamed of being married at St. George's in Hanover Square. And as I walked into the vestibule, my heart was singing. It was the happiest day of my life, Dane, and I was so certain it was just the beginning . . . The last thing I expected was that Thomas would not appear. But I waited and waited. Everyone in the church began to turn and stare. And whisper . . ."

Dane's heart went out to her, for she cringed with the memory.

"Yet even then I did not doubt Thomas. I was convinced an accident had kept him from me. But then his brother came, and I learned the truth. That Thomas had eloped to Gretna Green with another woman—Clarice Grey—the night before."

Dane uttered a furious exclamation. "That blackguard!"

But Julianna was shaking her head. "He is a good man. Truly. He is kind and compassionate, and perhaps that made it harder to understand, harder to accept. When they returned, Thomas came to see me, to explain. Clarice had come to him earlier in the day. She was carrying his child, you see. They'd known each other since childhood. It was a moment of weakness, he said, for both of them. He could not abandon her, and so they eloped. We—we both cried, Dane, for he knew how he'd hurt me. I felt like a fool for trusting him, for trusting my feelings—my heart! I thought I knew him so well! But then I felt like I didn't know him at all.

"I was so ashamed. Embarrassed. I hated the whispers, the stares, wherever I went. It was as if all of London knew. I wanted to hide from the world, and so I ran away to the Continent. I stayed for months. I was such a coward—"

"You are not a coward, Julianna. And I daresay, most women would not be so forgiving."

"Forgiving was easy. Understanding was not. I used to wonder . . . Perhaps I waited too long. Perhaps I should have agreed to marry him earlier. Perhaps he grew impatient. Perhaps I wasn't pretty enough."

Dane made a sound. "That is nonsense! You should hate him, but you don't, do you?"

"I did for a time," she admitted. "But Clarice was . . . *is* the mother of his child. It was only right that he marry her. His obligation, his duty was to them. He did the honorable thing. I respect his decision far more than if he had wed me knowing another woman carried his child."

So she said. But Dane wasn't so certain. For all her bravado, he sensed an elusive pain.

"You have no regrets? You do not wish you had married him?" Why it mattered, he didn't know. It shouldn't.

She hesitated. Her eyes avoided his.

An odd sensation gripped his chest. "You still love him, don't you? You still love Thomas."

Her gaze returned to his. Her lips parted. "No. *No!* But I miss what I will never have. I could never have married him knowing he betrayed me. I could never have married him knowing he had deserted Clarice. I could never countenance a man who lied to me. I would far rather be alone."

He persisted. "What then? What are you thinking?"

She took a deep breath. "A year later," she confided, her tone very low, "I was walking in the park. Thomas and Clarice were there. It was the first time I saw his baby, a boy. And I held him, his baby . . . *their* baby. I held him and I"—there was a tiny break in her voice—"I shouldn't have."

He toyed with her fingertips. "Why not?" he asked softly.

Her eyes squeezed shut. When they opened, they were dark and glistening. "I didn't expect it to hurt. But it did, Dane. It hurt so much I could have screamed aloud. And I'll never forget, as I cradled him in my arms, but one thing went through my mind."

He could almost feel the ache that battered her. "Tell me, sweet."

"That he could have been mine. That he *should* have been mine. And it wasn't that I wanted Thomas." Sudden tears glazed her beautiful blue eyes. "It was just that my arms were so empty. They'll always be empty."

"You are a beautiful woman, Julianna. It's not too late. You can still have babies—"

"No. *No.* I won't marry a man who doesn't love me, a man I don't love! I—I'm content with my life. I have my family for companionship. I have a home in London, a lovely house in the country. My finances are assured. A woman need not have a husband to be happy. And I don't want my child born out of duty. Out of obligation. I'd rather my arms were empty than wed a man I cannot trust. And I'm not sure I can trust any man again! A husband should be faithful and true. But how will I know? How will I know?"

This last was a stricken cry full of anguish.

Understanding dawned in a flash. She said she was content with her life. But was she? He admired her strength, her independence, her spirit, the way she had gone on with her life despite the shame and loss. But she refused to let herself love again. The experience had shattered her trust in others. Her faith in herself, whether she knew it or not.

And he'd been right. Sweet, lovely Julianna, whose gentle purity made him ache inside. Her features were helpless. Haunted. She was meant to have a family, to be a mother, laughing as her little ones clambered on her lap and gathered at her feet. God, he could almost see it! She had so much to give, yet she'd shut herself away.

A man would be lucky to have her as his wife, he decided suddenly. She was staunch and steadfast, bright and giving, her nature loving and generous.

I'm not sure I can trust any man again, she said.

But she had trusted him. She had trusted *him.*

A feeling of sheer, raw possessiveness swept over him. Yet all at once he felt he'd been seized by the throat. He couldn't breathe, couldn't even think. An unwanted voice reared up inside him. She wouldn't trust him if she knew how he, too, had deceived her.

Closing his arms around her, he brought her up tight against his chest. With a thready little sigh, she ducked her head and buried her face against him. Dane's lips brushed her chestnut waves. Stroking the shallow valley of her spine, he stared bleakly as the shadows crept across the timbered ceiling.

In time her body grew limp against him. Dane gathered her closer. A bitter tangle stole all through him. He should never have laid a finger on her, for she was irresistible. Impossible! He couldn't—shouldn't!—risk caring for her.

But it was already too late.

When Julianna woke the next morning, Dane was already awake. Fully dressed, he sat at the table. The sight of him made her stomach knot. His sleeves were rolled up, revealing the silky dark hair on his forearms. Julianna swallowed the dryness in her throat, her gaze trickling up over the strong brown column of his neck.

Faith, but he was handsome! The sun trickled over his profile. He appeared freshly shaven, and she could not help but recall the pleasantly rough friction of his chin and cheeks dragging against her belly. The memory made her body grow warm all over beneath the coverlet—and also reminded her that beneath the covers she was naked.

He must have felt her glance, for he looked up and smiled crookedly, a smile that made her heart turn over. "Good morning," he said softly.

"Good morning."

Their eyes caught and held immeasurably. It was Julianna who finally glanced away, retrieving her underclothing from the floor. Coloring fiercely, she turned her back and slipped on the garments. In light of their shocking intimacy, she shouldn't have been modest, but she was. Slipping from the bed, she donned her gown in much the same manner, then brushed her hair.

When she finally turned, it gave her a start to find Dane's regard trained fully upon her. His expression was enigmatic. What he was thinking, she had no idea. He stared at her so long and so hard she grew uncomfortable; it struck her that he seemed unusually somber.

Her fist closed on her breast. "Why do you look like that?"

He said nothing.

"Dane?" She stared at him dumbly.

What was wrong? The look in his eyes was almost sad. Perhaps even resigned.

He scraped his chair back from the table and came toward her. His gaze drifted down to her mouth, then back up, sending memories of the previous night flooding all through her.

With an effort she calmed her racing pulse. "You rose rather early. What are you doing?" she asked curiously. Her gaze lifted beyond his shoulder to the table. There was a pile of rags mounded there. A long metal rod lay atop them.

Her smile froze. Her breath caught.

He'd been cleaning his pistols; they lay there, next to the rags.

He bent and kissed her lightly on the lips. "Nothing that need trouble you, sweet."

He had seen where her gaze resided. Quickly he moved. Julianna couldn't tear her eyes away as he slipped the weapons into a small pouch.

An eerie, prickly sensation washed over her. All at once she felt chilled to the bone.

Her lips parted. Awareness washed over her like a cold rush of wintry air. "You're going out tonight, aren't you?"

His shoulders came up. All at once there was a marked tension in his stance.

"You are, aren't you? The Magpie will ride again?"

He said nothing.

She gave a short, brittle laugh. "I agree, a ridiculous question." She swept a hand at the two bulging sacks that still sat in the far corner of the cottage. "I've no doubt you've more hidden away somewhere. Isn't that enough for you?"

His eyes flickered, his expression guarded. He resolutely maintained his silence.

"Must I ask again, sir?"

A brow climbed high. He offered a mocking smile. "Sir? Come now. Surely we've progressed beyond such niceties, you and I, love."

Julianna's temper flared. She did not appreciate the reminder. "You avoid the question, Dane!"

"Very well then. It would seem that no, it is not enough." His tone was as cool as his appraisal. "Can a man ever have enough riches?"

His demeanor was one of utter calm. His mouth continued to carry the faintest of smiles. She was suddenly furious. "Why do you steal, Dane, why? Is it greed?"

Almost whimsically, he said, "What if I told you it was out of necessity?"

The way he looked at her, as if he were wholly without conscience . . . Oh, but it made no sense! How had she misjudged him so thoroughly? Had desire so blinded her to all that he was?

"Do not trifle with me!" she cried.

Something flickered across his face. "It's like a hunt," he said suddenly. "The thrill of the chase. Exciting. Tempting fate. Braving the odds and winning—"

"It's dangerous!"

His eyes glinted. He laughed, the wretch—he laughed! "Only if I'm caught."

"It's a game." Julianna felt sick inside. She gave a shake of her head, then looked up at him. "Dane," she said unsteadily, "would you stop if I asked you to?"

His smile faded. "What?"

"Would you cease being a robber, a highwayman—" she moistened her lips, almost afraid to give voice to the thought "—for me?"

She held her breath, held it forever, it seemed. Something that might have been regret flitted across his face, but then she heard his answer.

"You don't know what you're asking."

"I do. You can change, Dane. You are a good man. I know it. I *feel* it." She had witnessed first-hand his caring, his compassion.

But now a hollow band of tightness crept around her chest. "Don't you care that you could die?" she whispered.

He was suddenly directly before her, so close she could feel the heat of his breath. "Would you care?"

"Yes. *Yes!*" Warm, wet tears drizzled down her cheeks.

"Don't ask that of me." His tone was terse. "There are things you don't know—"

"Then tell me."

"Julianna, if circumstances were different. Another time, another place . . . If I were not the Magpie—"

"But you are," she whispered.

And how he wished he wasn't! Rent clearly in two, Dane stared at her. The plan was set in motion. He couldn't stop it now.

"Please, Dane. Don't go back. Don't *do* this. Stop. Please stop."

His jaw clenched. "I can't. Julianna, I *can't*. I can't have what I want. Not now. I can't change what I am—"

"You can change what you *do*. But you won't, will you?"

His silence stretched to a vast empty void.

Julianna gave a choked cry.

His hands curled around her shoulders when she would have lurched past him. "Don't!" A sharp denial ripped from her throat. "Please don't touch me!"

His mouth twisted. "What, will you shoot me again if I do?"

Her breath caught. That he could even say such a thing wounded her to the core. "Oh!" she cried. "That was cruel, Dane, and you know it!"

Time swung away. Their eyes collided endlessly.

Angry pride kept her head high. She struggled to keep the hurt from her voice. "I want to leave," she said, her tone very low.

His eyes seemed to spark. His grip tightened on her shoulders. "Julianna—"

"It's time. We both know it. You're well. There's no need for me to stay."

His hands fell away. He spoke through lips that barely moved. "Gather your things."

An hour later, they cleared the forest and followed a track alongside a rushing stream. As she rode in front of him on Percival, her nerves were stretched thin. She could feel the rigidity of Dane's arms about her waist. He had little to say, and Julianna knew not *what* to say. How she longed desperately for the closeness and camaraderie that had marked these last days.

When they rode past soaring, ivy-twined gates that guarded the entrance to a small estate, Julianna glanced back at the columned stone-and-brick façade of the house at the end of the drive. A wide, graceful portico guarded massive, double doors. Ahead of the circular drive a small pond glittered in the sunlight. Surrounding it were fragrant gardens abloom with brilliant yellow daffodils.

Determined to break the stifling stalemate between them, she glanced over once more. "How lovely," she ventured. "I wonder who lives there."

"I couldn't say." Dane's reply was curt.

There was an undertone in his voice that snared her attention. It was in her mind to query him further, but the relentless cast of his mouth encouraged silence.

Percival soon clattered over a bridge. A row of stocky cottages paved the way toward the inn. Blooms of riotous spring color spilled from the flower boxes below the windows in stark contrast to her mood.

Dane reined Percival to a halt, then reached up to help her down. The yard was deserted except for a leggy hound who bounded toward them just as he swung her to the ground. Julianna couldn't help it; a flicker of fear shot through her, and she shrank back. Dane's grip on her waist tightened ever so slightly.

"It's all right. He won't hurt you."

"I'm fine," she said in a rush, nearly falling in her haste to be free of him. Reaching down, she patted the animal's head. He was sniffing around her skirts. No doubt he smelled Maximilian. Maximilian . . . oh, she missed him so already!

She didn't see the shadow that flitted across Dane's features. He set her valise beside her. "I'll go see to your ticket."

Julianna looked up when he reappeared. "It shouldn't be long. Regular as clockwork, so I was told."

Everything inside her was suddenly wound tight as a knot. "Then there's no need for you to stay." Through some miracle, her tone was steady.

"Nonsense. I'll see you on your way."

"What if someone recognizes you?"

A ghost of a smile crossed his lips. "I wear a mask, remember?"

"I don't want you here," she said stiffly.

His smile withered. The air was suddenly leaping with currents.

His head came around. His gaze pierced her to the quick. "As you wish then."

Standing here with him was agony. There was a terrible, awful weight in her chest. She wanted to wrap her arms around him and never let go. Never in this world. Never in this life.

Her emotions betrayed her. Her *heart* betrayed

her. Fate had brought them together. But it was something else that had made her stay. As much as she adored her family, she had felt closer to Dane than anyone in the world. It wasn't just the physical intimacy; it was more. So much more. When it was just the two of them, alone in the cottage, life seemed so simple.

For so long now, on the outside she had been laughing and carefree, lively and vivacious. But inside, there was a void. There was something missing from her life, and now she knew what it was . . . him. This man. She was oddly reluctant to go back to the sameness of her dull, dreary life. But he left her no choice.

She could hardly enter into a life of lawlessness with him. She couldn't change what she was . . . and he *would* not.

If only she could stay. If only he would *stop* . . .

The situation was impossible.

A wrenching silence erupted. She willed herself to go numb. It was the only way she could stand to look at him.

Oh, God. Why did he linger? Why didn't he just go?

He was staring at her intently. "Julianna," he said, "you cannot reveal our acquaintance. You can't tell anyone what happened. Where I am. If you do . . ." He left the rest unspoken.

So that was why . . . She was stung. She refused to meet his gaze. "I won't tell." Her tone was scarcely audible.

He remained still as a statue.

She swallowed painfully. "Please, just go."

"Without a good-bye?"

He stepped close. Her throat clogged tight with the burning threat of tears. She looked away in confusion.

"Julianna," he said.

Her eyes swung back. "Go," she cried wildly. "Just—just go and leave me be!"

She could have sworn she heard his jaw clamp shut. With a muttered imprecation, he whirled around and stalked to Percival.

Her head bowed low, she waited for the sound of hoofbeats.

Instead she heard the staccato echo of bootheels rapping sharply on the cobblestones. Closer. Closer.

Her eyes flew wide. There was no chance for protest, no chance for anything but a faint, choked sound. Hard arms slid boldly around her back. She felt herself caught up against his length.

His mouth came down. He kissed her fiercely—ferociously!—lifting her feet from the ground. Suspended against him, Julianna could do naught but cling to him.

Her pulse was still clamoring as he rode off.

And she knew then. Knew what a fool she was! For she could almost believe she had fallen in love . . .

Not with a hero . . . but a highwayman.

Thirteen

London

It was raining, a steady leaden mist so reminiscent of London in the spring. Swirling gray fog shrouded the chimneys. A sudden gust of wind sent a sheet of raindrops spattering against the windowpanes.

Julianna sat in the sitting room of her London town house. Normally on such a day, she loved nothing more than to sit back and watch the blaze roaring in the fireplace, framed in gleaming rich mahogany, a cup of her favorite blend of steaming, fragrant tea at her side. It was a lovely room, a room that exuded both comfort and elegance; she had taken great pains to furnish it, searching the shops for weeks, looking for exactly the right pieces. The wainscoting and moldings were painted a creamy ivory that contrasted with the vivid blue of the damask-covered walls. A gilt-framed mirror set off the silk-patterned settee. But today her tea sat cold and untouched, the weather a dismal reflection of her mood.

Perhaps she should redecorate. Something. Anything to take her mind off Dane.

Two weeks had passed since she'd left him. She had resolved not to pine. To regret what might have been.

It was futile.

She had resumed her long-delayed journey to Bath. Her arrival at her home there hadn't been expected; she gave thanks that her maid Peggy had remained in London. But her anticipation for the country air was extinguished, her urge to linger in Bath vanquished. Chafing restlessly, she returned to London.

During the week she'd been back, she managed to busy herself with her usual activities, with the exception of her social calendar. But the nights spent alone in her bed were desolate.

For when he had come into her life, her world had changed, she thought achingly. Something came alive. Something long dormant. Her hopes and dreams, the ones she'd forsaken, the ones she'd thought dashed the day Thomas had deserted her.

Why had he kissed her? Touched her? Torn apart her well-guarded heart? Shredded what was left of her intentions? She'd closed off her heart, but being with Dane had pried her eyes wide open. For years she'd convinced herself she was happy. She had thought she had learned about herself. About what she wanted. What she needed. That it was possible to have one without the other.

But now she wondered achingly if she would ever be happy. How could she? Not now. Not after this. Not after him. It hadn't hurt like this when Thomas had wed Clarice. Now it was as if a piece of her heart had been chipped away.

A sudden commotion at the front door pulled her gaze from the flames. She moved to the entrance hall. Framed by an arch, the floor was patterned after a chessboard, polished squares of black and white. She watched as her brothers shook off the rain and stomped inside. Mrs. MacArthur, the housekeeper who had been in her employ for nearly three years, ushered them inside.

"Jules!" Justin hailed her. "We were just passing by on our way back from White's."

"And here I thought you were simply trying to escape the rain."

Sebastian bent and gave her a sedate peck on the cheek. "Hello, Jules."

Mrs. MacArthur straightened her apron. "I'll bring tea, my lords," she said brightly.

"Well," Julianna said dryly, "it appears you're staying for tea."

Her brothers followed her into the sitting room. Sebastian took his place at the other end of the settee, while Justin stuffed his long frame in the delicate white chair opposite.

Justin unbuttoned his coat. "Where the devil have you been? Arabella stopped by days ago and was told you'd adjourned to the country for a few days. I thought you'd have been back days ago."

"Yes, we haven't seen you in ages." Sebastian eyed her curiously.

"I decided to stay a little longer. I've been home for nearly a week now. I've simply curtailed my engagements a bit." It wasn't an out-and-out lie. Nonetheless, a sliver of guilt shot through her. She wondered what they would say if they knew she'd been in the company of the Magpie. Good Lord. Why, it would sound outrageous—and who would believe her? They'd likely consider her daft—or consider it a jolly good joke. Besides, she'd promised Dane.

It was a vow she would keep.

Mrs. MacArthur returned, sliding a tray onto the table before them. Justin flashed a devastating smile of thanks at the housekeeper, whose cheeks pinkened. The smile was second nature, she knew, but it was the same smile that had so captivated many a woman—for many a year. But not, however, his wife, at least not in the beginning; her sister-in-law Arabella had shocked her rakish brother by her failure to be impressed with him.

"Every time you are here," Julianna said lightly, "I swear Mrs. MacArthur whisks around beaming for days afterward. Perhaps I should apprise Arabella you've charmed yet another woman?"

"Oh, but there is only one woman in my life. Or rather—two," he amended. Satisfaction rimmed his smile. Julianna knew he was thinking about his infant daughter.

"And what about me?" Sebastian arched a black brow. "Am I such a troll then?"

Julianna wrinkled her nose toward her dashing eldest brother. "I do know one woman who is quite taken with you." She paused. "How are the twins?"

"Babbling incessantly. *Moving* incessantly. Devon and I are exhausted by day's end." He pulled a face but he fooled no one. He adored his children—and fairly worshipped his wife.

They chatted on for a time. Mrs. MacArthur brought in a selection of tea cakes and tiny fruit tarts. It was Sebastian who noticed Julianna's untouched plate.

There was a click as he replaced his cup in the saucer. "What's troubling you, Jules?" he asked quietly.

Julianna started. She'd grappled for strength these many days. But last night, she'd lost the battle. Images of Dane crowded her mind. The gold of his eyes burning through her brain. His heat surrounding her . . . how she longed for it. How she longed for *him*. God, would she ever forget the taste of him? The sleek, heavy texture of his skin? For a time the empty corners of her heart . . . her life! . . . had been full. That only made the emptiness all the more intense. All the harder to bear.

Something had broken inside her. She had turned her face into the pillow and wept. Sleep had not come till the first faint light of dawn colored the sky. When she woke, the ravages of the night had left their mark in the shadows beneath her eyes . . . *in* her eyes.

"Nothing," she denied quickly. "Why ever should you think that?" She took a sip of tea, nearly scalding her tongue.

His brows arose. His gaze traveled pointedly from her untouched plate to her face. "Those are your favorites. You never turn them down."

"I had a late luncheon," she lied.

Sebastian studied her. There was a void inside. She tried to hide it, but her brothers knew her too well.

"You look tired, Julianna."

She lowered her lashes but she'd already borne the brunt of Justin's sharp-eyed scrutiny as well. "You're different," he observed bluntly. "You've lost a bit of weight."

"Yes," Sebastian agreed. "And your spark is

gone. The sunshine in your voice." He frowned. "Have you been ill? Out of sorts?"

Julianna's chest had grown tight. A part of her longed to throw herself in their arms, seek their comfort, for she knew they'd have given it readily and willingly. But she salvaged her composure, shaking her head.

"Not in the slightest," she pronounced briskly. "It must be the poor light. It's such a dreary day, isn't it?"

It was Justin who spoke. "If I didn't know better," he said slowly, "I'd think—" He stopped, his green eyes assessing.

"I'm perfectly fine," Julianna declared, beginning to grow irritated.

"Prove it then," he challenged. "Come to the Farthingale ball tonight. I'm sure you received an invitation."

"Unlike you, I can resist a dare." To think she'd been convinced that marriage had tempered his bravado! "Frankly, I'd planned to spend a quiet evening here at home."

"But surely a night out won't hurt. And perhaps a nap would be just the thing so you'll be rested for tonight."

Now Sebastian had joined in. Julianna expelled a breath. She looked from one to the other. "You'll harry me until I say yes, won't you?"

"Never in this world!"

"Jules, you offend me!"

Sweetly, she asked, "Shall I see you out, dear brothers?"

Neither of them moved.

Her lips compressed. She'd never convince them all was aright unless she did as they asked. "Very well then. I shall see you there."

"Delightful."

"Devon will be most pleased to see you."

Julianna rose pointedly.

They finally followed suit. On his feet, Sebastian inclined his head toward Justin, his gray eyes agleam. "I congratulate you on your persuasive abilities."

Justin clicked his heels. "And I thank you for your gracious support."

Julianna muttered under her breath. Louts, the both of them!

At ten o'clock that evening, Julianna stood on the edge of the Farthingale ballroom. Across the floor, Justin was carrying Arabella's hand to his lips, making unabashed sheep's eyes at his wife. At times she was still a little amazed that he was such an adoring husband. Such a devoted father. Along with the rest of the *ton*, she'd once been convinced that her brother Justin was the quintessential rogue—the quintessential bachelor.

Her gaze slid to Sebastian, who was waltzing with her sister-in-law, Devon. They were staring into each other's eyes as if there were no one in the world but the two of them. The two had disclosed only tonight that in the autumn, there would be another addition to the Sterling family.

Julianna had hugged them both fiercely, for she truly shared their joy. But now—now a pang bit deep. Julianna did not regret their happiness, neither of her brothers. God knew they deserved it! But was it wrong to feel envious? To want what Sebastian shared with Devon? What Justin had with Arabella?

She sighed. She'd done her duty. She'd put in an appearance. Now she could go home.

But then a whisper snared her attention. Several women were standing nearby.

". . . the Magpie!"

Julianna turned her head. The musicians had struck the last chord and were putting aside their instruments. Carefully, she sidled backward behind a massive urn of fresh flowers, where she wouldn't be seen.

"They say he's very dashing. Very much a gentleman. For a highwayman, that is."

There was an almost wistful tone to the woman's voice. Julianna couldn't see her, and thus couldn't discern her identity. She held her breath, straining to hear.

The other was clearly disapproving. "Dashing! I vow he's an unscrupulous rascal! Do you know Loretta? Why, she was waylaid by the wretch a scant three weeks ago! He not only stole her purse, he stole a kiss and fondled her. And with her husband looking on, mind you!"

Julianna saw red. Oh, but she longed to march out and dispute the claim! Frankly, she doubted the woman's assertion, whoever she was. She wanted to make her presence known and snap that three weeks ago, he'd been with *her,* and in no condition to be pursuing his livelihood. Not only that, but it didn't sound like Dane to do such a thing with the woman's husband looking on. A kiss, perhaps . . . *perhaps.* But fondling? Never! Nor had she had seen any purses lying about the cottage—only those bulging sacks of coin.

"I wager he won't be so dashing when he's dangling at the end of a rope."

Julianna felt the blood leave her face.

"What?"

"Didn't you see this morning's papers? The price on his head has been doubled. He'll surely be caught sometime. And the lucky one who chances to catch the rogue and turn him over to the authorities will be richer by a considerable sum."

"Hmmmph!" said the first. "If his neck isn't stretched on the gibbet first!"

Julianna went dry with fear. She was still reeling when she felt a touch on her arm.

It was the Dowager Duchess of Carrington, a peremptory figure in red. With the tip of her infamous cane, the tiny duchess just barely lifted the hem of Julianna's gown. Fashioned of shimmering amber silk, it fell in soft pleats from beneath her breasts to swirl around her feet, emphasizing her slender form. Her maid had woven a shimmering strand of pearls through the curls on her crown. Snowy white gloves extended past her elbows, halfway to the dainty cap sleeves.

"That is a most becoming color on you, dear. It brings out the chestnut in your hair. And the pearls woven throughout—most charming."

Julianna barely heard. "Oh, good evening, Your Grace. And thank you." She would never have dreamed of being rude. One did not shun the dowager duchess. Besides, the duchess was practically family. "Ah, Your Grace, might I ask that—"

"I saw you watching your brothers earlier, my dear. You concealed it well, but I sensed your loneliness."

Julianna nearly gasped. "Your Grace, I am not lonely!"

The duchess nodded sagely. "Child, when one is my age, one sees many things." She paused. "You know, I consider myself responsible for bringing many a couple together—indeed, many a successful marriage. Why, it was I who foresaw that Justin would be the perfect man for Arabella—and in this very ballroom! And of course, there is Sebastian and Devon." Her mouth pursed. "My dear, I have restrained myself for some time now. But I would count it a pleasure were you to allow me to suggest a fitting gentleman." She laughed softly. "Perhaps the outcome will be the same."

Julianna nearly groaned. The duchess loved nothing more than to play matchmaker. She had always managed gently to dissuade the old woman.

"Your Grace," she began.

The duchess curled her gnarled fingers into Julianna's elbow. "Trust me, dear Julianna. I have much experience in these things, I assure you. Now then," she stated crisply, "the only question is who. I am exceedingly fond of you, you know. So the man in question cannot simply be eligible. He must be a man who is eminently suited to you. He must be a man of staunch reputation, of irrefutable character. I will countenance no less." Her eyes twinkled. "And handsome. Ah, yes, he must be handsome. Oh, but I know just the one for you!"

"Your Grace," Julianna said firmly.

"Now then, where the devil is he? I saw him just moments ago. There he is!" The duchess's cane came up and slashed in a vigorous circle. Julianna nearly shrieked, for it narrowly missed the arm of an earl striding by. The old lady paid no heed.

"Granville," she hailed. "Come here, I say!"

Drat! It was too late to retract gracefully. From the corner of her eye Julianna saw that a gentleman had halted. Perhaps she could just laugh it off . . .

Her eyes drifted away, then jerked back. The man was turning . . . turning.

Her heart lurched. There was something familiar about the angle of his shoulder, the way he carried himself.

What madness was this? Oh, God, now she was seeing him. Not just in her dreams. But in the flesh.

Beside her, the duchess stretched out a hand. He was bowing low over it. Straightening . . .

The dowager duchess was almost cooing. "It is my very great pleasure to present Lady Julianna Sterling. Julianna, allow me to introduce Viscount Granville."

Slowly Julianna raised her head. She confronted an impossibly broad chest. Her gaze trekked relentlessly upward, taking in a squarely chiseled jaw. Almost desperately she looked up into his face.

Heaven help her, he was real. He was *here*.

It was Dane.

Fourteen

It would have been impossible to say who was the more startled. Dane . . . or Julianna. Viscount . . . *viscount.*

The words seemed to pulse visibly in the air. Her tongue was all twisted in her mouth, and speech was quite literally beyond her capacity.

He was faultlessly—formally—dressed in evening clothes. Black coat, charcoal silk-embroidered waistcoat and impeccably creased trousers, shining, tasseled Hessians, his air no less than commanding, his cravat snowy white against his chin. His longish waves had been trimmed, yet despite his formal dress, he maintained a dark, rugged vitality that made it seem as if there were not enough air in her lungs to breathe.

Nonetheless, she took an almost perverse satisfaction in the shock reflected on his features. It was Julianna who recovered first, offering white-gloved fingertips.

"My lord. Your name again. It is Viscount"—an infinitesimal pause—"Granville?"

"Indeed, my lady. I vow, I am enchanted."

Julianna gritted her teeth. She could think of many names to call him—none of which she'd heard here. "And I, my lord."

Strong fingers had curled around hers. He bowed low over her hand. When he straightened, his eyes caught hers. "I fear you must forgive me—with this crush, I failed to catch your name as well."

Forgive him? Nay. Never. Why, the rake, the rogue, she could almost believe he was taunting her!

She matched that maddening smile. "Sterling, my lord. Julianna *Clare* Sterling."

The pressure on her hand increased ever so subtly. She tried to tug it back, but he retained possession.

And now it was his turn for triumph.

"Tell me—" an easy smile creased his lips "—are you by chance related to Sebastian Sterling, Marquess of Thurston?"

"Intimately so, sir, for he is my brother."

"Splendid!"

His eyes proclaimed otherwise, however. The

musicians had resumed their places. "Will you grant me a dance, dear lady?" He afforded no opportunity for refusal, for already he had handily tucked her fingers into the crook of his elbow and covered it with his own. He gave a little bow to the dowager duchess. "Your Grace, will you excuse us?"

"Of a certainty, my dears! Of a certainty!"

The duchess was beaming as he swept her onto the polished ballroom floor.

Shock was all that held Julianna upright. All that kept her on her feet. Only pride kept her from crying. Only his arm kept her from falling, or tearing herself away.

She had known something was amiss. She'd known something was off. His manners, his speech, his air of breeding. A part of her was overjoyed.

A part of her was devastated.

Why was he here? How dare he risk being discovered! If anyone should guess that he was the Magpie—

Something inside her wrenched. Who was he? Who was he really? Who was the real Dane? The daring highwayman? The elegant nobleman?

His head turned ever so slightly. The bristly hardness of his jaw brushed her temple. Her entire body was taut.

His arm tightened. "Relax," he murmured. "Relax."

She wanted to. Oh, how she wanted to! The scent of him was dizzying. She was as familiar with his smell as her own. And he felt so good. The warmth of his body next to hers in the dead of night, the powerful length of his body sheltering hers, the way his back shaped her spine and bottom. All this she remembered . . . and more.

But in truth, he was a stranger . . . or was he?

She didn't know. God above, she didn't know!

She tilted her head back to find him watching her, his mouth curled in a crooked half smile. "Why do you smile like that? Why do you look like that?"

"I believe you know, sweet."

Julianna stiffened. "Who are you? *Who are you?*"

He gave a shake of his head. "Don't do this," came his murmur. "Not here." For all his quiet, there was a note of steel in his tone.

"Tell me. Tell me now."

A muscle jumped in his cheek. "Julianna—"

"I'll make a scene."

His jaw tightened. His eyes seared her, but she would not back down. His lips tightening, he whirled her off the floor, onto the terrace, steering her down a winding pathway deep into the gardens.

He finally halted between two stone statues. The fragrant scent of lilacs wafted all around them. Julianna paid no heed. In the moonlight, his expression revealed nothing—nor did he.

"You bastard," she said feelingly.

His eyes flickered. "Hardly," he said coolly.

Her heart was near to breaking. *She* was near to breaking.

"Do not mock me. Do not *play* with me."

His smile vanished.

"Dane. *Dane.* Why, is that even your name—"

"It is."

"And you are Viscount Granville? You must be, for the duchess appears to know you well."

"I am."

"That is all you have to say?"

He simply looked at her.

"Tell me, Dane, or I swear I will—"

"Lower your voice! Dammit, Julianna, you're distraught."

"I am not distraught. I'm angry. You deceived me," she accused.

Still that brutal silence. Julianna lost her temper. Her hand shot out and delivered a stinging slap to his cheek.

He just stood there. Something sparked inside her; she would have done it again, but this time strong fingers encircled the fragile span of her wrist.

Dane was prickling as well. "Must I remind you that you deceived me as well, Miss Julianna *Clare*? I thought I'd seen you before . . . My God, the sister of a marquess. Why, if I'd known, I'd have delivered you straightaway back to London. Believe me, I'd never have laid a hand on you."

"I was afraid, Dane! I didn't know what you would do if you knew who I was. And then later, it didn't seem to matter. I didn't think we would ever see each other again. Besides, it wasn't as if you . . . as if we—"

She halted at his quelling glance. "Believe me, love, if your brothers knew what we'd done, they would gladly see me rotting in a cell in Newgate."

"Oh!" she cried bitterly. "Would it truly have mattered who my brother is? You're determined to land yourself in Newgate quite on your own."

He gave her a slow, deliberate smile. "Not if I can help it."

Of all the arrogance! "Unhand me, Dane."

"Not until I'm assured of your silence."

"Well, there's only one sure way of that, isn't there?"

He scowled. "I should have followed my instincts. I knew I shouldn't have come here tonight!"

Julianna caught her breath. Her eyes were flush with his chest. Flush with his heart. God, she thought wildly, did he even possess a heart, that he could fling hers to the depths of hell so easily?

He released her. "Christ," he muttered, "I'm sorry. I shouldn't have said that." He seemed to hesitate. "Julianna, please. I'm asking you to trust me."

Trust him. Trust him! Her mind was screaming. Was this nothing but a game? He played at niceties. He played at being a gentleman. He played at being a highwayman. Her heart wrenched. Had he played at the tender lover as well?

Whatever the truth, she would know it. She would not tolerate a blind acceptance.

She raised her head. "Perhaps it's you who should trust me," she said levelly.

"What do you mean?"

"Only this. We must talk, my lord."

His mouth tightened. She did not mistake the guarded tension in his stance. "Must we?"

"You are a master at fading into the night, Dane. But not tonight. Not now, for I will scream. I will scream this minute. And then I will tell everyone—everyone!—who the Magpie really is."

His eyes narrowed. "What makes you think I won't call your bluff?"

Julianna straightened her spine. "Will you?" was all she said. "I think not."

Dane was incredulous. He gazed down into snapping blue eyes, admiring her control, though he'd never been more furious in his life.

"Did you come alone?"

"I did."

His mouth twisted. "Then permit me to take you home."

Sitting on the rich burgundy velvet seat in his carriage, Julianna tucked her feet beneath her. Her head bowed low, she closed her eyes for a moment. Lodged fast within her chest was a world of turmoil. So much had happened, she was still reeling. It was almost too much to absorb. To believe. Perhaps she'd imagined it. Perhaps she'd conjured him out of her own wayward longing. Was it all a dream then?

No. He was still here. To her frustration, he appeared utterly calm.

Folding his arms across the broad expanse of his chest, he regarded her. "Are you quite recovered?"

"What do you mean?"

"I thought you were going to swoon. Then I thought you were going to succumb to hysterics."

"You were just as startled as I," she charged, her tone very low. "And I do believe you're trying to goad me."

His smile was almost lazy. "Perhaps I am."

The carriage bumped around a corner. All of a sudden everything changed. The carriage lamp swayed, throwing his profile into stark illumination.

His eyes were riveted on her mouth.

"Julianna." He spoke her name in a way that suddenly made her tremble. "Come here."

Julianna sucked in a breath. "No. *No!*" Neither the denial nor her tone was as determined as it should have been. She clasped her fingers tautly in her lap. It was the only way she could stop herself from reaching for him.

"Then I will come to you." In one spare movement, he transferred his long body beside hers on the seat.

He made no move to touch her, but she was aware of his gaze poring over her features. Unable to stop herself, her regard lifted. His lips were curved in a smile that was half-sad, half-tender.

"Don't." Her throat constricted. She had no hope of disguising the raw swell of her emotions. "Don't look at me like that."

"Kitten," he said. "*Kitten.*"

Her eyes filled with tears.

"I'm sorry . . . I shouldn't call you that, I know. But I can't help it."

Suddenly her hands were imprisoned within his. Impatiently he stripped away her gloves. He weaved his fingers with hers. His were twice as large, nearly twice as long, twice as dark as her fair skin.

"Your hands are like ice," he chided. He turned his mouth into her palm. "It will be all right," he whispered. "It will."

A low, strangled sound snagged in her throat. "I thought I'd never see you again. I thought I'd never see you!"

All at once she was sobbing, jagged sobs she couldn't withhold.

His eyes darkened. "Oh, God," he groaned. "Don't cry, kitten. Please don't cry."

He dragged her onto his lap. With unfaltering need, her arms wound around his neck.

"Dane," she cried. "*Dane.*"

His mouth was on the curve of her cheek. The slightest turn . . . her mouth angled into his. She did not surrender. She did not yield. Rather she sought . . .

His embrace was almost frighteningly intense, yet tempered with a world of restraint. Their kiss was molten; both succumbed to an almost frantic urgency driven by the undercurrent of desire. Sharpened by the time spent apart, escalating into a desperation neither could control.

With a muffled exclamation, he levered himself lengthwise down the seat and pulled her atop him.

She strained against him, into him. Her fingertips tore at the intricate folds of his cravat. His eyes burning, with a fingertip he traced the outline of the peak of her breast, a slow, ever-narrowing circle until her nipple grew taut. Lightning seemed to flash, there when his gaze centered. She made no outcry when he dragged her bodice down to her waist. Julianna tugged her hands free. She wanted to be free to touch, as he was free to touch.

His hands coasted up and down her bare back, stroking just the way she'd dreamed, warm against the valley of her spine. He bore her weight on his thighs, her sex against his. Her ball gown was thin, no hindrance at all to the rampant thrust of his arousal. Julianna's heart bounded forward as the pangs of awakening perception unfurled; she was unbearably aware of him beneath her, hard and thick.

She kissed the place where his jaw met his throat. "I want to touch you," she said, letting her tongue dance against his skin, warm and salty. "I want—"

He seemed to know exactly what she wanted. He tore open his trousers and freed his arousal. Julianna raised her head, wishing she could see what the darkness concealed—no matter. What she did see made her heart leap. She could feel his hunger. She traced the grid of his belly, loving the crisp texture of the hair beneath her fingertips. Her fingertips followed the line below the indentation of his navel, reveling in the way his muscles knotted beneath her.

And then she touched him.

Hot. She hadn't known that flesh could be so burning hot, hot as a brand. She snatched her hand away only to return in the very next breath.

She touched him again. She touched him *again*, and saw the way his jaw clenched, the way his eyes glittered. He muttered encouragement. Her fingers tripped along the length of his shaft, a tentative venture—yet still she did not withdraw, not even when she skimmed the helm of his member. Her heart seemed to stop. She could feel the tip, silken velvet, a shaft of iron.

"Dane," she heard herself say, "you feel like . . ." Words failed her. "And it's so—"

A harsh serrated sound scraped from his throat. His palms slid beneath her skirts, pushing aside her pantalets, catching her bare bottom. Through the night, his eyes gleamed dark and golden. She could feel the steely seam of his shaft searing her furrowed cove.

"Kitten," he said hoarsely. "Come here, kitten." He was lifting her, guiding, bringing her down onto him. She gasped as the swollen head of his member slipped inside her heat. Her maidenhead breached, he held her still, poised above him.

The carriage clattered around a corner. His fingers lost purchase on her hips. She clutched at his shoulders for balance. The motion drove her down, hard—sealing her to the hilt.

His expression was almost pained, his features strained. "Julianna," he grated. "Oh, kitten."

For an instant she stared at him in confusion. It hurt, more than she'd expected. He seemed impossibly hard . . . she seemed impossibly tight, impossibly full of him. And for a frantic instant she wasn't sure this was even possible. . . .

But her body was already adjusting to his possession, the burning sting of his entry fading. Her body stretched to accept him, clinging to his heat, as if it was meant to be. Wool chafed the inside of her thighs, but all she could feel was him . . . hard and deep inside her. Filling her as nothing ever had. As nothing ever would.

His hands renewed their grasp on the span of her hips. "Kitten," he said thickly. "I can't stop. I can't."

And she wouldn't. Her thighs gripped him tightly. Almost fiercely. Her bottom dug into her heels. Her palms flattened against the window of the carriage.

Wordlessly, she shook her head. Something passed between them in that moment. His eyes flared burning and gold and brilliant.

With a growl he covered her mouth. And she covered *him*.

Every inch of him.

She moved instinctively, tipping herself back, then forward. Squeezing her eyes shut, her movements directed solely by blind instinct. Dane's fingers dug into her flesh. The cords in his neck stood out as he caught her and brought her down on his shaft, spearing deep. Again and again, caught up in a frantic, white-hot frenzy. His fingers molded themselves to her scalp, tugging her forward. Her hair came down in a silken fall of curls and pearls around them both, his mouth taking hers in wild ferocity. Then she was crying out against his lips, until breath and voice and the world itself slipped away to nothingness.

Fifteen

$\mathcal{D}$ane's labored breathing eased to a trickle. Slowly, he raised his head, gradually aware that the carriage was rolling to a halt—and he was still inside her! Julianna was lying above him, dazed and limp, her white thighs a taut vise around his, her chestnut head still pillowed on his chest, a sight that was deliciously erotic.

He'd lost his mind. He'd lost control. He cursed furiously to himself. *At* himself. He'd just taken Lady Julianna Sterling on the seat of a carriage, their clothing thrust crudely aside! Not only that, he'd displayed all the clumsy technique of a randy youth anxious for his first taste of a woman. No finesse, no skill. Above all, no restraint! He hadn't even taken the time to properly undress her—or himself!

It was no way to take a virgin. No way to take a lady.

But it was done. There was no going back. No reclaiming the past. And if he was honest with himself—and he usually was—in all truth, he didn't want to.

He'd wanted her from the beginning.

He wanted her still.

"We've stopped, love."

He lifted her from his body. A spasm of regret speared through him. Pulling her skirts down, he glanced at her house, a red brick dwelling.

"Dane, why are you smiling like that?"

He shook his head. "You'll not believe this, sweet."

"Indeed I won't. Particularly not unless you tell me."

He chuckled, dragging her bodice back up around her shoulders. "I live just around the next corner," he stated blithely.

"You don't," she said immediately.

"I do. The house overlooking the square with the charming stone portico."

"Oh! I adore that house! I wanted to buy it, but it was beyond my means!"

He laughed. "It's just as charming inside."

The driver opened the door and offered a hand to Julianna. Dane leaped down behind her.

She was desperately trying to restore order to her curls. He settled a hand on her waist. "Sore?"

He lowered his mouth to her curls and inhaled deeply. He'd noticed how she winced once she was on the ground.

She was aghast. "No!"

"Liar," he challenged softly. "Permit me." He swung her up into his arms and strode toward the house. Her housekeeper was there, sweeping the door wide. Dane strode inside as if he had every right to be there.

The woman's recovery was admirable. At the sight of her mistress in his arms, she pointed toward the stairs. "Last door on your right, my lord."

Dane quirked a brow at Julianna. "Your housekeeper is a most insightful woman," he remarked. "I like her."

"You—you haven't even met her," Julianna sputtered.

He spun around the turn at the landing. "And you and I have only just been introduced formally tonight," he reminded her. "Our relationship has progressed most handily, has it not?"

"Are you a rake, sir?"

"Not anymore," came his brash rejoinder.

In her room a fire burned brightly. He crossed the gold-and-maroon-patterned carpet to place her beside the bed. He tossed his jacket across the footboard and rolled up his sleeves, baring strong, muscular forearms. She stood mutely while he divested her of her gown, stockings, and slippers. On the washstand was a pitcher of steaming water. Pouring a little into the basin, he wrung out a cloth and returned to her.

A hand on her shoulder, he eased her back on the crisp white counterpane. "Lie back," he said softly.

Julianna propped herself on her elbows. "What are you doing?" she asked weakly.

"Hush." He pressed the cloth between her legs, soothing her swollen flesh. He looked at her face. "Are you all right?"

Her hands lay alongside her head. Her fingers curled into her palms. "Yes," she said faintly. "Why wouldn't I be?"

He chuckled. "Sweet," he said almost cheerfully, "do you really want me to answer that?"

A vivid blush stained her cheeks. Dane wiped away the lingering traces of his possession. The cloth landed in the basin.

She shivered suddenly. "Chilly?" he murmured.

"A little."

"Then let me warm you." He stepped out of his trousers . . . and into her bed.

She inhaled sharply. "Dane."

"My prim little kitten." His body completely eclipsed her own. He bent his head and kissed her, his mouth sliding up the side of her neck. God, she tasted good. Of lemons and her own unique sweetness. She made his body ache. The feel of her made him dizzy. He wanted to plunge inside her once more, feel her body clamp tight around his flesh again and again.

"Stop," she said unsteadily. "I can't think when you do that."

"Your mind is far too occupied with thought, kitten."

"And your hands are far too occupied with me!"

He chuckled. "I do not deny it!"

She swatted away the hand that captured one round, sweet breast. "You are trying to trick me, aren't you? You think you can waylay me, don't you?"

"It would appear not," he said dryly. He stretched out beside her, propping himself on an elbow so he could look at her. Alas, she reached down to retrieve the sheet and drag it over her nakedness.

"You have much to explain, Dane. You postpone the inevitable."

He allowed a smile to curve his lips. "I suppose the sooner I explain, the sooner we can proceed to . . . a more pleasurable undertaking."

She took exception to his suggestiveness. "This is a serious matter. Pray do not trifle with me." Her diction was clipped and precise. Her obstinate little jaw thrust out as she regarded him.

All at once her gaze narrowed. "The day I

left . . . The estate we passed on the way to the village. Is it yours?"

A lone fingertip trailed along her cheek. "Very good, kitten. And yes, it's the family estate."

"And the cottage where you took me? That is yours, too?"

"A hunting cottage. Used by my family for years now."

"Your family," she repeated. "So you really have two sisters?"

"I do. Daniela is older than I by two years, Delphine by three. Both have three children."

"And your parents?"

"They died five years ago, my mother within a month of my father." He smiled slightly. "It was better that way, I think. It would have been hard for either of them to live without the other."

Her eyes had turned a stormy blue. "Why, Dane? Why would a man such as you ride as the Magpie? What possible reason could there be?"

"A very good one." He waited a moment too long to answer. His hesitation cost him.

She pounced. "You see! I knew it!"

He knew there would be no skirting her questions. "Julianna," he murmured, "what if I told you it was all a masquerade?"

She gestured impatiently. "I'm quite aware of that."

"What if I told you it was . . . necessary?"

"Necessary? Necessary that you resort to

thievery?" It was obvious how it pained her to say it. "Why? Why would a man such as you do such a thing? Are you a gambler? Are you in such dire need of funds that you must steal?"

He released a laugh. "Hardly."

"What then? A lark? A dare? You've taken silver, gold, jewels—"

"Do not be so dramatic! What has been taken has been only enough to maintain the façade."

"The façade! My God, Dane, you even dared to rob the Prime Minister's private secretary. The start of your illustrious career as the Magpie, was it not?"

"Nay, Julianna."

"Of course you did! I read the details in the newspapers . . ."

"Details greatly exaggerated, I assure you."

She scoffed. "You made no secret of your spoils in the cottage. Indeed you boasted of their value."

"Ah, those sacks in the cottage."

"Yes, *those*."

"I won't deny I took them, Julianna."

She made a sound.

He gave a half smile. "Kitten, which is it? Do you want me to be guilty or no?"

"Of course not."

"Then let me tell you what is in those sacks," he said softly.

"I know what's in them!"

"You think you know," he contradicted, then paused. "Julianna," he said softly, "the notes in those sacks are not real."

She stared. "What?"

"They're counterfeit, love. They've been forged."

"Counterfeit," she repeated, her confusion was evident. She looked at him blankly. "How could you know that, Dane. *How?*"

"The truth is, Julianna, we should not even be having this discussion. I risk much by telling you, both your safety and mine. But you have been drawn into this unwittingly. And while the circumstances do not compel that you know the truth, I cannot—I *will* not—hide it from you any longer."

Something changed in her expression. "Oh, Lord."

"I resigned my commission after Waterloo, sweet. I-I was so terrified of dying! Every time I thought of that blood-soaked field, a cold sweat broke out upon my brow. How could I continue being a soldier when I was so weak? Yet I felt . . . less than a man, so very much a coward! Those men at Waterloo . . . it was as if I had deserted them, turned my back on them. At times I felt I had walked away from my country. But I could not allow my fear to consume me—I *would* not!

I realized the best way to conquer my fear was to face it, not shirk from it! Indeed, for me it's been the only way.

"And then I discovered there was another way I could serve . . . by fighting the enemies on our own shores. A situation came up and an official in high offices approached me—during the war I had assumed a false identity and retrieved a document that proved invaluable to my superiors. They felt I had skills that might prove useful in certain endeavors . . . And my title gave me entrance to circles that might have been questioned otherwise."

Her fists had come up to curl beneath her chin. Another time, and he might have laughed at her dazed expression.

His eyes bored into hers. "Kitten," he said gently, "do you understand what it is I am saying?"

She did not relieve him of that unblinking stare.

"Dear God," she said numbly. "You're a spy."

Julianna felt as if the wind had been knocked out of her. Her mind teetered. Agents. High offices. False identities. All sounded so mysterious and dark.

"You are a spy," she said again, as if to convince herself. She heard her voice as if through a fog—and his as well.

"I confess, I have never been particularly fond of that term. It has such a devious quality. Agent has a much more palatable sound."

She was hardly about to quibble the point. She sat up, tucking the counterpane beneath her arms and pushing herself back so that she rested against the pillows. Her heart was racing so that she feared it would leap from her breast.

Dropping her head on her knees, she gathered herself in hand. She'd known something wasn't right about him. She just hadn't known what. But she'd never dreamed he was a spy.

Filling her lungs with air, she glanced at him. He had risen to a sitting position as well. He watched her intently, obviously gauging her reaction.

Where before her mind had been nearly wiped clean by shock, now a hundred thoughts crowded in, a furious encumbrance. "I would obviously never succeed as a spy—pardon me, an agent. For I can think of no reason why you would steal money that is counterfeit. And you say the Magpie is just a masquerade. How so? Why—"

He held up a hand. "One at a time, sweet. One at a time." He paused. "Some months ago, Julianna, a woman named Boswell came forward to the Prime Minister's office with a startling revelation concerning counterfeit currency."

Julianna's eyes widened. "Counterfeit?"

"Yes. It's existed throughout the ages, kitten.

Coins improperly weighted, even painted . . . Now, a skilled engraver and his tool does the trick. A plate and a press is all that's needed."

He continued. "Mrs. Boswell's husband, you see, had an intimate knowledge of this crime. Upon his release from prison, Mrs. Boswell disclosed that her husband was encouraged to make use of his knowledge—encouraged by someone in the Home Office. The idea might have been dismissed out of hand, but for one thing."

"What?"

"Less than a day later, Mrs. Boswell and her husband were killed," he said quietly. "Crushed beneath the wheels of a carriage as they crossed the street one night near their home. The driver was never discovered."

Julianna should have been prepared, but she wasn't. "Never say that it was—"

"Murder, not an accident."

She shivered. "No doubt," she said slowly. "What happened then?"

"Another agent—my partner Phillip—and I were assigned to investigate. As you can imagine, the scandal would be horrendous if the charges were true—if the public were to learn of such corruption in the Home Office itself. The need for secrecy was paramount, so we told no one, not even our superiors. Mrs. Boswell overheard the culprit reveal to her husband Daniel that the bogus currency was being sent via stagecoach from London. Primarily to Bath, where there is doubtlessly someone who distributes it from there."

"But first you had to discover if it was true?"

"Yes. We could not openly reveal the investigation, or word might get back to the man responsible. So I donned a mask and posed as a highwayman, and indeed, I found what we sought."

"Forged banknotes," she said slowly.

He nodded. "But there was another dilemma. If the perpetrator was aware he was under suspicion, he might stop his shipments, and we would never learn his identity. We had to beat him at his own game. Therefore, I elected to continue my guise as a highwayman to ferret him out."

Julianna's head was whirling. "You're trying to set a trap? Lure him out of hiding by stealing from him?"

"Precisely. If only his shipments were targeted, he would be onto us in an instant. He must believe the robberies are random, that the targets are random. That's why the newspapers have printed what they have. He dare not use his office to apprehend the Magpie. He cannot risk attracting too much attention to himself, lest he *reveal* himself. We must outwit him at his own game, lure him to the fore, bring him out of hiding. Make him angry. In time, he will make a mistake."

Her eyes widened. "You want to draw him out," she said, aghast. "You want him to come after you."

He nodded.

Julianna went cold to the tips of her fingers. "Dane," she heard herself say, "do you have any idea who this man is?"

His eyes flickered. "Not yet. But we will, I have no doubt."

"At what cost, I ask? The cost of your life?" Her stomach churned. "The newspapers are filled with your escapades. You were being talked about at the ball tonight. You chance your neck being stretched on a gibbet! And are you aware the price on your head has doubled?"

His brows shot high. "Indeed."

Julianna railed. "Will the Crown protect you if you are caught miles from London? No one knows who you really are! They'll think you're a brigand, a thief! You could be shot."

"Oh, come. Surely not *twice*."

His brashness was infuriating.

"This is not amusing!"

She would have lurched away. Dane trapped her, a heavy arm about her waist.

"I know, I know. I shouldn't jest." He leaned over her. "It's a chance I must take."

"What if you're caught? Captured? I'm afraid

for you." And she was. She was terrified that she would lose him again.

"Don't be. Kitten, look at me."

Their eyes tangled. Seizing her hand, he dragged it to his mouth and kissed her palm before carrying it to his shoulder.

"Put your arms around me, sweet."

Her fingertips curled into warm, satin flesh, whether to push him away or bring him close, she didn't know.

Dane entertained no such ambiguity. He shaped his hand around her neck. He kissed her until her breath dammed in her throat and there was no breath to be found in the world, until coherent thought fled to mindless sensation. Until the searing heat inside her obliterated all but the desire flashing through her veins.

Weakly, she sank back onto the pillows. His big body followed hers down as she clung to him.

"Julianna," he muttered. His brown hand was splayed upon her thigh. "I must know, kitten. Do you regret what happened tonight?"

Her heart leaped. She shook her head.

Their lips hovered but a breath apart.

"Are you sure? It wasn't because of Thomas? Simply that you wanted to know what it was like—"

"No," she heard herself say.

"To belong then. To—"

"That had nothing to do with it." Her heart

leaped. Her fingers scaled higher, twisting in the soft hair on his nape. "Are *you* sorry?"

"Only that it was too quick."

"Quick?" she echoed.

Dane made a sound. "Let me show you." He shoved aside the sheets. In slow deliberation, he trapped her knees between his. He was above her. Astride her.

"Your proximity is having a predictable effect on me, kitten."

Her eyes slid down his form. Her eyes widened. "Yes," she said shakily. "So I see." She gulped. "But it's only been a scant half hour."

Laughter rumbled in his chest. "I am in complete agreement, kitten. Much, *much* too long."

Much later Julianna found herself roused from a sound sleep.

"Julianna," came a husky male whisper against her temple.

Sighing, she stirred reluctantly. She had slept heavily, and she need not wonder why. Dane, she saw, was almost fully dressed.

"I must go, sweet." He pulled her from the bed and handed her the satin dressing gown draped over the foot of the bed.

Together they went downstairs. He chuckled when she stifled a huge yawn as they stopped in the entrance hall.

"What," she grumbled. "You are used to keeping such hours. I am not."

"That is true."

She tipped her head to the side. "Why are you smiling like that?"

"Like what?" A strong hand tucked a curl behind her ear.

"Like you know something I don't."

His hand trailed down the tip of her nose. "You imagine things," he told her lightly.

"Do I?"

"You do."

In the rear of the house a door creaked. Julianna bit her lip. "Dane, you must hurry. My staff is rising."

"And so is mine." Warm hands pulled her close and showed the truth of his statement, lifting her clear from the floor.

"Dane, you must go!"

"I cannot leave without a kiss from those lovely lips."

"Dane, you are the most brash—"

His mouth silenced her. She was still gasping and sputtering as his mouth closed over hers, a long, infinitely intimate kiss. Dazed, she felt her bare toes slide down to the top of his boots to the cold marble floor.

By the time she opened her eyes, the door had already clicked shut. Raising a hand, Julianna pushed aside the lace curtains beside the door, foolishly wanting just one more glimpse of him. A sound behind her drew her attention.

When next she peered through the glass, he was already gone.

Sixteen

"We have a most determined visitor, my lady."

Julianna looked up sharply as she stepped outside in search of her housekeeper. "A visitor?"

Mrs. MacArthur stood on the bottom step, clutching a broom. "Oh, aye. All morning I have been trying to shoo him off, but he is most persistent."

Julianna followed the direction of her finger. Slanted yellow-green eyes glinted in the sunlight.

It was Maximilian.

He sprang forward, his sleek black body curling around her ankles.

Mrs. MacArthur's jaw sagged. "Why, I'll be bound! The wretched creature wouldn't let anyone near him. I thought perhaps he was hungry, but he turned up his nose at the cream I offered him. Yet now he acts as if you are his dearest friend."

Julianna bit her lip. The memory of how Dane had once informed her Maximilian was most discerning suddenly flooded her mind. "Thank you, Mrs. MacArthur. I shall see to him."

"Very well, my lady."

Julianna picked him up. Maximilian immediately tucked his paws against her and rubbed his head beneath her chin. His throaty purr resonated through his entire body. His ears tickled, and she laughed, burying her nose in the soft fur of his neck.

"Oh, Maximilian, I missed you."

"And did you miss me as well?"

Julianna's heart leaped. She knew that low, husky tone, knew it well.

Dane stood before her, just beyond the little iron gate. He wore a navy frock coat with gleaming buttons and tight buff breeches that showed to advantage the lean, muscular length of his thigh.

The air was suddenly heated. She couldn't seem to summon her breath. And when she spoke, there was a faint catch in her voice.

"Hello."

"Hello." His gaze moved hungrily over her face.

"You shouldn't let Maximilian roam. He might get lost."

"He's not lost. He was here when I left this morning. Waiting for me. Now I rather suspect he's been waiting for you."

Neither of them had moved. Each watched the other with a rapt intensity that made it seem as if the world could have tipped on its axis and neither would have noticed—or cared. He stared at her mouth.

She stared at his.

"Will you come out with me?"

Julianna's throat had gone bone-dry. "Where?" As if it mattered.

"Away."

"When?"

"This afternoon." Something flashed in his eyes. "I have some things I must . . . attend."

The spell was broken. "Oh. About—"

"Yes." He paused. "One o'clock?"

Wordlessly she nodded.

"Until then." He gave a brief salute and was off.

Her gaze followed him long after he'd disappeared around the corner. Only then did she realize she still clutched Maximilian.

When the bell rang promptly at one o'clock, Julianna had to stop herself from rushing down the stairs. She heard the door swing open and Mrs. MacArthur's greeting. Pressing her hands against her cheeks, she stopped herself from hurtling down the hallway. *You're acting like a schoolgirl!* She chided herself. Yet, heaven help her, at her first glimpse of Dane in the entrance hall, she felt giddy and light-headed—as if she had indeed rushed down the stairs.

Outside, he helped her into a phaeton. As he guided the vehicle out of the heart of the city, Julianna's gaze strayed to his hands again and again, so capably curled around the reins. He had such wonderful, fascinating hands, his fingers lean and tanned, his wrists sturdy and wide and covered with crisp dark hair. Remembering the way he had touched her only hours before made her long to feel them roaming at will once more.

He glanced over at her. "What is it?"

"Nothing." She would not stammer like a schoolgirl. She would not!

She'd been filled with a nervous tension when she had first seen him again this morning. It faded away as her body bumped gently against his. She didn't try to hold herself distant. Being with him like this felt comfortably intimate and oddly soothing.

When they rolled to a halt, he swung her lightly to the ground. A path snaked away from the road into a forest of oak and elm trees. Wildflowers pushed their way through the earth here and there. The sun's rays dappled the grasses, lighting the world with fresh, vibrant color. In his hands were a blanket and small basket.

"Let us stop here."

Setting down the basket, he snared her by the waist and ducked her behind the tree, where he kissed her long and thoroughly.

"Dane," she gasped when he finally released her mouth, "you are being overly familiar, are you not?"

He threw back his head and laughed.

"Is this a tryst?" she asked pertly.

"Would you like it to be?"

Julianna bit her lip. A furious tide of color rushed into her cheeks. "I don't know," she answered honestly.

Dane said nothing, merely gave her a long, slow look. Pulling her down onto the blanket, he discarded his jacket and unpacked bread, cheese, and wine.

They shared the food. Once it was gone, he sat back against the trunk of the tree. With one booted leg against his chest, he glanced off into the trees. His long body filled the blanket from one corner to the other. A spear of the sun chased along his profile, casting it into golden silhouette. The curve of his mouth had taken on a rakish, lopsided slant that made her heart pound. Whether curved into a boyishly endearing grin or drawn into a thin line, his mouth captivated her.

It hit her like a blow just how arrestingly striking he was.

As if he sensed her gaze, he glanced over at her. Setting aside her glass, he reached for her hand. Julianna wet her lips as he ran his tongue along the tender web of flesh between her thumb and forefinger.

"If we were alone, do you know what I would do with you?"

"I believe I do."

Her prim tone made him laugh. She narrowed her gaze in return.

"You're smiling like that again," she told him.

"Like what?"

"The way you were last night."

"When?"

"When you . . . when we . . . after . . ."

"After what?"

"Are you laughing at me?"

"I am not, kitten. But I *am* smiling. As for why . . . something has occurred to me." He toyed with her fingertips. "When this whole wretched business with the Magpie is done, I think we should marry."

Julianna couldn't believe she'd heard him correctly. She snatched her hand back. "I do not find this amusing," she snapped.

"Nor do I."

"Dane! Why would you even suggest such a thing?"

A haughty lift of bold, black brows. "Why? Need I remind you what transpired last night? I took your virginity. It is the honorable thing to do."

Honor. *Honor.* Something constricted deep in her breast. It was honor that compelled Thomas to marry Clarice, she thought vaguely. It had taken a long time to see past her own feelings of anger and betrayal, but Thomas had done the right thing in refusing to abandon Clarice.

But Julianna wanted more than that. She *deserved* more than that.

"What's done is done. You took nothing, nothing that was not mine to give! And I certainly won't marry you because of a moment of madness!"

"Madness, is it? I remember it quite otherwise."

"Must I be blunt?"

His jaw bunched. "Please do," he replied pleasantly.

"We both succumbed to—to earthly delights."

"To *what*? Are we not being blunt? Sweet, there is no need to be delicate."

In the light of day, everything looked different. Granted, *he* did not look different. His hair was blowing in the breeze. The chiseled outline of his mouth was set in a harsh line. Yet he was as devastating to her emotions as always.

Her mouth opened, then closed. She had not

expected this. Her gaze was almost desperate. "I cannot deny the way we are drawn to each other, that we have been from the very beginning. But perhaps it was our circumstances, the fact that we were in such close quarters. In constant company. Yes, that is surely the case."

"You convince neither of us, kitten. We both know what drove us. We were hardly overwrought. Overcome, perhaps, but—"

"You said it yourself, Dane. It was quick. Heated. Intense."

"You think it was lust," he pronounced flatly.

"Yes, yes! Something wild and carnal."

"Carnal!" He made a sound of disgust.

"When I marry, if I ever marry," she stressed, "it will be for all the right reasons. Not because of a moment of madness."

She accurately read the disbelief on his features. Fire replaced it, burning and intent.

"You are refusing me?"

"I . . . It seems I am."

With a curse, he surged to his feet. Her head whirling, Julianna suddenly found herself standing before him.

"I could almost believe you seek to teach me a lesson. Is this because I was not candid?"

"It is not!" He towered above her, but she stood her ground.

"Sweet, if I were to go to your brothers and

divulge that we were acquainted in the *carnal* way, you are surely aware they would demand that we wed."

"They might demand it, but they certainly couldn't make me. Nor can you. My decisions are my own, Dane."

"We will marry, Julianna."

"What?" she cried.

He put his face just above hers. "We *will* marry, love."

Her chin raised aloft. "You may have a title. You may be used to giving orders. But you won't give orders to me."

There was a flash of white teeth. "Kitten," he drawled, "you are charmingly acrimonious."

"Oh, stop! If I had not seen you last night at the Farthingales, this would never have happened. The subject of marriage would certainly never have cropped up. Our paths would never have crossed again."

He caught her up against him. "I'd already set about making inquiries, Miss Julianna Clare—a task that might have proved easier if I had not had the wrong name."

"Oh, do not *dare* to upbraid me!" Her eyes flashed. Her gaze slid away, then back again, but she couldn't meet his demanding regard.

"I want to go home, Dane."

"Julianna—" He caught her chin and brought

her eyes to his. She looked at him then, her eyes swimming.

Her lips were tremulous.

Dane swore to himself, long and fluently.

Neither of them spoke all the way back into the city.

When at last they arrived at her house, darkness had begun to settle in like a shroud. He turned to her. "I'm coming in," was all he said.

"Please don't," she said, her voice strangled.

Julianna felt his gaze digging into her like a thousand tiny needles.

Slowly she raised her head. "It might be better if we don't see each other again."

She hadn't known she was going to say it until she did. She sat poised on the edge of the seat.

She felt the sudden tension that invaded his every pore.

He did not touch her. If he had, she thought wildly, she would never have found the courage to remain so still.

"Julianna, listen to me. I can give you the things you want. I *will* give you the things you want. The babies you want."

Her body trembled. And so did her heart. Ah, especially her heart!

She had told herself she would never know passion—desire—in a man's arms. But in Dane's arms, she had. So much it was almost frightening! Seeing him again . . . being with him. It felt so right.

He had feelings for her. Deep in her soul, she knew it. She'd felt it in the tender sweep of his arms around her back, in the compelling heat of his mouth on hers.

But so much of her was in turmoil! Being with him at the cottage, the dreadful way she'd missed him . . . She'd been a fool with Thomas, never guessing that he'd been seeing Clarice while they were engaged.

And perhaps she feared being so foolish once more.

She shook her head. Her eyes avoided his. "Please," she began carefully. All at once she broke off. Her gaze fixed on a point just beyond his shoulder.

"What? What is it?"

"That man across the way. He's just standing there. Dane, I think he's looking at us."

In one lightning move, Dane reached beneath the seat. When he vaulted to the street, there was a glint of steel.

The man across the street touched the brim of his hat and walked away.

"It's all right. I know him." Dane tucked the pistol into his breeches. He reached for Julianna and swung her down.

She blinked. "Oh, my God. All this time you had a pistol—"

"Yes."

The man had walked to the corner and stood there. "He's waiting for you?"

"Yes."

"Well, then, you'd best not keep him any longer."

His jaw might have been forged of iron. "This does not end here, Julianna."

"And I say it does."

Dane cursed. "I'll be back, Julianna."

"No, Dane. *No.* Please don't." She swallowed the rending ache in her breast. "It will be easier for me if you don't."

And then she walked away.

Dane nearly flung himself on the chair at the coffeehouse where he and Phillip had agreed to meet.

Phillip eyed him curiously. "You're in a mood, aren't you?"

Dane scowled and ordered a whisky.

"Does it have something to do with your ladybird?"

Dane raised his brows. "Clever, aren't we? I can see why you do what you do, Phillip. I just wish you would do it more quickly so I could have done with it."

Phillip laughed, then sighed. "The truth is, Dane, I am beginning to fear we shall never find this blackguard. It is proving an arduous process."

Long fingers drummed on the tabletop. "That is not what I wish to hear, Phillip."

Phillip grimaced. "I know. Yet we are doing all we can to force his hand." He eyed Dane. "Are you going out tonight?"

"It seems I have no choice, does it?" Dane picked up his glass.

His friend studied him. "Are you all right?"

"No."

Phillip watched him down the whisky. "You cannot afford to be distracted," he said softly. "This is dangerous business."

Dane's head turned. His bootheels rapped sharply on the wooden floor as he got to his feet. "You tend to your business"—he was unusually short—"and I'll tend to mine."

The ebony night was silent and sleepy. Overhead the darkness was almost impenetrable, thick and heavy, an ominous swell of clouds stifling the circlet of moon.

Dane swept a restless glance down the roadway. Beneath him, Percival shifted, pawing the damp earth and sending a scatter of leaves whirling with a sudden breeze. With a single word, Dane stilled his mount.

Phillip was right, he decided blackly. His mind was not where it should be. His mind was not on his work. Nor was his heart in it.

Hell. Bloody hell.

He did not want to be here. He wanted to be anywhere but here.

No, that was not right. He wanted to be with her. *Julianna*.

Almost from the beginning, he'd warned himself he could not allow his desire to rule him. Always before, the nature of his work had demanded he keep his heart intact, for what if his greatest fear should come to pass? To forfeit his life when he well knew the risks . . . It wouldn't have been fair to any woman . . . God knew, it wasn't fair to Julianna! There had been far too much heartache in her life already.

But desire had become much more. He couldn't stop what happened between them. He still couldn't. God above, he didn't want to!

Lord, he thought disgustedly, what a mess he'd made of things! What the devil had he been thinking? He'd been too confident. Just as she'd said—too arrogant! All that was male and swaggering within him still did not want to believe she'd refused him.

Not, he decided grimly, that it had been a very proper proposal.

No, it didn't come out as it should have. He should have courted her. Waited.

Her voice was sweeter than the sun shining through the blackest night. Pure. Bright and untarnished. Was it any wonder that he was impatient?

So what the hell was he supposed to do? He would not let her go. No, she wouldn't be rid of him so easily. She wasn't going to walk out of his life.

By Jove, he was going to walk right back into hers.

In the distance came the rumble of wheels. Percival's ears pricked forward. Dane laid a hand on his neck, feeling the powerful black's skin ripple beneath his touch.

When the coach came into view, the coachman beheld the ominous sight of a huge black beast stationed directly in the middle of the roadway, a masked, caped figure atop the muscled steed.

With a jangle of harness, the coach shuddered to a halt. The potbellied driver gaped.

"Hands up," Dane ordered smoothly. A middle-aged gentleman thrust his head from the passenger compartment. "What is it, man? Why have you stopped?" His eyes bulged when he glimpsed Dane's masked figure.

"It's him, Jane! The Magpie!"

There was a piercing scream from within.

"Rest easy, madam." Dane glanced inside as he slung a fat bag over his shoulder. "I have what I want."

He vaulted back into the saddle and seized the reins. A squeeze of his thighs and Percival was off.

Dane glanced back over his shoulder.

Damnation! The coachman was fumbling under his cape. Even as the realization ripped through his brain, a bullet zinged past his ear and splintered the bark from the low-hanging branch just above his head.

Phillip was right.

He could not be careless. That was entirely too close for comfort.

The woman in the corner lifted the folds of her veil. Roxbury was busy, reverently examining his latest piece, a long wooden box delicately inlaid with ivory and gold, wonderfully preserved. Reluctantly, he put it aside and regarded his visitor.

"Why do you stare, *madame*?"

"I have been wondering about the patch over your eye," she said suddenly. "I recall you did not have it when you were young."

"*Madame*, I wonder that you recalled me at all." He gave a short laugh.

"What happened?"

"An injury sustained while I served in the Royal Navy during the Battle of the Nile."

"The Battle of the Nile! I should have known!"

Her piquant brows slanted high. "Lord Nelson's ship?"

"No. The *Culloden*. You will recall the British soundly trounced the French."

She ignored the gibe. "I would have thought you well suited to the military life."

He touched the patch. "My commanders thought otherwise." His smile was tight.

"You are aware that François grows impatient for his gold. I cannot continue to make excuses for your lack of funds."

He feigned astonishment. "What! A man you cannot wrap around your finger?"

"You said the delay was because the highwayman—what is his name?"

"The Magpie."

"Yes, yes. The Magpie. That he had stolen your funds. But a man of your position . . . how is it you have acquired your wealth? It is not by legitimate means, is it?"

"Very good, *madame*."

"How then?"

A smile dallied about his lips. "Since you persist, *madame*, allow me to show you." Opening the drawer of the desk, he displayed two banknotes on the table before her.

"Look closely, *madame*. Look *closely*."

Understanding spread across her features. She inhaled sharply. "Do you mean to say—"

"Quite so. A nearly flawless execution, don't you agree? I daresay only an official of the Bank of England would know the difference. I ship the notes to a man who then distributes the bogus currency across England. Of course, like François, I prefer my payment in gold. But alas, the law of economy prevails. No production, no return. If my contacts do not receive my shipments, I cannot profit. And the Magpie is making that difficult. So I suggest you find a way to placate François, *madame,* for I've not yet finished with you. There are many who might be interested in learning that the late Armand was not your only husband—" he gave a grating laugh "—and hardly your first."

Her eyes flashed. "I may oblige you," she retorted, "but I do not have to like it."

Roxbury laughed softly. "Restrain your temper, *madame.* But come, I am a reasonable man. What would make you happy?"

"To return to Paris!"

"All in good time, *madame.* But I would know, what displeases you so?"

"I am tired of London. I am tired of England. And I am tired of the company of my maid!"

"Do not pout, *madame.* It's most unbecoming. I am, however, ever ready to accommodate you. So what would please you, I wonder. What would amuse you? A night at the theater?" He lit a cigar, sat back and stared at her through a haze of smoke. "Yes, I see that it would. We are alike, you and I. We both know how to get what we want, don't we?"

Seventeen

$\mathcal{D}$espite everything, Julianna half expected Dane to appear at her doorstep the following morning. He did not, and when she walked in Hyde Park later that day, she discovered why.

Lord and Lady Harrison stopped their curricle as Julianna stopped to retie the yellow silk ribbons of her bonnet. "You should not walk alone, my lady."

Julianna summoned a smile. "I often walk alone, Lord Harrison," she replied.

"Ah, but the Magpie was seen just outside of the city last night. I do believe the rogue grows bolder with each passing day."

Julianna's heart lurched.

"He's not such a dangerous sort," protested Eugenia, Lord Harrison's wife.

Lord Harrison sent her a startled glance. "And how would you know?"

Eugenia, who was quite the gossip, clasped her hands together, her eyes glowing. "I've heard he's quite . . ." She suddenly seemed to remember it was her husband she addressed.

"Handsome?" her husband supplied.

Eugenia bit her lip. "Well, yes."

A bittersweet pang shot through her. *That he is,* she affirmed silently. *That he is.*

Lord Harrison snorted. "Well, handsome or no, it's only a matter of time before the rogue is caught. The coachman hid a pistol in his coat, and when the Magpie rode off last night, he very nearly took off the scoundrel's head."

Her heart plummeted. She stood stock-still. Anger and fear warred like a tide in her breast. It was a precarious life that Dane led. How could he court danger so carelessly—and with such ease?

She did not understand it. She never would.

She was trembling as Lord and Lady Harrison bade her good day and rode off.

At the Farthingales' ball the night she had seen Dane, Julianna had agreed to attend the theater this evening with her friend Caroline and her husband. In truth, she had no desire to go. She had cried herself to sleep last night, and didn't know if she could appear bright and sprightly.

Not that she was about to explain. Indeed,

what could she say? She had half a mind to send a note round to Caroline explaining she could not attend. But if she remained at home, she was well aware what would happen. She would end up crying herself to sleep again.

The claret gown she donned lent her color and courage. Julianna put him from her mind as she entered the theater with her friends.

Of all the theaters in London, the Theatre Royal was Julianna's favorite. The theater had burned to the ground on four different occasions. She couldn't help but recall when it had reopened the last time, six years ago; she, Sebastian, and Justin had attended the opening performance of *Hamlet*.

The evening passed more quickly than she expected. Bidding good-bye to Caroline and her husband, she exited the lofty interior. Pausing around the corner on Russell Street, she glanced idly down the long procession of carriages, looking for her vehicle.

The throng streamed all around her. As she stood, a sizzle of awareness tingled its way along the back of her neck. She turned her head ever so slightly.

Splendidly attired in black coat and boots that showed off the beauty of his form, a man stood out above the others. She nearly gasped.

It was almost unnervingly like the other night at the Farthingales. There was something alarmingly deliberate in his unfaltering gait as he advanced. She turned, fighting a surge of panic.

Warm fingers curled into her elbow. "Going somewhere, love?" came his husky murmur.

Her heart knocked wildly in her chest. Julianna forced her gaze to his face, bracing herself inside. Her eyes flashed mutinously. "How did you find me?"

"Mrs. MacArthur proved most accommodating."

She stiffened. "I see. I shall have to speak with her. Unfortunately, you've made the journey in vain." She was proud of her aplomb. "Ah, there they are now. Please excuse me."

He didn't release her. Instead, his fingers caressed the inside of her elbow, there where her glove ended. A jolt of pleasure shot through her.

"I am leaving, Dane."

"Yes. With me." His tone was ever so pleasant, but beneath was a note of steel. There was a slant to his charming smile that did not bode well.

"No. I—I'm waiting for my friend Caroline and her husband. We're having a late supper—"

He was shaking his head.

Her lips compressed. "What? *What?*"

"You are undoubtedly the worst liar I have ever encountered."

"Coming from you, sir, I shall consider that a compliment!"

He maintained that damnable smile—and it

was vastly irritating. He tossed a greeting to someone. His gaze returned to her.

"I am not leaving with you, Dane."

"If you don't, I'll be forced to tell everyone here about those delectable dimples you have on your backside."

She gazed at him levelly. "Dane, what are you doing?"

"You threatened me at the Farthingales, love. It is not a pleasant feeling, is it?"

"I dislike demands."

"Except when you make them."

She glared at him. "You're late for the play," she said suddenly. "Did someone steal your pocket watch, my lord?"

His eyes narrowed. His grip tightened subtly, as if in warning. "Julianna," he began.

"Yes, yes, I'm quite aware. All in a night's work, I suppose."

He said nothing, merely watched her from beneath black brows.

Julianna swallowed. "Is it true what happened last night? That someone—"

"Yes." His lips barely moved.

"And you are well?" She couldn't help but ask.

"Of course."

Of course. *Of course?* Damn him! she thought wildly. He was not invincible. How like a man— how like him!—to be convinced he was.

By now her carriage had rolled to a halt, taking its place in line behind the others. George, the driver, pulled the door open. "My lady?" he said cheerfully.

Dane handed her inside and leaped up to follow her. Before she could protest, he'd swung up on the seat beside her. His thigh rode against hers, so much harder and longer than her own.

Strong fingers caught at hers. "You're running, Julianna. But you don't have to. You don't have to be afraid."

Was she? *Was she?* After Thomas, she had run, all the way to the Continent. But she didn't want to run from Dane. She wanted to throw herself against him, feel his arms lock tight around her back, and know the splendor of his kiss.

Her eyes were riveted by the sight of her hands trapped within his. She was achingly aware of his strength, his power, yet his touch was so very gentle.

Her gaze climbed high. Clear to his. Her eyes clung to his.

"Why are you here, Dane?"

He scanned her features. A tremor shot through her. Did he see it? Did he feel it? she wondered frantically. Did she even care? With his expression so heated and intense, it made her insides melt like wax beneath a flame.

"I can't stay away, kitten."

"This is madness," she whispered.

Never had she been so torn! To have happiness

within her grasp ... to have *him* within her grasp. She felt battered and bruised inside. He was right. She was afraid. She was terrified! What if she trusted him, and it was for naught? The hurt would be immense. Yet how could she deny herself? How could she deny him?

She had told herself she must forget him. But how, when he invaded her mind at every turn. She couldn't keep thoughts of him at bay. It appeared she couldn't keep *him* at bay! Oh, curse her stupid, foolish pride.

She drew a ragged breath. Her expression betrayed her. Did her heart? Dane must have read her struggle in her expression, for his gaze delved into hers. Fiercely intent. Indeed, it was as if he reached clear inside her. He saw what no one else saw. He saw what no one else ever had. He saw what *she* could not see.

"You claim you will never marry, Julianna. Is it an affair you want?"

"No!" she gasped.

"Nor do I," he said curtly. "So what is it then?"

A hot ache clogged her throat so that she could utter a sound. "I don't know," she whispered, unable to keep her voice from breaking. "I don't know!"

His gaze was almost accusing. "You care, Julianna. I know you do."

"And what if I do? Oh, don't you see? I don't want to."

His eyes darkened. "What the devil does that mean? We have lain together, Julianna. As a man and woman. As a husband and wife *should*. That is not something I take lightly, nor should you."

"Oh! Do not dare to lecture me, Dane! I meant it when I said I would not marry you because of duty or obligation, or out of any sense of honor. *My* sense of honor precludes it. I want more from marriage than that, Dane. I want more from a husband!"

He made a loud, impatient exclamation. "Julianna—"

Julianna was shaking from head to toe. "It's not just that," she cried. "It's not just that!"

Dane's eyes narrowed. "What then?"

Somehow she regained hold of her self-possession. "You say you will give me children and—and all the things that I want. But I want a husband who will be steadfast and true. I want a husband who will be there each and every day of their lives . . . each and every day of *my* life! I want a husband who will tell our children stories, and pick them up when they fall! Perhaps it's selfish, but I want a husband who will put me above all else."

"I will do that, Julianna. Let me prove it—

"No," she said wildly. "You can't. *You can't.*

You claimed you are afraid to die, but your actions say otherwise. I-I don't understand why you do what you do . . . Perhaps you are trying to punish yourself. Perhaps it's a question of daring, a question of courage! You said the best way to overcome one's fear is to face it. But I can't do that—I can't! I don't want a husband who—who dashes in and out of my life at his leisure! I shouldn't be able to survive knowing that when you left, it might well be the last time I saw you. I couldn't live like that. I hate the way you deliberately put yourself in jeopardy, Dane. I hate it!"

The speech was unflinching, straight from the heart.

Her outburst had startled him. She saw it in the way his mouth drew into a thin, straight line. She tried to wrench her hands away, but his grip tightened.

"Dammit," he said tautly, "I have no choice, Julianna. The game is not over. I must see it through. I cannot quit now."

"And therein lies the difference between us. It is a game to you. But to me it is your life!" She swallowed painfully. "I know you cannot stop now. I know it is a question of honor, of loyalty. I understand. Truly I do. But I cannot accept it. I cannot. I want a man, Dane, not a mask."

Dane sat back. "Hardly flattering," he said in a clipped, abrupt tone.

The silence in the carriage was stifling. He was scowling fiercely, his jaw clenched so hard it appeared he might splinter into a million pieces.

Finally, his gaze veered away. "Good God," he suddenly exploded, "why the hell haven't we moved?"

The very same thought was running through Julianna's mind. Outside, the patrons were still drifting from the theater. Theirs was on the corner, but with the endless procession of carriages, the narrow streets were jammed so that none had yet moved.

Julianna glanced through the window. A couple strode past. Half of the man's face was shadowed, yet there was something about him that drew her attention.

His companion wore a jaunty hat covered by a sheer red veil that matched the silk of her gown. They had stopped at the hired hack on the corner. The driver was there, a lantern in hand as he moved to assist her. She placed an elegant, gloved hand in the driver's. With the other she pushed back the veil.

It spun idly through Julianna's mind that the woman had undoubtedly been a stunning beauty in her day. Why, she still was. She was neither young, yet neither was she old. Her body was as trim as someone half her age.

Just before she entered the carriage, she paused and glanced back at the man.

The light from the lantern fell full upon her face.

Disbelief gripped Julianna's mind.

The world seemed to freeze. And for one perilous moment, her blood did as well.

"Oh, God."

Fumbling for the handle, she flung it wide and lurched through the opening. In her haste she landed hard on one knee, catching herself on her hands.

Her head jerked up.

The door of the hack clicked shut. It rolled smoothly away, the first of the night to do so.

An arm about her waist, Dane pulled her upright. "Julianna! What the devil!"

Julianna did not hear. "Wait," she cried. "Wait!"

His gaze swiveled sharply between the carriage that had just disappeared into the night and Julianna's white features.

"What is it?" he asked sharply. "Do you know that woman?"

Her gaze wrenched to his. Shock spilled through her, for the face she had seen was one she had barely known. A face she had never in all the world thought to see . . .

But one she could not fail to recognize.

"It was my mother," she said numbly. "It was my *mother*."

Eighteen

"**I** do not mean to doubt you, kitten. But weren't you just a child when you last saw your mother?"

Dane lowered himself to the gold brocade sofa in her sitting room. Dane would not soon forget Julianna's expression. It had sent an eerie prickle all through him once more. She had looked as if she'd seen a ghost.

There had been no hope of catching the veiled woman's vehicle, however. Dane had tried to follow on foot, but it was no use.

Julianna nodded. "I was three years old."

She was still visibly shaken. He filled two glasses of wine from the tray Mrs. MacArthur had just deposited on the table before them. Sitting back, he handed one to Julianna.

"Drink it. You're still pale."

She took a sip.

"Another," he bade her.

She obeyed. A smile grazed his lips. "There," he approved. "That's better."

She smiled back, then suddenly her gaze slid away. She bit her lip. "How can this be? How?"

"You don't know that it was," he reminded her. "You only saw this woman for an instant. And in the dark—"

"I know. I *know*. And yet when it happened, I had the strangest sensation . . . I'm not sure I can explain it. It was as if I knew she was a stranger, yet every sense inside me was suddenly screaming that she was familiar. That I should recognize her. And then I *did*."

"Julianna," he said gently, "if you were only three years of age, you may not remember her with any clarity."

Something flashed across her features. "It's true that I have no memories of her. I—I do not recall ever being sad because I had no mother. I had my brothers to love and—and who I knew loved me in turn. But there is a portrait at Thurston Hall, the family home, a portrait of me, Sebastian, Justin, and my parents. It was painted just before my mother left. It's said the artist's likeness is quite remarkable, the way he captured the essence of all of us. Sebastian's protectiveness, Justin's rebellion, my father's severity, my mother's frivolity. After she deserted us, my father had it removed to the attic.

"But I used to sneak up to look at it. And when my father died and Sebastian became marquess, he returned it to the gallery. But I was always fascinated by it. I rarely passed by it without glancing at it. When I was very young, I thought my mother was surely the most divinely beautiful woman ever." She touched a chestnut lock that lay curled on her breast. "I remember once, one of my friends remarked that it was a pity I did not inherit her green eyes and stunning coloring, as Justin did. But I was quite content with myself . . . I do not recall a time when I wasn't somehow aware that she had done something awful. I admired her beauty, but I did not want to *be* like her. *Or* my father.

"Perhaps I am a fool," she said, her voice very low. "Perhaps my sight has failed me. Perhaps my mind as well. Yet there is a part of me that tells me that the woman I saw was my mother." She shook her head. "Yet how can it be? How can it be?"

It was hardly compelling. Reason balked. A dead woman come to life after nearly a quarter century . . . It seemed unfathomable. And yet, Julianna appeared so convinced.

"Julianna," he said quietly. "You said she died years ago. Tell me again what happened."

"She ran off with another man. The ship they were on capsized crossing the Channel. Everyone on board drowned. That's all I know."

"What about Sebastian or Justin?"

"I'm not sure." Almost helplessly her eyes sought his. "Dane—"

He put their glasses aside. "You're trembling!" he exclaimed. For a moment he regarded her; he did not speak, but placed his fingertips gently on her cheek. Something flared in his eyes.

He pulled her up and into his arms. "Protest all you want," he told her, "but I'll not be leaving you tonight."

She buried her face against the side of his throat. She didn't want to protest. Nor did she want him to leave.

In her room he tugged off her gown. She obliged when he knelt to remove her stockings and slippers, balancing with a palm on his shoulders. His clothing was dispatched with the same impatient efficiency. When he straightened, she still hadn't moved.

Nor did he when she stretched out a hand, slim fingers tangling in the dark mat of hair on his chest.

Their eyes collided. A wordless entreaty. A wordless surrender. Did it matter? She was naked in the moonlight, naked in his arms. Her mouth lifted, seeking his. His insides turned to fire. The feel of her soft lips beneath his burned him.

He never broke the kiss as he lifted her to the bed.

She ran a hand over the supple muscle of his back. Perhaps it was the wine that made her reckless. She didn't want to think. She just wanted to feel.

And what she wanted to feel was him. *Dane*.

Shy fingertips strayed down the plane of his belly. She reached the place where the hair was rougher. Thicker.

His muscles clenched. He kissed the side of her neck. "Yes, kitten. Oh, yes."

His encouragement made her cheeks burn. Curling her fingers around him, feeling him leap and grow even hotter, she ran her thumb over the sleek, round tip of his organ.

"Impressive," she whispered.

"I know."

Her eyes widened.

He laughed.

She feigned outrage. Her fingertips retracted. She released him. "Do I not please you?"

"Impudent, cheeky wench." Husky laughter rushed across her cheek. Lean fingers closed around hers, guiding anew. Unbidden, she glanced down. His body was hungry—hungry for her. *For her*. And the sight of her hand wound tight around his flesh—the feel of him in her hand—was incredibly erotic.

Her eyes widened once more. He was hot. So very hot. But most of all, so very *hard*.

"But I beg you, lady, pray continue."

And she did, until he groaned and declared he could bear it no more.

He rolled her to her back. His hand drifted down to one knee, idly caressing the skin behind it, then slid up between her legs. His hand clamped possessively around the top of her thigh. He kissed her almost lazily, his touch hovering tormentingly near but not quite touching her cleft.

"What was it you asked?" he whispered. "Do I not please you?"

His thumb thrust just inside the heat of damp, pink folds, only to pull back. Her breath hitched in her throat.

"What, Julianna? Do I not please you?"

She pushed at his shoulders in mute frustration.

He lowered his mouth onto the hollow of her belly. Her brain flashed with stark, wanton images of that last night at the cottage, the way he spread her legs wide with the breadth of his shoulders. His dark head planted *there* between them, brazen thumbs parting the damp, tight curls to expose the nub of pleasure hidden high and deep in her cleft. . . .

"Will you tell me what you want, sweet?"

His tone was cajoling. His tongue traced a flaming line just above her triangle of chestnut curls. He raised his head to sear her with golden eyes.

"I—I can't say it." She was cold no longer. Her body was on fire.

"Are you still so shy? Of course you can. You can have whatever you want, love."

"Dane!" He knew, damn him. He knew. "I can't!" She turned her head aside.

She could feel his breath, moist and daring. Please, she thought desperately. She yearned to feel his molten caress *there*. Just once more. Just once . . .

"Tell me. Tantalize me."

She wet her lips. "Kiss me like you did before."

He was smiling. She could hear it in his voice. "How, sweet?"

"You know," she said faintly.

"Like this?" he whispered.

Like a brand of fire he touched the very heat and heart of her, the part that swelled and wept and ached.

At the first glide of his tongue, her body went taut, while everything inside went weak. The air sped from her lungs in a torrid rush.

She surged against his tongue. His mouth. Against him. Writhing until she was steaming inside, until a ragged moan caught in her throat. Unable to stand any more of the exquisite torture, she tangled her fingers in his hair and grasped his upper arms to clench him to her.

He reared over her. Their hands caught. His fingers locked tight with hers. His mouth tasted of unbearable sweetness, of raw possessiveness.

Only one thing would do. Only *he* would do.

"Now, Dane. Now."

She felt the vibration of his laugh. "Patience, kitten, will make it all the sweeter."

But he gave her what she wanted, what they both needed. A fluid twist of his hips and he plunged inside her. His penetration was deep. Hard. It resounded in every part of her.

He withdrew, keeping a scant inch inside her. Her wet channel clung to the helm of his member, as if she could not bear for him to leave her.

And she couldn't. "Don't stop." It was a ragged plea, a moan. "Don't stop."

When he kissed her mouth, she nearly cried out. "Kitten," he muttered. "*Kitten.*"

Slowly, he raised his head. The gold of his eyes flared hot, hotter than flames, blistering her with their heat. Julianna couldn't look away when he plunged again. And when he kissed her, she cried out.

Rampant pleasure spilled through her. To her very bones. Her fingers curled into his shoulders, thrilling to the resiliency of muscle and skin.

Climax hurtled close. It was there in the quickening, almost frantic tempo of his thrusts. And she was nearly there as well. Reaching. Seeking.

Her arms tightened. A wave of emotion broke over her. And she knew then . . .

This was heaven. This was bliss.

This was love.

Early the next afternoon, Julianna stepped into her sitting room. Her brothers had just arrived and followed her through the doorway.

"What's this about, Jules? Your note sounded rather urgent." Justin was a step ahead of Sebastian.

Dane was already there, lounging against the mantel. He straightened when they entered.

"Sebastian. Justin. This is Viscount Granville." Julianna made the introductions, her tone a trifle breathless.

The men exchanged pleasantries. Sebastian's gray eyes drifted to Julianna.

"We can return later if you like, Jules."

Julianna cleared her throat. "No. Actually, I've asked Dane to be present while I spoke to you."

His name slipped out before she realized it. The familiarity did not go unnoticed by her brothers, who exchanged a look. Her color was high as well; both gray eyes and green lingered.

Sebastian took the wing chair across from the sofa. Justin lowered himself to its mate, extended a long leg before him. Dane moved to stand near the chess table.

Julianna sat in her favorite Queen Anne chair and tucked her feet beneath her.

Sebastian frowned. "You're not in some sort of trouble, are you?"

She shook her head. Taking a deep breath, she lifted her chin.

"I saw Mother last night."

Her quiet pronouncement engendered a stunned silence.

Justin broke it with a terse laugh. "The devil you say! Jules, if this is your idea of a grand joke—"

Julianna shook her head. "I wouldn't joke about such a thing. I saw her getting into a carriage after the play last night at Theatre Royal."

"How can you be sure?"

"I can't," she admitted. "But the portrait at Thurston Hall . . . Justin, oh, I know how you hate it, but she still looks so much like you I vow it made my heart stop."

"Good God. I should imagine that seeing *her* would be enough to make one's heart stop."

"It was. Oh, God, it was! I know it's absurd. I know it's painful. I know it brings back so much we would all rather forget . . . yet it was uncanny. And if you had seen her, you would know, too . . . It was Mother. I felt it with everything inside me!"

Justin made no response. His brilliant green eyes lowered. There was no hint of what he was thinking—what he was feeling—reflected on his features.

Dane stepped forward. "If you wish, I am in a position to make certain . . . inquiries."

Sebastian's gaze sharpened.

"Discreetly? Our name has been dragged through the muck enough. I have no wish to put our wives and children through the nightmare the three of us endured when we were children."

"Unquestionably." Dane inclined his head. "Julianna has disclosed"—he sought to be tactful—"the circumstances of your mother's departure—"

The ghost of a smile curled Justin's lips. "Let us not mince words, man. Daphne Sterling, Marchioness of Thurston, left England with her lover. Their packet capsized in a storm off Calais. Everyone aboard went down with the ship." He turned and walked to the window, his gait stiff.

Dane looked between them. "So while it may be exceedingly improbable—and most incredible!—it is indeed possible that Daphne Sterling may have survived. But if so, where has she been all this time?"

Quiet descended. Neither Sebastian, Justin, nor Julianna said a word.

"She said she was going to the Continent," Sebastian said in an odd voice. "Paris. Venice. She said the weather would be lovely."

Justin pivoted. "What! Sebastian? How do you know?"

"Because I saw her leave. I saw her get into the carriage and leave Thurston Hall—the both of them. She and her lover."

Both of his siblings stared at him in shock.

"I know," Sebastian said quietly. "I was ten, wasn't I? She and Father quarreled so bitterly that night! I knew he would have been angry if he knew I'd seen her. At *her*. At me. Then came the news that she had died." He paused. "No one else knows but Devon."

Julianna was still stunned. For years, years he had kept the secret locked tight inside him. Her heart went out to him. It hadn't been easy for any of them, growing up with the scandal wrought by their mother's abandonment. Their father's harshness. That night had changed all of their lives . . . perhaps it had changed them all!

But never had she guessed that Sebastian had been there. That he had witnessed his mother walk away—walk from his life and never return. No child should have had to bear such a thing. Oh, how it must have hurt!

And how brave he had been. "Sebastian," she

whispered. Before she knew it, she was at his side.

"Don't look at me like that, Jules. It's all right. Really it is."

He gave her a quick hug, then drew back. Julianna smiled mistily. Her gaze slid to Justin, who watched them very gravely. He managed a semblance of a smile, but his expression was drawn, his posture wooden.

Julianna and Sebastian exchanged a troubled look, both aware of his strain.

"The man with her that night," Dane said. "Her companion. Who was he?"

Sebastian shook his head. "I have no idea. We were children. Do such things really matter in a child's world?"

True enough, Dane reflected soberly.

Justin had been strangely quiet. "Suppose she is alive," he said suddenly. "Suppose she *is* here in London. It's not just the question of where she's been all these years. Why has she suddenly returned? Why now?"

"A very good question." Dane advanced the thought. "Not only that, but who was she with last night?"

They all looked at each other.

It was Julianna who voiced the thought foremost in everyone's minds. "The man with her last night. Do you think he was her lover? The man she left with all those years ago?"

* * *

Julianna accompanied Sebastian and Justin to the entrance hall a short while later. Dane stood just to her right, near the vase of flowers on the table.

Sebastian turned to him and extended a hand. "It's good of you to lend your assistance." He engaged his eyes directly. "May I ask how it is you're acquainted with my sister?"

A slow smile crept across Dane's lips. "Certainly," he answered mildly. "I intend to marry her someday. Preferably soon."

Julianna gasped.

Sebastian arched a brow. "You might have told us, Jules."

"I gather," Justin added, "this comes as news to her."

"No," Dane said softly.

Sebastian hadn't missed the mutinous flare in Julianna's eyes either. "Ah," he said smoothly. "A source of ongoing debate then?"

The pair in question spoke at the same instant.

"Yes!" said she.

"No," said he.

"I see." Sebastian nodded, as if in perfect understanding.

Dane's smile widened. "She has yet to become accustomed to the idea," he supplied. Catching her fingers, he carried them to his lips.

"So noted," Justin observed dryly.

Mrs. MacArthur appeared with their canes. She opened the door.

"Well," Sebastian murmured, when they strode into the sunlight, "this has been a day of revelation, has it not?" He glanced at Justin. "What is your opinion of Granville?"

"A most confident chap."

"Yes, he is that, isn't he?" Sebastian looked back at the house. "And when we left, I noticed something different about Julianna. When she spoke to him, the sunshine was back in her voice."

"Is that what it was? I'd have called it something else entirely," Justin said with a low chuckle. "But you're right. Her spark is back. That alone would endear him to both of us."

"Indeed. I don't believe we should interfere, Justin."

"No," he agreed. "Our sister has a mind of her own."

Sebastian glanced at him. "Shall we walk for a while?"

"I could certainly use a brandy."

"Capital idea. The club then."

Once they were seated inside White's, Justin glanced over at Sebastian. "So," he said. "Do you think it's true? Do you think Julianna saw Mother last night?"

Sebastian could be no less than honest. "Damned if I know."

"I think she did. Sebastian, I feel the same as Julianna. I have this queer feeling that it *was*."

Sebastian sipped his whisky and eyed his brother. "Are you all right?"

"Why wouldn't I be?" Justin paused, his brandy halfway to his mouth.

"No reason, other than it *was* quite a blow to hear what Julianna had to say, wasn't it?"

"No. Not a blow. A shock, to be sure. It doesn't hurt to think of her like it once did. Until I married Arabella, I believed it was a curse to look like her. For so many years I was convinced I was *like* her."

"As if it's one's outward appearance that makes a man—or woman," Sebastian said with a quirk of his brow.

Justin smiled crookedly. "Yes, yes, I know. But it took my wife to show me that I wasn't."

Sebastian was puzzled. "What then? Surely you cannot doubt yourself again?"

"Lord, no!" Justin flexed his shoulders. "I'm just not sure I want to know if it's her," he admitted. "And yet I . . ."

He stopped short. Something flickered in his green eyes. "What's troubling you, Justin?"

Justin's throat worked as he swallowed the brew in his glass. "It's nothing. Really."

They moved on to their families. Sebastian mentioned how Devon seemed to understand perfectly their twins' babble, while it was totally beyond him. Justin laughed as he relayed how his daughter had wet his knee before his arrival at Julianna's.

No more was said of their mother, for he knew his brother well. If Justin was inclined to confide in him, he would, in his own good time. If not, there was nothing he would say or do that would change his mind.

Once the front door was closed and Julianna had bidden her brothers good-bye, she swung around, her lovely little mouth pinched tight.

Dane had meandered back into the sitting room. "What?" he murmured.

"Dane Quincy Granville—"

"Kitten," he drawled, "you sound remarkably like my mother and my sisters when they sought to give me a scolding."

"And I can well imagine the occasions were many when it was necessary to do so!"

"Oh, but I was an angel."

"You?" She marched across and prodded his chest with a finger. "Dane, how could you say such a thing? I haven't agreed to marry you, and you know it!"

"Well, I knew that *you* certainly weren't about to tell them. Besides, I sought to lighten the moment. The three of you looked as if you needed it.

And in my defense, I restrained myself. I merely stated we would marry someday. I could have said you were my betrothed."

"Oh," she countered sweetly, "but I am not. Why, I should have told them I shot you!"

"I should advise saving that particular bit of information for later, kitten."

"You are maddening!" She turned, stepping away to stare through the paned glass at the trees outside.

Maddening, was he? She hadn't said she *wouldn't* marry him, and he couldn't help but be rife with satisfaction. He wasn't sure why, but just moments ago, something had come to him in a rush. It wasn't just that she was wary after Thomas. What was it she had told him yesterday?

I want a husband who will put me above all else.

Seeing her with Sebastian and Justin—hearing them—he suddenly understood so very much. He suddenly understood *her* as he hadn't before. It wasn't so difficult to see. She wanted stability. She wanted what had never been hers as a child. She wanted what she and Sebastian and Justin had not had as children—a mother and father who stood together and fast. Who were there when they wept and when they laughed. Her brothers had found love already.

And now it was Julianna's turn.

Stepping up behind her, he brushed aside curling wisps of baby-fine curls and kissed her nape. His large hands closed around her narrow shoulders. She didn't resist as he turned her.

"Are you still angry, kitten?"

"It's difficult to be angry with you."

He couldn't help but laugh at her grudging admission. "Really?" Lightly, he traced the two tiny lines etched between her brows. "Then why do you frown so?"

She hesitated.

"Your mother?" he guessed.

"Yes," she admitted. "I must thank you for being here, Dane," she said, her voice very low. "Your presence has made it much easier to bear."

Her words pleased him. "But what?" he asked. "There is something else on your mind, kitten."

"There is," she said slowly. "You asked about the man she was with last night. My mind has been so filled with her, I've scarcely given him any thought. But I recall that when he walked by, there was something different about him. That's what drew my attention."

"What was different about him?"

Julianna took a breath. "He wore a patch over one eye."

Dane froze. *"What?"*

"It was the side closest to me. Yes, I'm quite certain of it." She nodded. "There was a patch over his right eye."

Nineteen

"Granville. We've not seen much of your face of late." Nigel Roxbury didn't sound surprised as Dane walked through the door of his office.

Good God! Surely Roxbury didn't know! The comment was enough to nearly make Dane stop short. He caught himself just in time.

He forced himself to relax. "Yes," he replied, "and more's the pity." He lowered himself to the chair across from Roxbury.

Dane had gone straight from Julianna's to the Home Office. Roxbury's quarters there were cramped, but the top of his desk was like the man himself—scrupulous, neat, and ordered. Roxbury had been his superior on more than a few endeavors. He'd never particularly liked the man, but that was immaterial.

"What, my lord, do you grow bored since we've not engaged your services for a while?" Roxbury looked across at him—with his left eye. His *left* eye.

Dane crossed his ankles and offered a faint smile. "I journeyed to the country for a time."

"An uneventful journey, I presume? With this wretch the Magpie haunting the roads one never knows, does one?"

"I have faith that the robin redbreasts will catch him soon. If not, perhaps we can put a man on it."

"Do you offer yourself?"

"It is a task I would undertake with the utmost enthusiasm, sir." Dane didn't bat an eye.

"Well, you have certainly proved useful in the past. And if you are anxious to put your talents to use again, I shall speak to Mr. Casey."

"I would appreciate it, sir." Reaching out, Dane picked up an Egyptian statuette on the corner of Roxbury's desk. "An interesting piece," he murmured.

"A reproduction. Remarkably well done, isn't it?" Roxbury reached for a stack of papers, a sign of dismissal.

Dane replaced the statuette and got to his feet. "By the way, sir, I believe I saw you outside Theatre Royal last night."

Roxbury looked up sharply.

"Your hack departed before I could reach you. A pity. I should have enjoyed meeting your wife."

"Oh, not my wife," Roxbury said immediately. "My sister."

"Ah. Forgive me."

"No harm done. I shall be in touch, Granville."

Dane closed the door to Phillip's office with the flat of his hand and swung around to face his friend.

"I need a favor," he said without preamble. "A personal favor. And you cannot reveal what I am about to tell you to anyone. Not a soul, Phillip."

The corners of Phillip's eyes crinkled as he smiled. "Yes, well, old man, that's the nature of the business, isn't it?"

Dane's mind was still whirling as he hauled a chair next to Phillip's desk. Very quietly he relayed all he had learned about the Sterling family.

When he'd finished, Phillip raised his brows. "He did not deny he was at the theater?"

"That is correct."

"Then it was he," Phillip said slowly. "As for the veiled woman Julianna saw last night—or thought she saw—you must admit, Dane, if she is their mother, it's strange for all those years to pass with no word of her."

"Yes, I know, Phillip. I know. But I believe her. And Roxbury was so glib. Almost *too* glib. Yet what possible reason could he have for lying? Unless it's true. Unless he has something to hide."

"An interesting consideration. So let us presume the woman who accompanied him last night is the Sterling siblings' mother. Let us presume that she *is* Daphne Sterling. That means—"

"That Nigel Roxbury lied," Dane concluded quietly, "and that woman could not possibly be his sister. Julianna would surely have known her uncle, wouldn't she?"

"Point conceded," Phillip acknowledged.

"How much do you know of him?"

"I've worked with him as much as you. He's been involved with the Home Office for some twenty years, I believe. To my knowledge his record is unblemished. But then, I wouldn't expect otherwise." He sent Dane a keen glance. "You say neither Julianna nor her brothers are aware of the identity of the man who was with their mother the night she left England?"

Dane nodded. "My first thought was that Nigel Roxbury was the man with whom she ran off that night. That perhaps they both survived—"

"Unlikely that it was Nigel," Phillip said thoughtfully. "He would have been some years younger than she."

"Yes." Dane's expression was grim. "I'd thought of that. At any rate, they were all children when it happened. It was a door to their past no one cared to open. That's why I cannot risk being too openly blatant about delving into this affair. I would spare the Sterlings any further scandal."

"It would take some time, but I might be able to find out the name of the ship she took across the Channel, the passengers who died. Though the fact that it's been so many years will make it more difficult," Phillip admitted. "But I'll see what I can discover."

Whistling a merry tune, Phillip strode across the floor of the coffeehouse later that afternoon. Dane sat in the corner, scowling rather fiercely into a whisky.

Phillip slid into the opposite chair. "Why so glum?"

"Not glum. Thoughtful."

"Ah," he said lightly. "I'm glad you made the distinction."

Dane signaled for a whisky to be brought to his friend.

"As a matter of course, I have more to add to the brew," he said.

Dane eyed him. "Meaning?"

"Meaning," Phillip stated very deliberately, "it is just as you said."

"I've said many things, man, and I can hardly recall all of them."

"Perhaps you will recall an assumption you made just this afternoon."

Dane sucked in a breath. "Phillip—"

Phillip leaned forward. "You were right, Dane. Roxbury doesn't have a sister."

Dane slid to attention.

"He had a brother."

Dane narrowed in on that one word. "*Had?*" he echoed.

"Indeed. James Roxbury died some twenty-four years ago. Perished"—Phillip paused for effect—"at sea."

"Sweet Lord. How the devil did you learn that?"

"A simple matter, really. Something kept nagging me after you left. So I managed to take a look at Roxbury's record of service. Born and bred in Westminster, he was. And my examination of the parish records proved most enlightening, wouldn't you say?"

Dane's laugh dissolved the severity of his expression. "My word, Phillip, you amaze me."

His smile died away, and he mulled for a moment. "It's odd. Damned odd. But now we know for certain that he lied. And if Roxbury lied about this, what if he has lied about other things? What if there are other things he wishes to conceal?"

"I agree, Dane. He warrants further scrutiny. I only wish I'd done it earlier."

"So," Dane said slowly, "in regard to the counterfeit scheme, you've not yet looked at Roxbury?"

Phillip shook his head. "No. I have been search-ing for someone whose circumstances appear to have bettered. A man whose dress is not the same. Perhaps someone who has made what appears to be an extravagant purchase beyond his means."

"Of course. Perhaps I should proceed on an-other tack. A methodical if highly unscientific manner."

"And what might that be?"

Dane hid a smile. "By order of the alphabet?"

Phillip blinked, then laughed. "Given the fact that there are no obvious suspects and *everyone* is suspect, that might not be such a bad idea," Phillip said dryly. "And if we were to find him that way, that would indeed be amazing, wouldn't it?"

The last rays of afternoon sunlight flickered off the wood-paneled wall as Roxbury poured a glass of wine for his visitor.

"I'm glad I found you at home," she said.

She laced her fingertips together in her lap. His gaze lingered on the movement.

"You appear nervous, *madame*," he observed. "And you are empty-handed. Have you no pret-ties for me? It is most ungracious of you. Particu-larly after our night out at the theater."

"I have a message for you from François. There will be no more of your 'pretties' until he receives his gold."

Roxbury's lips continued to smile. His eyes did not. "As imperious as the little Corsican upstart, isn't he?"

"He is a businessman," she said coolly. "He merely tends his affairs."

His hand fisted and unfisted. "The Magpie plagues me," he muttered. "He steals from me. I could almost believe he *knows*."

Her chin lifted. "Our liaison. I would end it now."

"Our liaison will continue until I have what I want. Do not tell me when and where it will end."

"I want no part of this."

"My dear, you are already a part of this."

"No. I want out."

"I deal harshly with those who cross me."

"I am not afraid of you."

"Perhaps you should be."

"What do you mean?"

Oh so pleasantly he spoke. "The man who assisted me greatly in my endeavor . . . His wife interfered. She dared to taunt me that she would have told tales on me! But the lady . . . Well, her husband had served his purpose. And let us just say she'll be telling no tales from the grave. Nor will her husband."

His eyes delved into hers. His laugh was cruel. "Yes, I see you take my meaning, *madame*."

She pressed her lips together, watching as he lifted a sack from behind his desk and dropped it on top. Opening a drawer, he rummaged around inside.

The very next instant, a long, sinister-looking pistol lay next to the sack.

He glanced at her. "Go back to your hotel. Send a message to François that I will have his gold. I will be back in London in two days." He strode to the door and flung it wide.

"Where are you going?" Somehow, she managed to conceal her shock.

A hard light shone in his eyes as he grabbed the sack. "Why, just as you say, *madame*. I'm off to Bath. A man must tend his affairs, mustn't he?"

It was late in the day, and the building was nearly empty as Phillip made his way back to his office.

A thin-faced young clerk stepped forward.

"There's a woman waiting for you in your office, sir," said the clerk.

Phillip frowned. "A woman?"

"Yes, sir. She said she had information we'd be very interested in hearing. She refused to tell me what it was. Insisted she had to speak to an agent."

He frowned. "Thank you."

He stepped inside. He saw her immediately, though she was hidden in the shadows. She was incredibly petite, immaculately dressed. Her spine primly erect, she perched just so on the edge of the chair, her gloved hands arranged delicately on the reticule in her lap, her tiny feet shod in kid boots tucked beneath the chair. Everything about her spoke of a certain elegant flair.

The door clicked shut. "Good evening, madam. My name is Phillip Talbot. I'm told you wished to speak to someone."

Only her head turned as she beheld him. "I do," she announced, her diction was clear, concise, cultured. "I have done many things in my life of which I am not particularly proud. But I will not be a part of murder."

Phillip's gaze had fixed on the jauntily plumed hat atop her head. A sheer veil hung from the brim, obscuring her features. His conversation with Dane earlier in the day washed through him, jarring his consciousness. No, he thought in amazement. Surely it wasn't . . .

His heart was suddenly pounding. "Your name, madam?"

She paused. For all her air of haughty poise, Phillip had the strangest sensation she didn't know what to say . . .

Her chin lifted. She pushed aside the veil that covered her face.

"Sterling. My name is Daphne Sterling. And I was once Marchioness of Thurston." The comment was accompanied by the rise of a slender black brow. "Perhaps I still am."

Twenty

The misty haze of twilight had just begun to cling to the distant rooftops. Julianna sat near the window in the sitting room, her eyes downcast, her chin resting on her knuckles, her gaze fixed on the gold braiding that edged the carpet. The tea that Mrs. MacArthur had brought an hour earlier was cold, the biscuits untouched on her plate. So much had happened today that she found it an impossible task to quiet her mind.

She didn't hear the knocker, nor did she hear Mrs. MacArthur's pronouncement that she had a visitor. Indeed, she was not aware of another presence until she chanced to glance up. Precisely what made her do so, she wasn't sure. But she did . . . and, well, there he was.

Her heart began to thud with hard, almost painful strokes.

He presented a most devastating picture, an air of surety about him, his cravat very white against his strong throat. A long-fingered hand had carelessly pushed aside his jacket and rested on one narrow hip, the muscled length of his thighs set off by tight black trousers. It was quite apparent from the arch of one dark brow that he'd been there for some time.

Crossing the floor, he pulled her to her feet. And if she hadn't been thinking clearly before, she most certainly couldn't do so now. The rhythm of her heart was gauged solely by his presence. His nearness provoked a piercing awareness. Her pulse skittered. She was all at once beset by the memory of that mouth brushing the very tips of her breasts, the heat of that very same hand clamped tight between her legs.

Their eyes met. His sudden, crooked, half smile made her heart catch.

"I do hope that I am not the cause of that fretful, anxious expression."

"Not today." A hint of dry laughter surfaced in her voice. "Actually I was hoping you'd come back."

His mouth quirked. "Ah, a welcome I like."

Raising a hand, he brushed his knuckles down the curve of flushed cheek, eyeing the frown gathered between her brows.

"You appeared lost in thought. What is on your mind? Your mother?"

"Yes," she admitted. "But mostly my brother."

"I can see why, of course. But Sebastian strikes me—"

"Not Sebastian. Justin." She paused. "He looked so odd for a moment. And he seemed rather subdued before they left, Dane. Like a shadow swept over him. Sebastian saw it, too." She pondered a moment. "I'm so glad Justin has Arabella."

"Arabella?"

"His wife. He worships the ground she walks on. And if you had known him before—" She gave a shake of her head. A slight smile rimmed her lips. "Tamed the beast, that's what she did. And I suppose it's foolish to dwell on matters about which I can do nothing."

"You're a compassionate woman. It's natural to care about those you love."

Their eyes held. "Thank you," she said softly, "for understanding." A pause. "Will you stay for supper?"

He hesitated. "I should like to," he said carefully. "But I fear I must be elsewhere."

The Magpie would ride tonight. His guarded tone gave it away. "I see." She willed the tremor from her voice.

He studied her for a moment, his regard oddly penetrating.

"What? What is it?"

"There's something you should know," he said slowly. "The man with your mother last night, Julianna, the man with the patch. I know him. His name is Nigel Roxbury. I've worked under his direction on numerous assignments."

Julianna inhaled. "What? But how—"

"Phillip and I believe it's possible it was Roxbury's brother who left with your mother all those years ago. We haven't yet figured out the puzzle, if there's a connection with the culprit at the Home Office. But there's something peculiar going on." He spoke, as if to himself. "We're getting close. I can feel it."

A shiver slid down her spine. She stared at him uneasily. "Dane," she said unsteadily, "you're scaring me."

"I don't mean to," he said immediately. "I'll be fine. Truly I will."

His eyes darkened. He stepped close. A hand came up to gently touch her hair. "I know you don't understand. But I couldn't leave without seeing you."

A finger beneath her chin, he tilted her face to his. His gaze scoured hers, his features solemnly intent. "I love you, kitten."

A scalding ache filled her throat. Heaven help her, she was going to cry. "Oh, God," she whispered.

He smiled crookedly. "I do, sweet. I love you."

The battle was lost. Her tears spilled into her voice. "Dane," she said helplessly, "you can't tell me that and—and leave."

His smile ebbed. With his thumb, he traced the shape of her mouth, the tiniest caress. "I can't *not* tell you and leave."

Lightly he kissed her.

And then he walked away.

Before she knew it, she was standing at the narrow window in the entrance hall, staring at his back. His head was high, his spine straight, the set of his shoulders wide and square.

A clamp seized hold of her heart. This was her every fear come to life. She wanted to cry out in despair, to beg him to stay. But this was about pride and honor—not just his, but her own. She could be brave, as brave as he. She *would* be brave.

She struggled against a sob, and wrenched the door wide.

"Dane!"

He turned, halting before the next house as she burst outside. Julianna flung herself against him. She lifted her face. "Be careful," she cried. "Be careful and—come back to me!"

He caught his breath—and caught her up against him. His eyes darkened. His arms closed tight around her back.

His mouth came down on hers, hard and fierce.

She kissed him back, there on the streets of London. She didn't care if the entire world saw.

It would surely be the longest night of her life.

He'd been gone no more than ten minutes, and she was pacing back and forth before the fireplace in the sitting room.

Her stomach churned. How, she wondered desperately, could she stand to wait? Wait and wonder, without knowing? How could she bear knowing he was in danger? That he might—

In the midst of that thought someone pounded on the door.

Mrs. MacArthur was already hastening briskly to the door.

A chill went through her. "Wait!" Julianna nearly shrieked. She snatched a vase from the table in the hall. Holding it high, she stationed herself just to the side of the door.

The pounding continued. "Hello!" a man was shouting. "Is anyone there?"

Mrs. MacArthur's mouth formed a little "o" of shock, but she recovered quickly. Julianna nodded for Mrs. MacArthur to open the door.

It swept wide. The man on her doorstep saw her.

"For pity's sake, it's all right! My name is Phillip Talbot. I'm from the Home Office."

Phillip. Dane's partner. She sagged with relief,

lowering the vase to her side. She was shaking, she realized. *Shaking.*

"I must find Dane! Is he here?"

Her lips parted. "No." She hesitated. "He's . . . gone."

Phillip understood. He cursed. "Dammit, I was afraid of that!"

Ice ran through her veins. "There's something wrong, isn't there?"

"There is a passenger on the coach. A man who hopes to put a stop to—"

"Roxbury?" she breathed.

Phillip shot her a look.

"I know," she cried. "I *know!*"

"He's armed," Phillip said curtly. "He wants the Magpie. If Dane stops him, he's prepared."

That was all she needed to hear. A trembling foreboding washed over her. Fear clutched at her insides—a fear quite unlike anything she'd ever known.

Phillip headed for the door. Julianna caught his arm. "Wait! Where are you going?"

Phillip shook his head. "Dane may need help. I'm going for a horse and some men."

She was scarcely aware of his departure. She stood on the bottom stair, unmoving, her mind racing. Dane was in danger. Roxbury intended to kill him.

She couldn't let that happen. She *wouldn't.*

* * *

After buying her ticket at the booking office, Julianna walked across the cobbled stones toward the coach. Several boys had just finished harnessing the team. Another held the door wide while Julianna stepped inside.

The man with the patch was already aboard—Roxbury.

Her pulse hammering, Julianna seated herself, her back to the horses. Drat! It would have been better if she faced forward, so that she could see ahead of them.

But she also wanted to be able to see Roxbury.

He was not what she imagined. He was tall, almost distinguished-looking, though the coat he wore was on the shabby side. She could imagine him behind a magistrate's bench, for there was an air of authority about him. She guessed his age at somewhere in his forties.

The crunch of bootheels reached her ears. "All aboard!" shouted a voice.

"Wait!" cried a high, feminine voice. "Do not leave yet!"

A little girl clambered inside, followed by her mother. Julianna scooted aside to make room for them. She longed to warn them not to journey this night, but she didn't dare.

The vehicle shifted with the weight of the driver climbing on the box. The inn yard's gates scraped open. With a flick of the whip and a jangle of harness, they were off.

The little girl promptly peered up at Julianna. Beneath the brim of her little bonnet, huge brown eyes sparkled. "My name's Annabelle," she announced cheerily. Her pixie features exactly matched her pixie voice.

Julianna guessed her age at somewhere around six or so. She returned her smile. "Hello, Annabelle."

"We're going to see Mama's sister. My aunt Prudence."

Her mother offered an apologetic smile. "You'll have to forgive her, I fear. Annabelle is a bit of a prattle-box."

"I don't mind," Julianna said softly.

The little girl had turned her attention to Roxbury—and so did Julianna. He gave no sign that he'd seen or heard any of them. His manner was distant; his gaze remained trained outside.

Julianna caught at the strap as they rattled around a corner. Before long they began to gain speed. The city was left behind.

It was strange, how much like before it was . . .

The darkness settled in. She found herself peering out the window, anxiously scanning the side of the road, seeking to see behind every tree and bush. Each second was like the passage of a year.

And then it happened.

The coach was hurtling around a sweeping curve. From outside there came a shout and the squeal of the wheels. And just as before, Julianna couldn't stop herself from tumbling to the floor. But this time she managed to avoid cracking her head hard against the side of the coach. She groped for the cushion, and was about to heave herself up when she heard the sound of male voices punctuating the air outside.

The door was wrenched open. She found herself staring at the gleaming barrels of twin pistols. Swallowing, she lifted her gaze to the man who possessed it.

Garbed in black he was, from the enveloping folds of his cloak to the kerchief that obscured the lower half of his face. A silk mask was tied around his eyes; they were all that was visible of his features. Even in the dark, there was no mistaking their color. They glimmered like clear, golden fire . . .

Her lover's eyes.

A gust of chill night air funneled in. She knew that voice, knew it well . . . So softly querulous, like steel tearing through tightly stretched silk, she recalled dazedly.

Goose bumps rose on her flesh. She couldn't move. She most certainly couldn't speak. She could not even swallow past the knot lodged deep in her throat. Fear numbed her mind. Her mouth was dry with a sickly dread such as she had never experienced.

But this time it was not fear *of* him . . . but a great deal *for* him.

* * *

Dane guided Percival through the grasses and ferns beside the road and settled back to wait. As always, Percival sensed the coach before Dane heard the rumble of wheels in the distance. Percival's ears pricked forward. Dane tightened his fingers on the reins. Adjusting his mask, he drew his hat down low over his brow. And when it was time, his shout echoed in the clear crisp night.

"Stand and deliver!"

He slipped from Percival's back, moving even as his feet hit the dirt.

"Throw the blunderbuss and the gun in the bushes," he advised the coachman tersely. "Then reach high . . . higher, man."

The coachman, shaking and blubbering, did what he was told. Dane rifled through the boot. Damn, there was no sack! He yanked open the door of the coach. "Step outside, if you please."

Three figures were pushed roughly—rudely—through the opening by someone inside. A woman. A mother and child. A ripple of shock went through him as his gaze skittered over them, then swung sharply back.

His heart surely stopped in that moment. Julianna! What the devil was she doing here?

Even as the realization washed through him, her eyes cleaved to his. Her expression was strange, her eyes wide and dark. Desperate somehow. As if she were pleading. Imploring . . .

Another figure emerged.

It was Roxbury.

In his hand was a pistol—leveled straight at Dane's chest.

Roxbury smiled. "The Magpie," he said smoothly. "Oh, but I was hoping we'd meet."

The instant the passengers were clear of the vehicle, the terrified coachman grabbed the reins. With a crack of the whip, the coach jolted around the bend.

Roxbury's face contorted with rage. Vile curses blackened the air. He yelled at the three females.

"Stay where you are, all of you!"

Dane gave a sputter of laughter. "Well, well, Roxbury, could it be the driver has just left with your property?"

Shock skittered across Roxbury's features. "Who the devil are you?" he demanded. "You coward, show your face!"

Dane ripped off the mask.

Roxbury's lips flattened. "Granville!" he spat. "So it's you!"

Dane offered a tight-lipped smile. "You seem surprised. But you've been caught, Roxbury. The Prime Minister himself knows what's afoot."

"The Boswells, I suppose." Roxbury sounded disgusted.

"Yes. She overheard you and her husband. We were already aware someone in the Home Office was involved. We knew how it was being transported. We just didn't know who was responsible."

"That blathering bitch." His soft pronouncement was a curse. "So. Your disguise as a highwayman . . . the robberies. Put into play, I suppose, by you and Talbot so that you could conduct your investigation?"

Ten paces stood between them. Moonlight glinted off both weapons. The three females stood frozen, off to Dane's right, to Roxbury's left.

"What I don't understand is why, Roxbury. Why involve yourself in forgery?"

Roxbury touched his patch. "Nelson at least acquired a title and glory. I was not so lucky. I was granted a dismissal and sent packing. Yet still it was never a question of loyalty to king and Crown."

"Why then?"

"Oh, come. *Think*, man. I am hardly so well breeched as you!"

Dane's eyes narrowed. "What do you mean?"

Roxbury's smile was gloating. "It was there beneath your hand, man. Beneath your fingertips. There beneath everyone's noses, and no one even suspected."

Something echoed in Dane's mind. *I have been searching for someone whose circumstances appear to have bettered*, Phillip had said. *A man whose dress is not the same. Perhaps someone who has made what appears to be an extravagant purchase beyond his means.*

He sucked in a breath. "The statuette in your office." It suddenly made perfect sense. "Where did you get it?"

"An old friend in France, who is well acquainted with an assistant curator who, like me, has no doubt found his extra funds—useful, shall we say."

"Daphne Sterling," Dane stated flatly.

Roxbury's eyes narrowed. "Well. It seems I must give you more credit than I thought. But I do believe the Crown will thank me for ridding them of the Magpie."

"You'll be caught. Surely you know that."

"Witnesses can be disposed of. Perhaps Talbot will meet with an accident, much like the Boswells. And now, enough talk, Granville. Throw down your weapons."

Dane's eyes glinted. "I think not."

Roxbury moved before Dane could stop him. Before he could get off a shot.

He snatched the child against his chest.

The muzzle now rested on the little girl's temple.

Her mother screamed. "Annabelle!" The child began to whimper.

Roxbury's gaze drilled into Dane. "Do it, I say!" he barked.

Fury and fear pumped through Dane. He wanted to lunge for Roxbury's throat, even as dread coiled sickly in his belly.

"All right. All right!" Slowly he tossed aside the pistols, first one, then the other. They landed with a dull thud, off to his right. "Let the child go."

Roxbury released the little girl. Weeping, her mother sank to the ground, clutching her to her breast. Julianna hadn't moved. Dane sensed her terror.

Tersely he spoke. "Are you truly such a monster, Roxbury? If you're going to kill me, do not do it in front of them. Do it elsewhere."

"As you wish," Roxbury replied pleasantly. "I will spare their sensibilities." He hitched his chin toward the copse of elm trees where Percival was tethered. "There. Behind you, near your mount. Face me and walk back."

Dane's gaze flitted to Julianna. For a fraction of a second, their eyes collided. Hers were huge, her features panicked and half-wild. His hands held high, he began to step back.

"That's far enough!" Roxbury barked.

The moon slipped out from behind the clouds, casting a milky glow over the earth below.

Roxbury smiled. A fingertip caressed the trigger. His tone was silky. "I do hope you realize this is going to give me a great deal of pleasure."

Roxbury never saw the rise of the shadow behind. But Dane did. His gaze shifted to a point just beyond Roxbury's shoulder, an almost imperceptible movement of his eyes.

"Shoot," he said softly. *"Shoot."*

Twenty-one

It was not a time for reflection. Not a time for fear. Nor was there time to think.

Most certainly not to waver, either in the mind or in the heart. . . .

Sparks and fire flashed from the barrel of the pistol. A shattering roar filled the quiet of the night, magnified by the stillness; the sound echoed eerily through the treetops. A cloud of smoke hung in the air.

Roxbury pitched forward without a sound.

Dane knelt at his side, feeling for his pulse. Then he leaped up.

Julianna clenched the pistol so tightly he had to pry it from her grasp. He shoved it into his breeches.

Julianna's knees weakened. She would have

fallen if he hadn't reached out and pulled her against his length. Dane's voice was a low murmur against her forehead.

"Steady now."

Julianna couldn't tear her gaze from Roxbury's form. "Is he . . . ?"

"Yes. What about you, kitten? Are you all right?"

Her nod was jerky. "My God," she said numbly. "My God, Dane." Reaching up, she touched the plane of his cheek. "He was going to shoot you . . . he would have . . ." Her throat closed. She couldn't bear to say it aloud. A shudder tore through her.

With his hand he cupped the back of her head. Her hair had come unpinned. He combed his fingers gently through the chestnut mass.

"My brave, brave girl," he soothed.

She sagged against him. Dane's arms tightened. Julianna squeezed her eyes shut and clung. Their embrace was both reassuring and almost desperate, for both sought the comfort of body and heart and warmth that only touch could give.

The pounding rhythm of hooves made him look up. Phillip and two other men leaped from their horses.

"I heard the shot," Phillip said, striding forward. "Anyone hurt?"

"No," Dane murmured. "But there's also a

woman and a little girl. Someone should see to them."

Phillip nodded to one of the other men.

"I should have known I'd miss the excitement!" Phillip glanced at Roxbury's body and whistled. "Nice shot, old man."

"No," Dane said with a rise of brow. "Not me." He drew back and nodded at Julianna.

Phillip cocked his head. "A crack shot. I don't suppose we could persuade her to join us?"

He was promptly given a withering look.

Phillip sighed. "I thought not."

Dane's hands dropped on Julianna's shoulders. "Julianna," he said almost sternly, "while I thank you for saving my life, I should like to know what the *hell* you were doing on that coach."

Julianna bit her lip. Her gaze flitted to Phillip.

Dane's eyes narrowed. He looked from one to the other.

Phillip cleared his throat.

"It's a bit of a long story. But there's a woman locked in my office with a clerk standing watch." He paused. "I think perhaps you should meet her."

The night was not yet over.

She sat on a bench in a narrow hallway in the Home Office. Sebastian and Justin were there as well, Sebastian on the end of the bench, Justin with his shoulder propped against the wall. They had been apprised of the night's events. An hour earlier, Dane, Phillip, and another tall, austere man named Barnaby had walked through the door on the opposite wall.

The three were not privy to what was unfolding inside that room.

There was no denying the sizzle that hung in the air. It wasn't tension, Julianna decided curiously, so much as . . . expectancy.

Their mother was in that room. The mother they had not seen or heard from in twenty-four years.

Now they waited.

The door slid open with a *whoosh*. Phillip stepped out, slanting them a faint smile, followed by Mr. Barnaby. Dane was last.

While the other men moved down the hall, Dane stepped before the three Sterlings.

Justin swung around to face him. Sebastian and Julianna got to their feet.

Sebastian broke the silence. "What's happening?"

Dane's hesitation was obvious.

"Please don't try to spare us," Justin said with a faint smile. "The truth is best."

"Apparently she was aware of Roxbury's counterfeiting scheme. For that reason, any charges brought against her will be very serious.

Granted, the fact that she *did* come forward will play in her favor."

"Does she know we're here?" he asked.

"She does."

"We'd like to see her."

He nodded. "Actually, she asked to see you. But I fear you may only have a few minutes before Barnaby comes back for her."

Dane opened the door and Sebastian stepped inside. Julianna followed.

Last was Justin.

She sat behind a small table, white-gloved fingertips folded before her. As small and delicate as she appeared, there was a sharpness about her vivid green eyes—something about her manner that portrayed a seasoned worldliness.

Silence filled the room, a silence that seemed to go on forever.

It was Daphne who broke it. "Well," she said lightly. "This is rather awkward, isn't it? I certainly never imagined that we would meet again under these circumstances."

"I should imagine you didn't think we would meet again at all," Sebastian said quietly. His observation was not meant to be confrontational; it was merely a statement of fact.

"No," she said with a lift of her brows. "Frankly, I hadn't."

At least she was honest.

"You look exceedingly well. All of you."

It was Justin who voiced the question in all of their minds.

"We thought you were dead. All those years . . . Why did you never come back?"

Her smile wavered. "Oh, but I couldn't. Never in this world! It wasn't that I didn't think of the three of you. But your father and I . . . well, he stifled me. And . . . I am what I am. I realize that. I am not perfect. But he could never accept that. We would surely have torn each other apart. We would surely have destroyed each other. And once I left . . . once it was *done*, it could not be *un*done.

"James Roxbury understood me, in a way your father never did. He loved life as I did. But when he drowned, well . . . It was my chance to begin life anew, to change who I was forever. I couldn't go back. I couldn't *look* back. I *didn't* look back. Yes, there were times I wanted to see you. Times I wondered . . . But I knew the three of you would be taken care of. You had your nurses. You had each other. But I had no one. And I had to go on. If I was to be happy, it was up to *me*."

Oddly, Sebastian understood. Perhaps it was because he was the eldest. Perhaps because he'd known her as she was, a frivolous, beautiful creature.

He didn't see the shadow that sped across

Justin's face. His head was bent down, but suddenly it came up.

"Wait," he said, his voice very low. "I haven't thought of this for a long, long time. But now you're here and . . . and I have a question only you can answer."

She regarded him, her head tipped to the side.

"It's no secret there were other men in your life. James Roxbury. The man you married in France. And others before that, I presume."

She neither confirmed nor denied it.

Justin's tone was strained. "The night Father died, I goaded him. I goaded him with how his wife had left him for her lover. That perhaps *he* was not my father, or—or any of ours. Yet he must be forever saddled with your children, wondering if any of them were his own. That he had to claim us, because he just didn't *know*."

"Didn't he?" The merest smile creased her lips. "Always the fool, wasn't he?"

Sebastian had sent Justin a sharp glance. Julianna sucked in a breath.

"Is he?" Justin went on. "Is William Sterling our father? Or is it possible we are not his? All of us. Any of us. *One* of us."

There was a sharp rap on the door. It opened. A grim-faced guard stepped inside. "Time's up," he announced. He came around to take her arm.

Justin turned as she was whisked around the

desk. He stared at her. "Do you even know?" he asked quietly.

She was at the door now. Her expression held an almost curious whimsy as she looked back over her shoulder. Then something flared in the brilliant emerald eyes so like his. "Justin—"

"This will have to wait." The guard sent him a glare. "Mr. Barnaby wants her removed to the magistrate's office immediately."

Her gaze broke with Justin's; it swept the three of them. "*Adieu*, my little ones. *Adieu*."

Perhaps they were still reeling—still in shock, the three of them, for so much had happened! For they could only watch as their mother disappeared from sight. . . .

When Dane, who had been standing at the end of the hall with Phillip, stepped up, Julianna could only look at him, her eyes huge.

"Dane," she said faintly, "what will happen to her?"

His hand curved around her elbow.

"There's nothing any of you can do right now. Go home and rest"—lightly he squeezed—"and wait for me there."

In truth, Dane had a very good grasp of the situation. . . .

And he would do whatever he could.

Whatever must be done.

Twenty-two

Later that morning, Sebastian climbed the steps to Julianna's town house. Justin followed a short time after. They had all bathed and changed; Mrs. MacArthur had laid out a light breakfast in the morning room. It seemed none of them was very hungry, and it wasn't long before they moved into the sitting room. No one had much to say, but Justin had been particularly quiet; Sebastian and Julianna exchanged a worried look as he preceded them into the sitting room. Julianna sat down next to Sebastian and took a deep breath.

"Well," she said, "it's time we talked about Mother, isn't it? I fear it may be a rather messy situation, at the very least."

"I fear the family name is about to be dragged

through the muck again, isn't it?" Sebastian's face was grim. "We must acknowledge the very real possibility that she may go to prison. I honestly cannot imagine how she'll survive there. But I think we should lend whatever support we can to see that she is defended."

Julianna ran a fingertip around her teacup. "I think you're right. She may have abandoned us. But we can hardly abandon *her* at such an hour."

Sebastian's regard slid to Justin. "Are we in agreement then?"

For the first time that morning, a genuine smile flirted at the corners of Justin's mouth. "What, did you think I wouldn't? She is still our mother."

"Frankly, I wasn't sure," Sebastian admitted. "Mother was always so capricious. So damned impulsive. And Father was . . . impossible, wasn't he? I do not make excuses for what she did, any of it. She wanted to be adored. She wanted to be admired. But she loved us in her way. And perhaps I am a fool, but I ceased judging her years ago. And somehow, regardless of what she may have done now, I cannot believe she is truly evil."

Justin shook his head. "You're not a fool, Sebastian. You are . . . in a word, the best man I know."

Sebastian's smile was crooked. "Thank you." His smile faded. He searched his brother's face. "May I ask you something?"

"Of course."

"What you said to Mother earlier. About Father. I always knew something happened . . . I just wasn't sure." He watched him closely. "You were there the night he died, weren't you?"

"I was *with* him when he died."

Sebastian was puzzled. "Why did you never say anything?"

"I blamed myself for his death, Sebastian. For years. Indeed, until I married Arabella. I was ashamed." He rested his hands on his knees, his hands linked together. "I was young. I was wild. And we'd had that terrible row."

"About Mother."

"Yes."

"I always knew you were the one who hurt the most when Mother left," Sebastian said softly. "But you never showed it."

"Before that night," he confided, his voice very low, "I had never doubted what we'd always been told—that Mother never strayed until after Julianna's birth. Until we were older . . . But after that night with Father"—something crept across his features—"I wondered if it was true. *Was* she unfaithful before we were born? Did Father hate me because my resemblance to Mother was so strong? Or was it because perhaps he was *not* my father at all?"

Listening to him—hearing him—Julianna's heart began to ache. "Justin," she said gently, "it wasn't that he hated you. He punished us because he couldn't punish *her*. He simply didn't know how to love."

"His life was consumed by bitterness," Sebastian added. "By duty. I don't believe he ever really knew how to be happy."

Justin's features had gone very pensive. "Perhaps you're right. Perhaps that's what it was."

They all sat for a moment, steeped in the whirlwind of all the day had wrought. Their own private thoughts—and memories.

It was then that a knock on the door sounded.

Julianna was on her feet immediately. "It's Dane," she said urgently.

And so it was. He strode into the room with long, purposeful strides.

"Well," he said quietly. "It's over. The situation regarding your mother has been—resolved."

Julianna's eyes hadn't left his figure. "What happened?" she asked. "Did Barnaby decide not to pursue the charges?"

"Not precisely."

Sebastian looked at his siblings, then at Dane. "What then . . . precisely?"

Dane chose his words with careful deliberation. "How shall I put this? . . . I persuaded the guard to allow me to escort her to the magistrate's office in his stead. On the way there . . ."

"What are you saying?"

"What I am saying is this. Should I be asked, I should respond that your mother proved a most resourceful woman. During the transport, she was able to evade my escort and . . . escape. It was the damnedest thing, really. One minute she was there. The next she was gone." He paused. "Should I be asked, of course."

During his speech, Dane looked each of them in the eye, one by one. Julianna stared, along with Justin and Sebastian. *Escape*, he said. *Escape*.

She set aside her cup. "My word," she said unsteadily, "are you saying—"

"I might even dare to suggest that she is doubtless on her way back to France."

Dear God, he had looked the other way. No, more than that, she realized dimly. He had helped her. He had let her go. Somehow he had helped her *escape*.

It was very clear—not from the words themselves—but from all that lay beneath them.

And in rescuing her, he had rescued all of them—her, Sebastian, and Justin.

Oh, Lord, how she loved him!

"She'll never be able to return to England, will she?" she asked.

"No." Dane spoke very quietly. "She would likely be arrested and charged as an accomplice. And in the course of things, her bigamy would probably be revealed as well. But I should like to make it clear . . . What happened with Nigel Roxbury will not go beyond the Prime Minister's office, and the Home Office. No one need know what happened with him—and with your mother."

"So to the world," Sebastian said slowly, "Daphne Sterling is still dead."

Dane's eyes held his. "Yes. No one ever need know any differently."

"You have our gratitude," Sebastian said quietly.

Julianna tipped her head to the side and addressed her brothers. "We won't see her again, you know," she murmured.

"No," Sebastian agreed. "But that's all right. She'll be fine." A slight smile curved his lips. "I think Mother has established that she is well able to take care of herself."

Julianna glanced over at Justin. He was sitting on the edge of the settee, one strong wrist resting on his knee. He hadn't said a word since Dane had entered. His handsome features were half-pained, half-relieved . . .

Julianna's hand slipped into Dane's. Lightly he squeezed it, but he didn't look at her.

Dane cleared his throat. "She asked me to give you this." Reaching into his jacket, he emerged with a sealed, neatly folded sheet of parchment. "She had a request. She said this letter is for all of you." He looked at Justin. "But she said you might want to be the first to read it."

He walked back to the door. "I'll leave the

three of you alone. I believe this is a family matter." Quietly, he withdrew.

Justin had accepted the letter gingerly, almost as if he were afraid to take it.

He looked up at Julianna and Sebastian. "My God," he said in an odd, strangled voice. "You know what this is, don't you?"

Julianna bit her lip. All at once her throat was achingly tight. This was so uncharacteristic of Justin, who was always so confident. So sure of himself. Never had she seen him so torn!—and somehow the sight wrenched at her insides.

"It seems you'll have your answer after all." Sebastian's tone was bland, his posture completely at ease as he propped an elbow on the chair and folded his big hands in his lap.

Justin looked at him. "Sebastian! Don't you want to know? Don't you want to know the truth about our parents? Our father?"

Sebastian shrugged.

Justin's gaze slid to Julianna.

She gave a tiny shake of her head. "Justin," she said gently, "it's not whether *we* want to know. It's whether *you* want to know."

Justin rose numbly to his feet, the letter gripped in both hands. "Damn," he said hoarsely. "Damn! I thought I wanted this. I thought . . ."

Before he knew it, he was standing in front of the fireplace. He swallowed. His gaze lowered slowly, his regard utterly fierce as he stared at the lump of wax that sealed the letter.

Silence descended.

Both Sebastian and Julianna were keenly aware that Justin was searching. Seeking. Desperately reaching into the deepest corner of his heart . . . his very soul . . .

For an answer only he could find.

They waited—waited forever it seemed!

Turning, Justin bent low. Gently, he pushed a corner of the parchment into the flames, watching as the fire licked along the edge; it smoldered, then suddenly flared high and bright.

Warm, wet tears drizzled down Julianna's cheeks. Her throat tight, she wiped them away with the back of her hand.

When nothing remained of the letter, Justin turned.

"She was right," he said very softly. "Mother was right. We had each other, didn't we? I don't think I ever realized it in quite the way I do now . . . But we're stronger—the three of us— because she was gone. Closer for it—for only having each other. By God, I can't regret that. And the contents of that letter—no matter *what* it was—could never, *ever* change the way I feel about the two of you."

He looked at Julianna, his eyes a clear, brilliant green.

"I love you, Jules." His eyes swung to Sebastian. "And you, brother."

His tone was grave. But he was smiling faintly, a smile that went straight into Julianna's heart. And then she couldn't help it. A ragged sound tore from her throat, and she began to sob uncontrollably, her emotions too vast to contain.

Her brothers were beside her immediately, Justin to her right, Sebastian to her left. Justin slid an arm around her. "Jules, don't cry! It's all right. It's never *been* so right."

"I know. I *know*. That's just it, don't you see? And these are happy tears!" She gazed up at him, her smile watery but blindingly sweet. Reaching out, she slipped an arm about both of them.

Justin laughed, the sound rather rusty. Lowering his head, he kissed her cheek. "Then may all your tears be happy tears," he whispered.

When he raised his head, his eyes were misty— and so were Sebastian's.

Together they stood, a circle of three. A circle unbroken . . . a circle of love.

It was Justin who gave a low chuckle. "And now, I fear I must be off. I suddenly find I have a most urgent need to go home and hold my wife and daughter."

"I was thinking the very same," Sebastian murmured.

At the door, Justin cocked a brow. "Supper tomorrow?" he asked. "Sevenish?"

Sebastian inclined his head. "Wonderful idea."

Justin glanced over at Dane, who had bolted toward the sitting room at the sound of Julianna's sobs. Having ascertained the crux of the situation and the fact that he was not needed, he'd started back into the morning room. Hearing the trio exit the sitting room, he'd stopped.

Julianna had already crossed the floor and slipped an arm through his.

Justin addressed Dane. "You'll come, too, won't you? It's time you met the rest of the family."

"But be warned," Sebastian put in, "with three little ones, it will be exceedingly noisy."

Dane had settled his fingers over Julianna's. Now he glanced down at her in silent inquiry.

Justin and Sebastian looked at each other, smothering a laugh. Both were aware of the trace of the other's thoughts—he was acting like a husband already!

Julianna gave a tiny nod.

"Then I shall look forward to it." Dane accepted graciously.

The instant they were alone, Dane tugged her around to face him. His hand stole upward. With his thumb, he blotted the dampness from the curve of one cheek.

"Are you all right?"

"I'm fine."

His eyes probed deep. "Are you sure?"

"I have never been more certain of anything in my life," she whispered. "Dane . . . what you did for my mother . . . I do not know how to thank you—"

His fingers on her lips stilled the flow of words. He shook his head. "I had to, kitten. I had to. I do not know if she is guilty. It's not my place to judge her. But without knowing for certain if she would have come to trial . . . I couldn't allow it to go that far. I could not allow the mother of the woman I love to go to prison. It wouldn't have been right. One chance was all I had, kitten. It was all *she* had."

Her heart thumped. There. He'd said it again. *He loved her.*

"I only wish you'd had the chance to say good-bye, the three of you."

"Oh, but we did, Dane! We did say a kind of farewell. We are at peace now. All of us, and—and there is no sadness!" She laid a hand on his chest. "But what about you? Won't Barnaby be angry that you let her escape? Will it jeopardize your position at the Home Office?"

A smile rimmed his lips. "No."

Julianna was puzzled. "Why not?"

"Kitten," he said very gently, "the Magpie has made his last ride. As for the Home Office . . . Well, that is a part of my life that is behind me, as of today."

She was stunned. "Dane," she said, with a shake of her head, "you did not have to—"

"Yes, I did. I *do*. Julianna, I had already made up my mind. I intend to devote myself to my wife and our children."

"Ah," she said lightly, "but you do not yet have a wife. Or children."

"Not yet," he said with a boyish grin. "But as soon as I *have* a wife, I predict the children will quickly follow. I will certainly make every effort to see that they do."

Her eyes flew wide. "Oh!" she cried. "But you sound very certain of yourself."

"And you have yet to give me an answer."

"You mean an answer you like," she said playfully.

"True. But I will accept only one answer."

"And what might that answer be?"

He was eyeing her in that way that made her feel hot and giddy inside. His arms tightened, lifting her clear from the floor. His mouth hovered just above hers.

He countered with a question of his own. His gaze was suddenly dark and intense. "Do you love me, kitten?"

Her heart never faltered. "I do," she whispered. "I love you quite madly!"

"Then say yes, love. Say you'll marry me."

"Yes," she whispered. "Oh, yes, I'll marry you . . ."

He kissed her then, sweetly, fiercely, with all the love held deep in his heart. Julianna wound her arms around his neck and clung.

But all at once he drew back with a laugh.

Julianna was not pleased. "What?" she grumbled. "What is it?"

"I nearly forgot. I have something to show you."

To her surprise, he led her outside and around the corner. Julianna looked up at the sprawling brick house with graceful Grecian columns. This was *his* house, the one she'd always admired from afar. And now she was finally going to see it for herself. Not that she really cared right now, she thought with a laugh. All she wanted was for him to carry her up the stairs, to feel the hard weight of his body as he made love to her . . .

But he did not lead her to the door. He did not lead her up the stairs to his room.

Instead, he led her around the side of the house, through a lovely garden, to the stable in the rear. Stepping into a stall, he tugged her forward.

She blinked. "Dane! What—"

He pointed to the corner. Julianna stared in astonishment. There, on a blanket spread against the wall, lay a green-eyed, yellow-haired cat. Nestled against her belly were three tiny, pure black balls of fur.

Something rubbed against her ankles. Julianna looked down.

Understanding dawned. "Maximilian! You devil!" With a laugh she glanced between Maximilian and the yellow cat.

"Apparently Maximilian had been prowling around for some time when I wasn't aware of it," Dane said dryly.

"I've never seen anything so adorable," she exclaimed. "Do you know if they're—"

"Two boys and a girl," he supplied. His mouth curved. "And I had a thought."

"What?" Julianna stretched out a hand toward the kittens and their mother.

"Perhaps they'd like it in Somerset. In the country, I think, somewhere they can romp and play. And perhaps we could name them—"

Her heart tripped. Oh, Lord, surely he didn't remember . . .

"Alfred, Rebecca, and Irwin," he said softly.

Moved beyond words, beyond measure, Julianna walked straight into his arms.

His fingers tangled in warm, honey-colored hair. He tilted her head back so he could see her. "What do you think?" he whispered.

Blinking back tears—oh, but they were such happy tears indeed!—she smiled. "I think," she whispered, "that I will love you forever!"

*   *   *

It was much later that night when Dane heard the echo of hoofbeats on the street below. Rising, he pulled on a dressing gown, pressed a kiss on his future bride's lips—and went outside to meet Phillip.

"All is well?"

"It is," Phillip confirmed. "Daphne Sterling— or Madame Lemieux—is on the ship and bound for France once more. And I must say, spiriting her away was damned exciting!"

"So it's excitement you crave, eh?"

Phillip laughed gustily. "Don't we all?"

"Do you remember how you once said you wished that you could take my place?"

"I do."

"Well," Dane said mildly, "I do hope you meant it." He slipped his hands into the pockets of his dressing gown and smiled at Phillip's bemused expression. "Because I suggested it to Barnaby when I gave him my resignation. He intends to speak to you about it tomorrow—rather, today."

Phillip was incredulous. "You're serious!"

"I am."

Phillip was practically crowing. "I am a spy. I am *truly* a spy!"

Dane threw back his head and chuckled. "My word, do I dare think of it?" he teased. "Will the shores of England ever be safe again?"

"Ha! Safer than ever," Phillip retorted brashly.

"So you're pleased?"

"Need you ask? But what about you, Dane? Are you quite sure this is what you want? No more midnight escapades. No more secret rendezvous."

"No more danger."

"But . . . what the devil will you do? How on earth will you fill your days and nights?"

Dane chuckled. "Oh, but I shall be doing something much more exciting."

"And what is that?"

He smiled. "Making little Granvilles."

Epilogue

Their wedding took place one month later in St. George's in Hanover Square, a far different occasion than Julianna's last appearance there. Yet there were no memories of the past, for her heart was too full of the future.

She stepped into the vestibule on Sebastian's arm, clutching a bouquet of lilies and roses in one hand. Little by little, the guests' whispers fell to a hush when the music began. And when it was time for Julianna to glide down the aisle, every eye in the church was upon her . . . and hers was on her husband-to-be, waiting at the altar.

The hold of his gaze was tender and wholly captivating.

She had thought there might be tears, for indeed there was a monstrous lump in her throat.

His eyes were so tender her heart surely melted. But as her fingers weaved through his, they heard the Dowager Duchess of Carrington behind them, whispering loudly how *she* had brought this pair together.

There was surely not a soul in the church who did not hear.

Julianna bit back a laugh. Her gaze slid to Dane, who was struggling very hard not to smile. It was a moment so wondrously precious she knew she would remember it forever.

And there was more.

Her niece Sophie, who—at the tender age of two—must be forgiven for neglecting to strew the flower petals before the bride, suddenly remembered her basket in the middle of the ceremony. She dumped the petals at her feet—then sat down to play with them.

Her brother Geoffrey joined her.

Their father sighed. He gave a little cough and beckoned with a fingertip when the pair glanced up. Geoffrey, his eyes agleam, stood upright, dusted his hands of rose petals—then darted between Julianna and Dane when Sebastian crooked his finger once more. Sophie shrieked and dashed after him.

It was utterly chaotic. Utterly unforgettable . . .

And utterly perfect.

* * *

It was nearly one year later when Dane heard the cries of their son in the nursery adjoining their room. His wife stirred and turned to her side. Pressing a kiss on her mouth, he rose from the bed and walked into the nursery.

The fretting infant quieted the instant he felt his father's hands lifting him from his cradle. Lighting a candle, Dane kissed the babe's dark scalp, then settled Christian Elliot Granville— fondly called Kit by his parents—into the crook of his elbow and settled himself into the chair nearby.

The babe's fingers curled strongly around his father's thumb and held fast. His features tender, Dane captured a plump fist and carried it to his mouth, brushing his lips over dimpled knuckles.

"So, my little lad, you think there are better things to do in the midnight hour than sleep, eh?"

The babe made that sweet little sound that so enraptured his mother—and made his father's heart swell with pride. And then he crinkled up his brows and gave a tiny little grin.

Dane laughed softly. "What, you ask? Ah, but let me tell you a tale, my boy. There once was a highwayman who rode through the night alone and fearless. The Magpie, he was called. Oh, and a most bold, dashing fellow was the Magpie, my boy. But all was not as it appeared, you see. For the Magpie was not such a terrible fellow, as the world was convinced."

His son regarded him raptly.

"One night, the Magpie rescued a lady. Oh, but she was a beauty, with chestnut hair and eyes that glowed like sapphires, why, just like yours, my boy! The highwayman spirited the lady away to a cottage not far from here. He waited and waited and waited for the lady to wake. And when she did, he beheld the woman of his dreams, his one, true love! As for the lovely lady, well, do you know what she saw?"

So engrossed were father and son in each other that the rustle at the door had gone unnoticed.

"She saw her husband . . . her hero."

And from the doorway, Julianna smiled.

She had indeed.

Author's Note

Dear Reader,

I hope you've enjoyed the conclusion of the Sterling family trilogy. Writing this series was an unforgettable experience, and I hope you'll find it as memorable as I have. Sebastian, Justin, and Julianna came alive in my heart in so many ways . . .

Writing is a revealing process, sometimes as much for the author as for the reader. Indeed, in the course of writing this trilogy, it proved a truly spontaneous endeavor. Plotlines cropped up that I never expected—and so did several characters! And I discovered things about the Sterling family that took me completely by surprise.

I refer, of course, to the issue of their paternity.

Yes, Sebastian, Justin, and Julianna shared the same mother. But did they share the same father? That they did was never in doubt as I wrote book one, A Perfect Bride. *But then Justin posed the question in book two,* A Perfect Groom, *and then even I began to wonder . . . Should they know the truth? What would happen if they did?*

There is no question, I put these three characters through their paces. Because of that, in my mind, no one deserves a happy ending more than these three.

As for the resolution of the Sterling siblings' paternity, I must confess . . . I wrestled with this issue—oh, how I wrestled with it!

But, ultimately, this was their story. And in the end, it was Sebastian, Justin, and Julianna who stepped forward and guided me. Who spoke to me and told me what they wanted and needed . . . What mattered most . . . and how their story should end. They knew the bond they shared as children could never be shattered—it could never be any different. It could only grow stronger. And so the message throughout the trilogy really never changed.

It's all about family . . . all about love.

My very best wishes,

Samantha J

"I need a hero!"

Imagine that you are the heroine
of your favorite romance. You are
resilient, strong, intrepid.
You rule a country, own a business,
or, perhaps, run a drafty country house
on a shoestring budget. You *can* do it all . . .
and, usually, you do.

But every now and then a gal needs
some help—someone to vanquish
the enemy soldiers,
keep your business afloat . . .
or just plain offer to keep
the servants in line.

Sometimes you need a hero.

Now, in three spectacular new romances by
Kinley MacGregor, Samantha James and
Christie Ridgway—
and one delicious anthology
by Stephanie Laurens, Christina Dodd
and Elizabeth Boyle—
we meet heroines who can
do it all . . . and the sexy,
irresistible heroes who stand
by their side every step
of the way.

"Well?" Queen Adara asked in nervous anticipation as her
senior advisor drew near her throne.

Xerus had been her father's most trusted man. At almost
three score years in age, he still held the sharpness of a man in
the prime of his life. His once-black hair was now streaked
with gray and his beard was whiter than the stone walls that
surrounded their capital city, Garzi.

Since her father's death two years past, Adara had turned

to Xerus for everything. There was no one alive she trusted more, which didn't say much, since, as a queen, her first lesson had been that spies and traitors abounded in her court. Most thought that a woman had no business as the leader of their small kingdom.

Adara had other thoughts on that matter. As her father's only surviving child, she refused to see anyone not of their royal bloodline on this throne. Her family had held the royal seat since before the time of Moses.

No one would take her precious Taagaria from her. Not so long as she breathed.

Xerus shook his head and sighed wearily. "Nay, my queen, they refuse to allow you to divorce their king. In their minds you are married and should you try to sever ties to their throne by divorce or annulment they will attack with the sanction of the Church. After all, in their eyes they already own our kingdom. In fact, Selwyn thinks it best that you move into his custody for your own welfare so that they can protect you . . . as their queen."

Adara clenched her fists in frustration.

Xerus glanced over his shoulder toward her two guards who flanked her door before he drew closer to her throne so that he could whisper privately into her ear.

Lutian, her fool, crept nearer to them as well and angled his head so that he wouldn't miss a single word. He even cupped his ear forward.

Xerus glared at the fool.

Dropping his hand, Lutian glared back. A short, lean man, Lutian had straight brown hair and wore a well-trimmed beard. Possessed of average looks, his face was pleasant enough, but it was his kind brown eyes that endeared him to her.

"Speak openly," she said to her advisor. "There is no one I trust more than Lutian."

"He's a half-wit, my queen."

Lutian snorted. "Half-wit, whole-wit, I have enough of them to know to keep silent. So speak, good counselor, and let the queen judge which of the two of us is the greater fool present."

Adara pressed her lips together to keep from smiling at Lutian. Two years younger than she, Lutian had been seriously injured as a youth when he'd tumbled from their walls and landed on his head. Ever since that day, she had watched over him and kept him close lest anyone make his life even more difficult.

She placed a hand on his shoulder to silence him. Xerus couldn't abide being made fun of. Unlike her, he didn't value Lutian's friendship and service.

With a warning glare to the fool, Xerus finally spoke. "Their prince-regent said that if you would finally like to declare Prince Christian dead, then he might be persuaded toward your cause . . . at a price."

Closing her eyes, she ground her teeth furiously. The Elgederion regent had made his position on that matter more than clear. Selwyn wanted her in his son's bed as his bride to secure their tenuous claim to the throne, and the devil would freeze solid before she ever gave herself over to him and allowed those soulless men to rule her people.

How she wished she commanded a larger nation with enough soldiers to pound the arrogant prince-regent into nothing more than a bad memory. Unfortunately, a war would be far too costly to her people and her kingdom. They couldn't fight the Elgederions alone and none of their other allies would help, since to them it was a family squabble between her and her husband's kingdom.

If only her husband would return home and claim his throne, but every time they had sent a man for him, the messenger was slain. To her knowledge none of them had ever reached Christian and she was tired of sending men to their deaths.

Nay, 'twas time to see this matter closed once and for all.

"Send for Thera," she whispered to Xerus.

He scowled at her. "For what purpose?"

"I intend to take a lengthy trip and I can't afford to let anyone know that I am not here to guard my throne."

"Your cousin is not you, Your Grace. Should anyone learn—"

"I trust you alone to keep her and my crown safe until I return. Have her confined to my quarters and tell everyone that I am ill."

Xerus looked even more confused by her orders. "Where are you going?"

"To find my wayward husband and to bring him home."

June 2005
It's a special treat

Hero, Come Back

Three unforgettable original tales
Three amazing storytellers:
Stephanie Laurens, Christina Dodd, Elizabeth Boyle

Imagine, the return of three of the characters you love best—Reggie from Stephanie Laurens's *On a Wild Night* (and *On a Wicked Dawn*)! Jemmy Finch from Elizabeth Boyle's *Once Tempted* (and *It Takes a Hero*)! And Harry Chamberlain, the Earl of Granville, from Christina Dodd's *Lost in Your Arms*!

Now you get to meet them all over again in this delicious anthology of heroes who were just too good *not* to have stories of their own.

Lost and Found
Stephanie Laurens

Releasing Benjamin, Reggie looked at Anne. He'd recognized her soft voice and all notion of politely retreating had vanished. Anne was Amelia's sister-in-law, Luc Ashford's second sister, known to all family and close friends as highly nervous in crowds.

They hadn't met for some years; he suspected she avoided tonnish gatherings. Rapid calculation revealed she must be twenty-six. She seemed . . . perhaps an inch taller, more assured, more definite, certainly more striking than he recalled, but then she wasn't shrinking against any wall at the moment. She was elegantly turned out in a dark green walking dress. Her expression was open, decided, her face framed by lustrous brown hair caught up in a top knot, then allowed to cascade about her head in lush waves. Her eyes were light brown, the color of caramel, large and set under delicately arched brows. Her lips were blush rose, sensuously curved, decidedly vulnerable.

Intensely feminine.

As were the curves of breast and waist revealed by the tightly-fitting bodice . . .

Jerking his mind from the unexpected track, he frowned. "Now cut line—what is this about?"

A frown lit her eyes, a warning one. "I'll explain once we've returned Benjy to the house." Retaking Benjy's hand, she turned back along the path.

Reggie pivoted and fell in beside her. "Which house? Is Luc in town?"

"No. Not Calverton House." Anne hesitated, then added, more softly, "The Foundling House."

Pieces of the puzzle fell, jigsawlike, into place, but the picture in his mind was incomplete. His long strides relaxed, he retook her arm, wound it with his, forcing her to slow. "Much better to stroll without a care, rather than rush off so purposefully. No need for the ignorant to wonder what your purpose is."

The Matchmaker's Bargain
Elizabeth Boyle

"Oh, this cannot be!" Esme said, bounding up from her chair. "I can't get married."

"Whyever not? You aren't already engaged, are you?" Jemmy didn't know why, but for some reason he didn't like the idea of her being another man's betrothed. Besides, what the devil was the fellow thinking, letting such a pretty little chit wander lost about the countryside?

But his concerns about another man in her life were for naught, for she told him very tartly, "I am not engaged, sir, and I assure you, I'm not destined for marriage."

"I don't see that there is anything wrong with you," he said without thinking. Demmit, this is what came of living the life of a recluse—he'd forgotten every bit of his town bronze. "I mean to say, it's not like you couldn't be here seeking a husband."

The disbelief on her face struck him to the core.

Was she really so unaware of the pretty picture she presented? That her green eyes, bright and full of sparkles, and soft brown hair, still tumbled from her slumbers and hanging in long tangled curls, was an enticing picture—one that might persuade many a man to get fitted for a pair of leg-shackles.

Even Jemmy found himself susceptible to her charms—she had an air of familiarity about her that whispered of strength and warmth and sensibility, capable of drawing a man toward her like a beggar to a warm hearth.

Not to mention the parts, that as a gentleman, he shouldn't know she possessed, but in their short, albeit rather noteworthy acquaintance, had discovered with the familiarity that one usually had only with a mistress . . . or a hastily gained betrothed.

He shook that idea right out of his head. Whatever was he thinking? She wasn't interested in marriage, and neither was he. Not than any lady *would* have him . . . lame and scarred as he was.

"I hardly see that any of this is your concern," she was saying, once again bustling about the room, gathering up her belongings. She plucked her stockings—gauzy, French sort of things—from the line by the fire.

He could imagine what they would look like on her, and more importantly what it would feel like sliding them off her long, elegant legs.

When she saw him staring at her unmentionables, she blushed and shoved them into her valise. "I really must be away."

The Third Suitor
Christina Dodd

Leaning over the high porch railing, Harry Chamberlain looked down into the flowering shrubbery surrounding his oceanfront cottage and asked, "Young woman, what are you doing down there?"

The girl flinched, stopped crawling through the collection of moss, dirt and faded pink blossoms, and turned a smudged face up to his. "Shh." She glanced behind her, as if someone were creeping after her. "I'm trying to avoid one of my suitors."

Harry glanced behind her, too. No one was there.

"Can you see him?" she asked.

"There's not a soul in sight." A smart man would have let her go on her way. Harry was on holiday, a holiday he desperately needed, and he had vowed to avoid trouble at all costs. Now a girl of perhaps eighteen years, dressed in a modish blue flowered gown, came crawling through the bushes, armed with nothing more than a ridiculous tale, and he was tempted to help. Tempted because of a thin, tanned face, wide brown eyes, a kissable mouth, a crooked blue bonnet and, from this angle, the finest pair of breasts he'd ever had the good fortune to gaze upon.

Such unruliness in his own character surprised him. He was, in truth, Edmund Kennard Henry Chamberlain, earl of Granville, the owner of a great estate in Somerset, and because of the weight of his responsibilities there, and the additional responsibilities he had taken on, he tended to do his duty without capriciousness. Indeed, it was that trait which had set him, eight years ago, to serve England in various countries and capacities. Now he gazed at a female intent on some silliness and discovered in himself the urge to find out more about her. Perhaps he had at last relaxed from the tension of his last job. Or perhaps she *was* the relaxation he sought.

In a trembling voice, she pleaded, "Please, sir, if he appears, don't tell him I'm here."

"I wouldn't dream of interfering."

"Oh, thank you!" A smile transformed that quivering mouth into one that was naturally merry, with soft peach lips and a dimple. "Because I thought that's what you were doing."

Julianna felt herself tumbling to the floor. Jarred into wakefulness, she opened her eyes, rubbing her shoulder where she'd landed. What the deuce . . . ? Panic enveloped her; it was pitch black inside the coach.

And outside as well.

She was just about to heave herself back onto the cushions when the sound of male voices punctuated the air outside. The coachman . . . and someone else.

"Put it down, I s-say!" the coachman stuttered. "There's nothing of value aboard, I swear! Mercy," the man blubbered. "I beg of you, have mercy!"

Even as a decidedly prickly unease slid down her spine, the door was wrenched open. She found herself staring at the gleaming barrel of a pistol. In terror she lifted her gaze to the man who possessed it.

Garbed in black he was, from the enveloping folds of his cloak to the kerchief that obscured the lower half of his face. A silk mask was tied around his eyes; they were all that was visible of his features. Even in the dark, there was no mistaking their color. They glimmered like clear golden fire, pale and unearthly.

The devil's eyes.

"Nothing of value aboard, eh?"

A gust of chill night air funneled in. Yet it was like nothing compared to the chill she felt in hearing that voice . . . So softly querulous, like steel tearing through tightly stretched silk, she decided dazedly.

She had always despised silly, weak, helpless females. Yet when his gaze raked over her—*through* her, bold and ever so irreverent!—she felt stripped to the bone.

Goose bumps rose on her flesh. She couldn't move. She most certainly couldn't speak. She could not even swallow past the knot lodged deep in her throat. Fear numbed her mind. Her mouth was dry with a sickly dread such as she had never experienced. All she could think was that if Mrs. Chadwick were here, she might take great delight in knowing she'd been right to be so fearful. For somehow Julianna knew with a mind-chilling certainty that it was he . . .

The Magpie.

Dane Quincy Granville did not count on the coachman's reaction—nor his rashness. There was a crack of the whip, a frenzied shout. The horses bolted. Instinctively, Dane leaped back, very nearly knocked to the ground. The vehicle jolted forward, speeding toward a bend in the road.

The stupid fool! Christ, the coachman would never make the turn. The bend was too sharp. He was going too fast—

The night exploded. There was an excruciating crash, the sound of wood splintering and cracking . . . the high-pitched neighs of the horses.

Then there was nothing.

Galvanized into action, Dane sprang for Percival. Leaping from the stallion's back, he hurtled himself down the steep embankment where the coach had disappeared. Scrambling over the brush, he spied it. It was overturned, resting against the trunk of an ancient tree.

One wheel was still spinning as he reached it.

The horses were already gone. So was the driver. His neck was broken, twisted at an odd angle from his body. Dane had seen enough of death to know there was nothing he could do to help him.

Miraculously, the door to the main compartment had remained on its hinges. In fury and fear, Dane tore it off and lunged into the compartment.

The girl was still inside, coiled in a heap on the roof. His heart in his throat, he reached for her, easing her into his arms and outside.

His heart pounding, he knelt in the damp earth and stared down at her. "Wake up!" he commanded. As if because he willed it, as if it would be so . . . He gritted his teeth, as if to instill his very will—his very life—inside her.

Her head fell limply over his arm.

"Dammit, girl, wake up!"

He was sick in the pit of his belly, in his very soul. If only the driver hadn't been so blasted skittish. So hasty! He wouldn't have harmed them, either of them. On a field near Brussels, he'd seen enough death and dying to last a lifetime. God knew it had changed him. Shaped him for all eternity. And for now, all he wanted was—

She moaned.

An odd little laugh broke from his chest, the sound almost brittle. After all his careful planning that *this* should occur . . . But he couldn't ascertain her injuries. Not here. Not in the dark. He must leave. Now. He couldn't afford to linger, else all might be for naught.

The girl did not wake as he rifled through the boot, retrieving a bulging sack and a valise. Seconds later, he whistled for Percival. Cradling the girl carefully against his chest, he lifted the reins and rode into the night.

As suddenly as he had appeared, the Magpie was gone.

August 2005
We're going to make you
an offer you can't refuse in
Christie Ridgway's

An Offer He Can't Refuse

The first in her delicious new Wisegirls series

Téa Caruso knows what everyone thinks about her
family . . . her very large, very powerful family. After
all, she grew up in the shadow of her grandfather—
The Sun Dried Tomato King—and her uncles, with
their mysterious "business." And, of course, there
are her aunts, who don't ask too many questions.
She's spent a lifetime going legit, and now her past
comes back to haunt her when she falls for John
Magee. He's a professional gambler, the worse kind
of man, one who'd make the family proud . . . or
is he?

Téa Caruso had once been very, very bad and she wondered
if today was the day she started paying for it. After spending the morning closeted in the perfume-saturated powder
room of Mr. and Mrs. William Duncan's Spanish-Italian-
Renaissance-inspired Palm Springs home, discussing baby
Jesus and the Holy Mother, she emerged from the clouds—
both heavenly and olfactory—with a Chanel No. 5 hang-

over and fingernail creases in her palms as deep as the Duncan's quarter-mile lap pool.

Standing on the pillowed limestone terrace outside, she allowed herself a sixty-second pause for fresh air, but multitasked the moment by completing a quick appearance check as well. Even someone with less artistic training than Téa would know that her Mediterranean coloring and generous curves were made for low necklines and sassy flounces in gypsy shades, but her Mandarin-collared, dove gray linen dress was devised to button up, smooth out, and tuck away. Though she could never feel innocent, she preferred to at least look that way.

The reflection in her hand mirror presented no jarring surprises. The sun lent an apricot cast to her olive skin. Tilted brown eyes, a slightly patrician nose, cheekbones and jawline now defined after years of counting calories instead of chowing down on cookies. Assured that her buttons were tight, her mascara unsmudged, and her hair still controlled in its long, dark sweep, she snapped the compact shut. Then, hurrying in the direction of her car, she swapped mirror for cell phone and speed dialed her interior design firm.

"She's still insisting on Him," she told her assistant when she answered. "Find out who can hand paint a Rembrandt-styled infant Jesus in the bottom of a porcelain sink."

Glancing over at the Madonna blue water of the pool, Téa was reminded of the morning's single success. "The good news is I talked her out of the Virgin Mary in the bidet bowl." Surely the Mother of God would appreciate that fact.

Still on forward march, she checked her watch. "Quick, any messages? I have lunch with my sisters up next."

"Nikki O'Neal phoned and mentioned a redo of her dining room," her assistant replied. "Something about a mural depicting the Ascension."

The Ascension?

Téa's steps faltered, slowed. "No," she groaned. "That means Mrs. D. has spilled her plans. Now we'll be hearing from every one of her group at Our Lady of Mink."

A segment of Téa's client list—members of the St. Brigit's Guild at the posh Our Lady of Mercy Catholic Church—cultivated their competitive spirits as well as their Holy Spirit during their weekly meetings. One woman would share a new idea for home decor, prompting the next to take the same theme to even greater—more ostentatious—heights.

Three years before it had been everything vineyard, then after that sea life turned all the rage, and now . . . good God.

"The *Ascension*?" Téa muttered. "These women must be out of their minds."

But could she really blame them? Palm Springs had a grand tradition of the grandiose, after all. Walt Disney had owned a home here. Elvis. Liberace.

It was just that when she'd opened her business, filled with high artistic aspirations and a zealous determination to make over the notorious Caruso name, she hadn't foreseen the pitfalls. Like how the ceaseless influx of rent and utility bills and the unsteady trickle and occasional torrent that was her cash flow meant she couldn't be picky when it came to choosing design jobs.

Like how *that* could result in gaining woeful renown as designer of all things overdone. She groaned again.

"Oh, and Téa . . ." Her assistant's voice rose in an expectant lilt. "His Huskiness called."

Her stomach lurched, pity party forgotten. "What? *Who*?"

"Johnny Magee."

Of course, Johnny Magee. Her assistant referred to the man they'd never met by an ever-expanding lexicon of nicknames that ranged from the overrated to the out-and-out ridiculous. To Téa, he was simply her One Chance, her Answered Prayers, her Belief in Miracles.

An offer you won't want to refuse!

USA Today bestselling author of *The Thrill of it All*

Christie RIDGWAY

An Offer He Can't Refuse

"Pure romance, delightfully warm and funny."–Jennifer Crusie

Interior decorator Téa Caruso is an ordinary woman with one tiny difference. Her grandfather isn't just in the mob . . . he is the mob! But Téa's legit and plans to stay that way–until Johnny Magee shows up. The Caruso family destroyed Johnny's dad and now it's payback time. Intent on using Téa for revenge, Johnny hires her to redo his home. But then she makes him "offers" he can't refuse–of her body, of her heart, and soon, he's falling in love. When all the secrets are revealed, what will Téa–and her family!– do?

Buy and enjoy AN OFFER HE CAN'T REFUSE (available August 2, 2005), then send the coupon below along with your proof of purchase for AN OFFER HE CAN'T REFUSE to Avon Books, and we'll send you a check for $2.00.

- -

 AuthorTracker

Don't miss the next book by your favorite author. Sign up now for AuthorTracker by visiting www.AuthorTracker.com

OHC 0705